ALSO BY KAT & STONE BASTION

No Weddings Series

No Weddings · One Funeral

Two Bar Mitzvahs · Three Christmases

For Valentine's

Unbreakable Series

Heartbreaker · Rule Breaker · Lawbreaker

Forthcoming: *Ball Breaker · Icebreaker*

Highland Legends Series

Forged in Dreams and Magick

Bound by Wish and Mistletoe

Born of Mist and Legend

Found in Flame and Moonlight

THE TRAVELER: Initiate Years

Veil of Realms · Secrets of Alexandria · Panther Rising

Stones of Power · Highland Magick

Half-Baked Holidays

Half-baked Holidays:

A Romantic Comedy Holiday Collection

PRAISE FOR KAT & STONE BASTION

No Weddings and
THE NO WEDDINGS SERIES

"One of the best romantic comedies of the year!"

— *AGENTS OF ROMANCE*

"The No Weddings series is one of the best I have read that follows one couple. Cade and Hannah are both lovable characters, the storyline is real and entertaining, and the banter is fun and witty."

— *LIVES & BREATHES BOOK BLOG*

"I loved it, and I mean REALLY loved it!"

— *ORCHARD BOOK CLUB*

"This is an exceptional series... You find yourself fully engrossed in their world and can't put the book down."

— *BOOKS -N- KISSES*

"The No Weddings series has a group of such amazing characters; you can't help but relate to them and feel the emotion in every situation they encounter. It has been a long time since a story has made me feel that way let alone an entire series!"

— *UNDER THE COVERS BOOK BLOG*

"The story of Cade & Hannah's relationship is realistic, heart-warming, and filled with real-world connections that shook me in a way that few titles I've read this year have managed...I have loved every minute of the No Weddings series."

— *THAT'S WHAT I'M TALKING ABOUT*

Heartbreaker

"This book has definitely earned its five stars and I am just floored right now. The passion is explosive, the story itself is beautiful, and the emotions are so real my heart is ready to burst. Beautiful book. Absolutely breathtaking."

— *ONE PAGE AT A TIME*

"Heartrending, passionate, and captivating! *Heartbreaker* is a riveting page-turner that will leave you breathless with raw emotions, and the need to hold tight to the ones you love!"

— *BENEATH THE COVERS BLOG*

AWARDS & PRAISE FOR KAT BASTION

Forged in Dreams and Magick

First Place – Unpublished Beacon Award
Best Paranormal Romance

First Place – Hold Me, Thrill Me Award
Best Paranormal Romance

Chosen by FreshFiction.com as their
Fresh Pick for October 22, 2013

"A beautifully woven tale about love, choices, courage and destiny, *Forged in Dreams and Magick* is one of the best time-travelling novels. Fans of Gabaldon's *Outlander* will love it."

— *BOOKISH TEMPTATIONS*

"I was gripping my iPad like a crazy woman and fanning myself from the smoldering romance. Lawdy!"

— *THE FLIRTY READER*

"Bastion's debut is pure perfection, a combination of romance, magic, emotion, adventure and surprising twists and turns. This is a truly unique romance that should not be missed!"

— *THEBOOKQUEEN*

"HOLY HELL!!! I am so... um... wow! FABULOUS-NESS. *Forged in Dreams and Magick* definitely makes my BEST OF list for 2013..."

— *THAT'S WHAT I'M TALKING ABOUT*

"A story guaranteed to enthrall with lushly detailed travels into times long gone by. Woven with love, passion, magic and legend, the story had me hooked from the very first chapter."

— *READ-LOVE-BLOG*

"Kat Bastion's wonderful debut brings a new voice to the fore. Her voice is strong and unhesitating, very human and real, sometimes young and delicious in her treatment of intimacy and relationship development."

— *FANGS WANDS & FAIRYDUST*

"OMG, Bastion hits all cylinders in this supernatural tale. The layers in the book were fascinating, and I devoured the fun, adventuresome read."

— *LITERATI LITERATURE LOVERS*

Bound by Wish and Mistletoe

"I LOVED it! *Bound by Wish and Mistletoe* is, to my mind, a perfect entry in the historical / paranormal fiction genre and has quite a bit to offer."

— *FAB FANTASY FICTION*

"Kat Bastion has done it again! ... Excellent holiday novella, perfect for a cup of cocoa and snuggling under a blanket in front of the fireplace this holiday season."

— *THAT'S WHAT I'M TALKING ABOUT*

"Move over, Julia Quinn and Sabrina Jeffries! Kat Bastion is an absolutely gifted author and deserves to be recognized for her talent."

— *LOVESHISTORICAL BOOK REVIEWS*

TWO BAR MITZVAHS

TWO BAR MITZVAHS

KAT & STONE BASTION

To those who love with all that you are...

1. BLISS INTERRUPTED

"Hannah..." I kissed her temple.

Our bodies were wrapped together. What an incredible way to wake up.

Her lips curved into a smile. "Cade..." She let out a low moan that turned into a purr right before she turned and snuggled her sexy ass back into me.

I groaned. My cock stiffened further, aching. And it had nothing to do with morning wood. But even though I wanted to bury myself balls deep back into Hannah, I only pulled her closer, held her tighter—grateful she was in my arms.

I'd been waiting five months for this moment. *Five*. For a guy like me, that's a lifetime. A fucking monumental achievement. But it wasn't just about the sex. We were great friends who'd wanted more, even with the risk. So we'd taken things slow. And I'd do it all over again. I sighed and tightened my arms again.

She wriggled, loosening my hold. "I have to pee."

"No." I pulled her back to me.

"Yes." She smacked my hip. "Pee. Coffee. Work."

I let out a low grunt. "Reality sucks. Bed all day better." Sometime in the middle of our wild night, we'd stumbled out of the mosquito-netted tent in her backyard and made it into her house, knocked her mountain of throw pillows onto the floor, and tumbled into her bed.

She turned in my arms and smiled at me. "Bed all day sounds perfect." Her dark hair tumbled over her shoulders, the ends teasing her breasts. Bright light streamed through her windows, making her hazel eyes vivid green. Her gaze dropped to my mouth, and she bit her lower lip.

Growling, I launched up and tugged that lower lip away from her into my own mouth. I kissed her hard at first, then long and slow, until her body relaxed into my hold again. "So it's settled, then."

She smiled against my lips but pulled back. "No. I need to get into the bakery. Chloe and Daniel promised to open, but I have a business to run. So do you." Chloe and Daniel were dedicated employees, but Hannah's sense of responsibility was admirable. Her other point was dead on. I did have a business to run. And my commitment to everyone at Loading Zone, the bar I co-owned with my best friend Ben, was unshakable.

I gave her a hard nod, finally releasing her. "You're right. Reality doesn't suck that much."

When she stood from the bed, the sheet drifted from her body. I swallowed hard, staring at her gorgeous backside.

"Oh? Why's that?" She turned, giving me a half smile.

I let out a slow exhale. "Because you're in it."

The corner of her mouth kicked up in a smirk. "Good answer."

A noise hummed. She leaned toward her nightstand,

grabbed a lit up phone, and handed it to me. "Here. Your phone has been vibrating on and off all morning. Somebody wants you in an urgent way." After another slow kiss, she left and walked around the bed toward the bathroom.

Irritated that I hadn't turned the damned thing off and the noise had bothered Hannah, I pressed the control button to light up the screen again. Several alerts were stacked in a list. A couple of them (two missed calls and a voicemail) were from my oldest sister, Kristen, all from the last few hours this morning. One call and voicemail came from Ben. The third call was from an unknown number. That caller had also left a voicemail.

I pushed up, then sat on the edge of the bed as I listened to the voicemail from Kristen. Something about a messed up order with our family's event-planning company, Invitation Only, but my brain was too hazy to follow all the details. Ben's message was a reminder about Loading Zone's quarterly meeting today. The third voicemail was from...a familiar, sultry voice.

Warning bells fired adrenaline into my veins. I jolted awake, heart racing, recognition hitting my body first. My brain lagged a few seconds behind.

"...shocked as hell to hear from me. I know we left on horrible terms. But I was hoping we could get together. Talk."

I blew out a hard breath.

Madison.

My ex. The one who'd dumped me when I proposed to her two years ago, admitting she cheated on me repeatedly when we'd been together.

Pissed the fuck off, I shot up from the bed and threw the phone onto it. Of course, my ex would surface after so long, as if nothing had happened. *During a date with Hannah.*

I caught Hannah staring at me from the entrance to her bathroom, her eyes wide. "What's wrong?"

With concentration, I relaxed my scowl. "Nothing." So *not* nothing. But fuck if I was going to ruin this date for Hannah too.

Her brows drew together, and she dropped her hands onto her hips. "Doesn't look like nothing. You're angry."

I took a deep breath, willing my out-of-control head to calm the fuck down. I shoved the disturbing voicemail out of my mind, doing my damnedest to compartmentalize that shit. My past didn't matter. It didn't belong in this room. Only the most important person did—Hannah.

She stood there naked, hair rumpled with that sexy just-been-thoroughly-fucked look, skin flushed a beautiful pink. She was what I needed to focus on. "You're all I need to calm down." I crossed the room and gathered her in my arms.

She pressed her hands on my chest, pushing back from my hold. "Who called?"

Not giving up on it, then. I sighed. "A few people."

"Like?"

"Ben. Reminding me of today's meeting."

"And?"

"Kristen. About some issue she's dealing with."

"And that made you mad?"

I released her and took a step back. "No."

She crossed her arms over her chest. "Why won't you tell me? I thought we were past keeping things from each other." Her eyes darkened.

I blew out a breath. "We are. Damn, Hannah. I didn't want to ruin this morning for you. Our first morning waking up together should be free of shit from our past."

Her brows raised. "Shit from your past called?"

I gave her a brief nod. "Selfish Bitch, to be exact." Never ceased to amaze me how fitting the nickname was that Hannah had given my ex. Or how damn good it felt to say it. A benefit from the cleansing bonfire therapy a few months ago after I'd dubbed hers Dumbfuck.

Hannah gasped. "What did she say? What did she want?"

I shrugged. "Not much. She wants to get together to talk."

A hurt expression crossed over her face. "And do you want to? Are you going to?"

Her pained look killed me. "No. I don't. And I'm not. Now do you see why I didn't want to tell you? I've ruined our first *real* date."

She shook her head, the harsh lines in her forehead softening. "No, Cade. You didn't ruin anything. But please, don't keep things from me." On a shaky inhale, she stepped into my arms again. "With the betrayal from my past, and with how you suffered from yours, we're both damaged when it comes to trust."

I brushed her hair out of her face. "I'm sorry." My gut instinct had me wanting to deal with Madison on my own, protecting Hannah. "I know we're fucked up with those issues. I hesitated because last night and this morning was amazing. I was angry that she'd called. That I hadn't turned my damned phone off. That my reaction upset you. Ruined our morning, at the very least."

She gave me a gentle smile. "No not ruined. Remember our *first* first date? The one I thought was a disaster? That I was convinced I'd ruined?"

"You didn't ruin it. And it wasn't a disaster." Had she been a little nervous? Yeah. And *way* too much in her head about her ex—nothing a little on-the-spot fantasizing and a few sessions of professional therapy hadn't been able solve.

"Semi-disaster," she countered. "And you're missing my point."

"That I've only semi-ruined it?"

She slapped my chest. "No. What did you do to get me out of my head?"

"Got you to think of a happy place."

"And what did I picture?"

I grinned. "A field of cupcakes. With me naked. Covered in icing."

With slow steps, she walked backward. "Icing can be sticky. We're sticky right now."

"From mind-blowing sex." I stalked after her, matching her step-by-step. I definitely liked the direction she was headed.

"So do you think maybe we can go to a happy place here in my bathroom? I'm sticky. You're sticky. We both have to go into work clean, don't we?" She bit her lip as she stepped into her shower and turned on the spray.

I growled low, following her in. "I *love* your idea of therapy."

Hair slicked back, she stepped out from under the water and grabbed a shampoo bottle. "Good. Because therapy is about to get very hands on."

I stepped under the spray and did my best to block out the negative vibe from my ex. Hannah caught my gaze and held it. Doubt reflected back at me for a split second, like she'd read my mind, could see my struggle to get settled back into us. But then she tilted her head, gave me another sexy smile, and wrapped a soapy hand around the tip of my cock.

I groaned, leaning into her hold as her hand slipped

from tip to base. Her face tilted up as I closed my eyes. Soft lips pressed against mine.

I gave myself over to her touch, her kiss. Relief washed through me. Her medicine, her kind of therapy, helped to fade the image of the earlier look of hurt in her eyes. I didn't want her to worry. I needed her trust. Needed her.

2. CAUGHT OFF GUARD

After a shower that rivaled all others, we stood in Hannah's kitchen. She tapped her fingers on the chrome coffee maker as it dripped into the carafe. Drawn to her, unable to keep my hands to myself, I pulled her into my arms. She smiled, and I bent down, kissing the top of her head. "Damn, you smell good."

She gave out a soft laugh. "You smell like coconut mango too. Just...in a manly way."

I grunted. "Tropical is never manly. I need to bring over guy shampoo."

Over her head, I gazed out her windows. The sides of the white tent we'd left in her backyard rippled in the wind. "You okay with leaving that stuff out there for now?" Last night, my sisters pulled through for me in setting up the perfect date for us. Iced wine. Candles everywhere. A tent with a luxurious bed inside.

Hannah turned in my arms, following my gaze. "What's that bright color by the corner of the tent?"

"Ahhh, yes." I grabbed my coffee and pressed my hand

to her back. "I'd forgotten. It was a surprise for you last night, but it was too dark to see."

Hannah rushed out her back door before I finished talking. I hurried after her.

Once we were a few feet away, she jerked to a stop and spun around, eyes widening. "Snapdragons!"

I grinned. On our first attempt at a date a couple of months ago, I'd brought her a single rose. She'd pulled off a petal, then revealed her other flower obsession: making snapdragons *sing*. Nothing in the world would've stopped me from trying to make that happen on our first *real* date.

She knelt down in front of them, blinking. Her voice fell to a whisper. "You remembered how much I liked snapdragons."

"I did."

Unable to see what she was doing with her fingers, I squatted beside her. She gripped the back joint of the flower and pinched her finger and thumb together. The two halves opened like a jaw. When she released the pressure, they closed.

She proceeded to pinch the flower open and shut to the rhythm of her exaggerated operatic voice. "La, la, la, la, la, laaa."

I burst out laughing. She looked up at me, pure joy in her eyes.

My heart warmed at how easily she was her raw, true self with me. "Damn, I love you."

I blinked hard. What the fuck was with my spewing out words without thinking? I blamed the snapdragons.

Yet I did love her. And no part of me wanted to take back the admission.

She gave me a wide smile until her lips twisted into a

smirk. Probably because if my expression matched what I felt, I looked shocked as hell at my revelation.

But her gaze held mine. "I love you too." A whispered confession.

I grasped her hand, pulled her up, and held her tight. "You don't have to say it just because I did."

"You seemed surprised you'd said it." She placed a soft kiss along the side of my neck.

"I was." It's what happened when love blindsided a guy enough for him to run at the mouth without considering the consequences.

She pulled back to look at me, tilting her head with a tender smile. "I knew last night. Maybe I'd felt it for a while, but last night, I knew."

"We've come a long way in a couple of months after burning bad memories of our past, in this very backyard, to give us a chance at a future together. And now here we are."

Shit. Memories of my past. Of Madison. The only other woman who I'd ever loved was the person who'd shattered my heart. And that same ghost from my past showed up to haunt me the morning I told Hannah I loved her?

The two were unrelated. Had to be.

I focused back on the woman in my arms.

Her smile was breathtaking, but her brows suddenly drew together. "You okay? You look like you're deep in thought."

"Yeah. Sorry. Exorcising a ghost."

She took a deep breath. "Selfish Bitch?"

I gave her a curt nod. "I guess I'm just rattled today. Her call threw me. And it's not every day I tell someone I love them."

She stared at me for a beat, her expression turning hard.

"You told her you loved her. But what you feel for me is different, right?"

I gave her a fierce stare. "*So* different. Beyond compare. I...I've never felt this before."

The corners of her lips twitched, and her eyes narrowed for a split second. Then she poked a finger into my chest. "That's right. You *looove* me."

I smiled down at her. "Yes, Maestro. I *looove* you." And I did. That she saw me spiraling again and pulled me out with her quirky humor made my heart ache.

Hannah *was* different. Madison might've gotten the best part of me back then, but Hannah made me feel like the best version of myself all the time.

She tugged me back up to the house. "C'mon. I need to go make the cupcakes, and you're going to be late to your meeting." We climbed her back steps, and she turned around as she opened her back door. "What are you doing tonight? Will you come back later?"

I dropped a serious look at her. "Nothing could keep me away."

She gave me a devastating smile, then tilted her head to the side. "I had the most wonderful time last night."

I topped off my coffee as I looked out toward the tent. "Camping à la Cade has a certain appeal, doesn't it?"

"Not sure I'd want to camp any other way."

"You ever been camping before?"

She shook her head. "No. You?"

"Yeah. Couple times in college. Group of friends. Keg. Loud music."

She nodded absently and gazed out the window toward the tent with a sad expression.

"That's it. We're going camping."

"Really?" Her face lit up.

I pulled her toward the front door. "Yeah, really. Talk to those two employees of yours and clear your schedule as soon as you can."

When we reached her car, she turned and kissed along my jaw until her lips found mine. I deepened the kiss, then groaned when my body decided in firm terms that it wanted to stay.

———

A FEW MINUTES LATER, and after a dozen more kisses that would have convinced me to stay on any other day, I finally eased my motorcycle out of her driveway and headed straight to my bar.

I walked through the back door and into Ben's office. He glanced up from his desk, then put down his cell phone as he stood. "About time you got here. Was just calling you."

"Sorry, man. Got waylaid." Or laid. Repeatedly.

"Don't sweat it. You're here. Everyone is except your dad. He said to start without him."

My dad was a mostly silent partner with Loading Zone. We invited him to the quarterly meetings, which he attended, silent but interested.

Ben paused as a look of understanding washed over his face. "That's right. Last night was your date with Hannah. How'd it go?"

With a deep breath, I gave a nod and a happy-as-fuck look that said it all. Because words never could.

He grinned and clapped me on the shoulder. "Awesome, man. Hannah is gold."

"Yeah, she is." Made a guy feel invincible with the love of a woman like Hannah. I stowed my keys, phone, and electronic tablet in his bottom drawer. "Cool if I steal your office after the meeting for an hour? I'm behind on emails for Invitation Only events."

He grabbed a stack of envelopes and a single sheet of paper from his desk before we left his office. "Sure. I'm gone as soon as we're done."

We headed out to the main floor where everyone had gathered for our fourth quarterly meeting and the first annual report of our fledgling company. Loading Zone had twenty-three employees, from the bartenders to the waitresses, the security team to the barbacks. Even our DJ, Darren, was here. Every face popped up, full of anticipation, as Ben and I walked in from the back. I exhaled slowly, glad to be able to focus on business.

I leaned back against the bar. "As you all know, we decided to do something different with Loading Zone. We undercut the competition and acquired the best staff by overcompensating you. How do you feel about that?"

"I think I love you, man." Mark, our floor manager and head of security had a dead-serious tone. No one laughed. They all nodded, expressions fierce.

Ben stepped forward right as my dad walked in the front door. "When Cade first suggested sharing the profits with every employee, I have to admit, I thought it was a great idea to incentivize but wasn't sure how it would work in reality. I'm happy to say, we've blown our one-year revenue projections through the roof."

The room exploded into whistles and shouts.

"Most of you have been with us since the beginning. All of you have worked hard to make Loading Zone an amazing place. I hope you understand how much you all mean to us in being a part of our team. A family, really."

I nodded toward the envelopes Ben held. "We wanted to show our appreciation for all you've done. Each of you has an extra bonus in there, beyond your profit-sharing percentage."

Hushed whispers and gasps spread across the floor.

"That's not all. You know how important giving back to the community is to us. Your support at our occasional softball games has been incredible in helping us raise money for charity, but what we haven't shared until now is that a percentage of every net dollar earned at Loading Zone is also donated."

I glanced at Ben. He nodded in support before I turned back to the group. "What do you say to our hosting a charity event for Loading Zone's one-year anniversary at the end of the month?"

Jillian, one of our lead waitresses, stood from the chair she'd been sitting in. "You mean donate our time for the night?"

I tilted my head toward her. "Only if you want to." Scanning their faces, I saw determination and pride in their expressions. "Each of you can decide. Loading Zone will be donating all the liquor and every penny of profits for the one night. We'd love for you to be a part of it, but only if you can swing it. We totally understand if you can't."

One by one they all stood beside Jillian, forming a tightknit group.

Mark spoke for them. "We've all made more money in the profits we share here than at any other job we've had. A lot of us have been trying to figure out a way to thank you. This is it."

Without hesitation, they all nodded.

"We're in." Darren crossed his arms.

Jillian took a step forward and gave a hard nod. "I'll even donate all my tips that night too. I'll work my ass off."

I smiled at her. "You always do. All of you do. Thank you

for everything you've done for us, for being dedicated to Loading Zone as something more than just a job you punch in at."

From across the room, my dad swept his gaze over the animated group before it landed on me. He stared hard at me with immense pride. I gave him a slight nod. Were it not for him, I wouldn't have had such a passion for business at a young age, when even the wildest ideas seemed possible.

Ben waved his fistful of envelopes at our group. "Time for the fun part."

He handed me the stack. I called out the names, and as each person came forward, they shook my hand in appreciation. Then Ben read off the sheet of paper he'd brought, rattling off random information about costs and profit. Not that he needed to.

This wasn't a shareholders' meeting. The employees didn't own a slice of the company. We shared the profits with them as inducement to performance. And as Jillian had so eloquently phrased it, they worked their asses off in return. Because when each customer was happy, they showed it with their wallets, which fattened ours, and enabled us to give liberally to those in need.

After everyone left, including my dad, who slipped out the front door before we handed out the last check, I made my way back to Ben's office.

In the calm silence, I fired off a group email to my three sisters and Hannah about the bar's anniversary event, formally enlisting the help of Invitation Only. Since Kiki was the artistic one who'd actually been the drive behind Loading Zone's industrial-grunge vibe, I asked her to create and send out the invitations. I outlined all the details we'd just discussed at the bar's employee meeting and suggested to Hannah to use them as inspiration for the cake.

After I sent it, I smiled, wondering what Hannah was doing. Probably icing a batch of cupcakes. I imagined her with colored flecks of frosting on her arms and that ruffled apron over her tiny T-shirt and short shorts. I took a deep breath, clearing my head. If I didn't concentrate on something *other* than Hannah, I'd never get anything else done. I'd race over to her shop, kidnap her away from work, and we'd dive back into her bed. And then neither would she.

I scanned through the several dozen emails in my inbox that had come in since Friday and began replying to them from the top down. A handful were late congratulations to me on my recent graduation from the Wharton MBA program. A couple were from Kristen related to early event bookings in the fall. And the alcohol distributor we used for both the bar and for scheduled Invitation Only events had sent us order confirmations.

Then I reached an email that had been sent four hours ago from another key vendor regarding a high school graduation party scheduled for next week.

"What the fuck?"

Confused as hell, I read it through again. It talked about the forfeiting of our substantial deposit. I grabbed my phone. I sure as shit wasn't about to email a reply on such an urgent matter.

He picked up on the third ring. "John. I just read your email and have no idea what you're talking about. We didn't cancel."

A sigh on the other end. "I thought it was strange. You've never canceled before."

"Well, I know *I* didn't call you. And I was the one that placed the order. What made you think we'd canceled?"

"One of your sisters called first thing this morning."

I shook my head. No way in hell. Unless one of them had

an aneurism, we didn't operate on our own. Group decisions were made. Tasks were delegated and carried out. End of story.

"Which sister?"

"I'm not sure. Kristen I think."

I put him on speaker while I fired off a text to Kristen.

> URGENT! Did you cancel tent and furniture rental for next week?

Focusing on damage control, I pinched the bridge of my nose and prayed things hadn't gotten royally fucked up. "John, is the order still available?"

Kristen's text alerted through.

> No! That's what my voicemail was about.

John replied, "Yeah, I haven't done anything yet."

I exhaled sharply, remembering Kristen's indecipherable message. Now her anger threaded through it made sense— we Michaelsons had a touch of Irish fire flowing through our veins.

"Good," I replied to John. "Book it again. And don't change a thing unless you hear directly from me. I don't know what the fuck is going on, but that wasn't us who called you."

"Okay, man. Great to hear."

Yeah. Because pissing off a vendor at the last minute didn't lose only a huge deposit—it threatened our reputation with a reliable supplier.

Kristen texted me again.

> We good?

I took another deep breath, trying to calm the fuck down, and typed a reply.

Yeah. Crisis averted.

But had it been? I didn't believe in coincidence, which is how other people might explain Madison popping into the picture on the same day we got anonymously fucked with. Growing up together, I'd witnessed rare moments of her manipulation. Never thought I'd be at the receiving end of it. But a stunt like this had her MO written all over it and was typically her weird way of getting attention.

Initially, I hadn't planned on responding to Madison. But now it was clear that avoiding her wasn't the answer. Confronting her was.

3. THE BENEFITS OF DISCLOSURE

D inner that night was at my place, like it was every Monday. After a long afternoon of straightening out emails and starting on Loading Zone's second-year business plan, I walked through the front door.

My mouth watered the moment I inhaled. "Oh my God. What is that?"

Hannah texted an hour ago to say she was heading over to make dinner and wanted it to be a surprise instead of the usual, where I played kitchen assistant to her chef. I dropped the keys to my bike in the front entry bowl and followed the scent.

When I stepped into the kitchen, she glanced up from the stove. A smile lit up her face. "How do you feel about bacon bison barbeque burgers?"

I grinned, walking over to her before wrapping my arms around her. "Like I just fell in love with food without ever tasting it."

She leaned up and gave me a soft kiss. "Grab a plate. Mase was just about—"

"—to steal all the damned burgers for himself." My

roommate walked in as he interrupted her. "Jesus Christ, Hannah. Are you *trying* to ruin us for all other food?"

He tried to press in as Hannah transferred the burgers from the grill top to a platter, but I palmed a hand on his bare chest and pushed back. I stared at the shorts barely hanging on his hips, scowling. "Put a shirt on, idiot. Show some respect."

His eyes narrowed, but he glanced at Hannah and nodded before disappearing down the hall.

I dropped my face to her ear. "Sure you still want to come over to cook for these heathens?"

The front door opened and slammed shut, the other heathen arriving. "Holy shit!"

Hannah and I laughed at Ben's shout. She nodded. "I love hanging with the guys. You included."

What a lucky fucker I was. I had a great girl who liked hanging with the guys. A girl who liked *being* one of the guys when the table talk turned...well, guy.

I grabbed the burger platter and brought it to the table already set with four plates, napkins, and silverware. French fries were in four small bowls at the corner of each plate. I set the burgers next to another platter piled high with toasted buns.

Ben barged into the kitchen, took one look at the table, and tackled Hannah into a bear hug. "I think I love you."

Her brows shot up. "Only think?"

Mase returned with a faded T-shirt on. "He knows he loves you. But Cade'll beat the shit out of him if he comes on too strong."

I shrugged as I opened the refrigerator. "True." I slid beer bottles between the fingers of each hand and brought four of them to the table.

Manners were lost as everyone sat and it became a free-for-all. We grabbed buns, forked burgers onto them, and loaded up with mustard, tomatoes, lettuce, and onions.

Hannah nudged me with her elbow. "I can break away for camping Wednesday."

I grinned. "Nice. I'll check with Kristen, but that should be doable. Ben, can you cover for me at the bar?"

He gave a brief nod as he stuffed a handful of fries into his mouth.

Mase whined. "Who'll feed us?"

I shot him a warning glare. "Fend for yourself. Oh, we'll need to borrow your gear."

He gave a tired sigh. "Fine. Pizza it is. And no problem."

Conversation stalled the moment we bit into the burgers. I groaned. So did the guys. When I finally came up for air, I gave Hannah a hard look. "Best burger I've ever tasted."

She snorted. "You're so easy. You told me your weakness: bacon."

Ben gave her a matter-of-fact nod as he took a pull from his beer. Then he set it down. "Everything's better with bacon."

Mase raised his bottle high. "A-*the-fuck*-men."

Hannah fought a smile. "So now it's a religious experience?"

He dropped her a deadpan look. "It has been. I've been on my knees ever since you started cooking for us, thanking the kitchen gods. It's like Cade and his contractor made this gourmet kitchen just for you."

"Build it, and she will come," I mumbled.

Hannah shot me a heated glance.

Mase tossed a fry at her. "No. No sexy shit at the table. We have to eat here."

Ben shook his head. "Finish your food, then get the hell out of here. We'll clean up."

They usually did. But as I looked at my half-eaten burger and hers, I'd suddenly lost my appetite for anything but her.

Hannah and I scraped our chairs back at the same time, then I chased her down the hallway. The guys' laughter was muted when I slammed my bedroom door shut.

She spun around, her chest heaving. The tiny purple T-shirt clung to her breasts with every sharp inhale. Her cheeks were pinked, eyes glinted with amusement.

But instead of jumping onto my bed like usual, she stood her ground between my desk and bed, waiting for me to make the first move. After our first time together last night, my bed suddenly had a greater purpose than our usual post-dinner studying.

I took a deep breath. "Before we do anything, we need to talk first."

Her expression fell.

"No, it's good. Well, not exactly 'good.' But it's me not keeping things from you. I have to tell you what happened today."

With that disclosure, she nodded and sat on the edge of the bed.

I sat in my desk chair and updated her on the malicious phone call, the resulting cancellation email, and my suspicions. "I plan to call Madison back. Agree to meet with her."

Hannah's expression remained steady, attentive. "How do you feel about that?"

"Irritated. Pissed. Determined. But oddly, relieved to get it over with. If she wants to meet me—whether or not she had anything to do with canceling our order—I'll see what she wants. I hate getting a tetanus shot too, but it's a necessary evil."

She nodded but said nothing.

Worried about the whole disclose-everything idea, I frowned. "How do *you* feel about it?"

On a heavy sigh, she crossed her arms. "You meeting *Madison*? I don't like it at all. You've been through hell with her. But I see why you feel you need to meet with her. Being informed is better than being left in the dark." She shrugged one shoulder.

Yeah, she didn't need to connect the dots for me. I got off the chair and knelt in front of her. "Hey. Don't worry about me. I'll be careful, Maestro. She's only a nuisance. But she won't be for long." *I sure as fuck hoped.* "Now, enough talk about what irritates both of us. Let's shift the mood in here."

"Oh?" She tilted her head. "What mood are you going for?"

I worked my way in between her knees, then pushed up, forcing her back on the bed. "Bad. My mood is getting very bad."

She collapsed back onto the center of the bed, her dark hair fanning around her head. "How bad?" On a deep inhale, she tugged her lower lip into her mouth with her teeth.

I growled and dipped down, sucking her lip into my mouth. Then I slanted my head, kissing her hard. By the time I pulled away, she'd gone breathless. Her lips were red. Her eyes sparked with lust. "Hannah. I'm going to strip you naked and flip you into every position I've imagined while you innocently studied on my bed."

She sucked in a sharp breath. "Which positions?"

I shook my head. "No. No itinerary." Taking a deep breath, I pulled back and stood. I grabbed the front of my T-shirt and yanked it over my head. In the next few seconds, I popped open the buttons of my fly and shoved off my jeans.

Hannah swept her gaze from my face, down my chest, to

the erection jutting out toward her. "Beautiful," she whispered.

Primal. Blood thundered in my ears as I lunged forward.

Her jaw dropped open as I stripped off her shorts and thong together. I crouched over her, reached behind her back, and unclasped her bra with the flick of a finger and thumb. Then I clutched her top and bra and ripped them over her head before tossing them across the room.

Eyes wide, she swallowed hard and scooted, rotating into a missionary position, head toward the pillows. I gripped her hips, flipped her over, and tugged her down.

She gasped, face on the comforter, arms spread wide. But her hands clutched the fabric. And when I spread my palm across her ass cheek with a light touch, she let out a soft moan.

Oh yeah. The anticipation amped her up. "You like this, Maestro?"

A quick nod of her head.

"What about this?" I smacked her ass.

She sucked in a sharp breath, but that was it—no answer.

It wasn't a no. So I slapped her skin again, this time the other cheek, harder.

The response I got was a groan as she exhaled.

I smiled, rubbing skin that pinked right before my eyes. "You trust me, don't you?"

"Yes, Cade. I trust you."

Stretching my body over hers, I pressed a gentle kiss to her shoulder blade. "Good. Then trust me to make you feel good."

For the first time in my bedroom, I didn't need to reach for the condoms in my nightstand. We'd already established she was on birth control, and we'd both been safe (or in her case, infrequent) with our sexual encounters.

I moved to the side and dragged my fingertips down her back before gently palming over her ass cheeks, one, then the other. The entire time, I gauged her reactions—when she took a deep breath, how long she exhaled. My fingers trailed lower, between her thighs, up into her cleft that had already become wet. Her responses grew hotter: gasps every time I surprised her with a touch to her clit, a fingertip pressing inside, lightly lifting; low moans on each exhale as I pressed and rubbed, finding out what she liked, how she needed it.

I took my time. Pulled her to the brink. Balanced her there before shifting my touch. And as my teasing dragged on, her soft cries and moans grew louder.

I stopped, resting my fingertip on her clit, another finger pausing its strokes inside of her. "Careful, Maestro. I'll give you what you need, but unless you want the guys to have a ringside seat, you'll need to keep it down."

She nodded and pulled the corner of a pillow toward her face. Then she squirmed her hips.

"Ah, ah, ah. No grinding. *I* take you there." Once she stilled, I began circling and stroking, slow, steady. With every muffled cry and moan, I brought her to the brink again, then kept her there. Teasing. Taunting.

She dragged out a low moan into the pillow, then turned her head to the side and whispered, "Please, Cade. Please."

Her begging undid me. I slid my finger deeper and stroked her harder, faster.

Her breath caught. Her muscles tensed. She pressed her head down into the pillow.

The second I felt her first hard pulse, I moved between her legs, spreading her thighs wider with my knees. I pressed my tip to her entrance, slid further, over her clit, then pulled back and slowly plunged deep.

She screamed into the pillow as her orgasm continued around me.

Fully seated, pulsing heat wrapped around me, I sucked in a shaky breath. Then I pulled back and thrust forward, hard and slow, taking my time, extending her pleasure. Soon the ache grew too intense for me to hold back any longer. I leaned back and lifted up onto my knees, grabbing her hips as I pulled her ass up against me. She buried her face into the comforter, muffling her loud moans. Her arms extended straight forward and clutched the corners of the pillows.

Gripping her hips, I pushed them forward and pulled them back, crashing her body into mine with every hard thrust. Then on a sharp inhale, I drove deep and paused, balls pressed against her. I dropped my mouth to her back, muffling the harsh growl that tore through my throat as I came hard inside her.

In slow motion, I collapsed onto her, bracing my weight with my arms and legs, trying to catch my breath. I pressed a kiss to her shoulder again, then gathered her in my arms as I rolled us to the side, still connected. I shifted slightly inside her, and she moaned low.

Our breaths were the only sounds left, slowing, deepening. My mind spun with the incredible experience it was to be with Hannah.

She blew out a slow breath. "Wow."

I grinned, lips pressed into the crook of her neck, grateful she trusted me to take her there.

4. LIKE A TETANUS SHOT

Wednesday morning, I went to my favorite coffeehouse. Madison knew the one. But it was my turf, a place I was comfortable. I spotted her in line.

She hadn't changed a bit. Tall. Blonde. Fit. High-dollar clothes, not off the rack.

Not wanting to startle her, I swung wide and carefully stepped into her line of sight, as if she were an animal in the wild.

Her eyes brightened when she saw me.

I sighed, ready to get the damned meeting behind me. Nodding over to the empty tables by the window, I said, "Go grab us a seat. I'll get this."

She smiled. "Sure. I'll have a skinny caramel macchiato."

When she left and the line moved, I turned to the barista. "One skinny caramel macchiato. One quad espresso." Fitting. Two drinks diametrically opposed. *What the hell did I ever see in her?*

I brought our drinks to the table and slid hers in front of her before taking a seat.

She pulled the top off hers, then swiped her tongue through the whipped cream, never taking her gaze off me.

I leaned back and crossed my arms, unimpressed. "Thought you were in Europe. How long have you been back?"

She shrugged. "I got bored over there. I've been back a little while. Saw a picture of you at Dwight Cavanaugh's party in the paper."

Invitation Only publicity. It had brought out Hannah's ex a few months ago. Guess I shouldn't have been surprised that Madison resurfaced. I gave her a nod, waiting.

"Look, Cade, I know things ended horribly for us. I get why you're tense right now."

"Tense isn't even close to what I'm feeling."

She sighed. "I know. I screwed up. I didn't appreciate you like I should have."

Another understatement. "No. Apparently you were too busy appreciating many others."

"I'm here to apologize. I'm sorry."

"For which part?"

"All of it. Not being faithful. Rejecting you. Hurting you." Her gaze dropped down to the tabletop while she took a deep breath. "I know this is no excuse, and it's coming very late, but I found out I have a problem. Well, *had* a problem."

Unused to Madison being humble under any circumstances, I waited.

"I—" Her voice lowered, and she leaned forward as she met my gaze. "I am a recovering sex addict."

Holy shit. I blinked. Not what I'd expected her to say. Then again, our relationship had been highly sexual. Speechless, I stared at her.

An awkward silence stretched between us. She glanced down at her coffee, then up at me again. "It got pretty bad in

Europe. Until one of the men I was with insisted I needed help." An unreadable expression flickered across her face.

"And you got help?"

She nodded. "Believe it or not, they have rehab for sex addiction, just like any other addiction. And afterward, there are support meetings, similar to Alcoholics Anonymous."

Wow. I didn't even know what to say to that. My mind spun. So she only cared about her next "fix" when she cheated on me? Couldn't help herself?

I had to focus to get back on point. There was a reason I'd agreed to meet with her. Two of them, actually. "What do you want from me?"

"I just needed to apologize to you; it's part of my recovery. You don't have to accept it." The corner of her mouth tugged up then fell, her expression sad. When she glanced up at me, she looked hopeful.

Fuck. I sighed. I wasn't cruel. "I'll accept your apology, Madison." Didn't mean I had to like her. Or suddenly become friends with her.

Or forget.

"Thank you." Her tone was genuinely vulnerable, a first from her.

I took a swallow of my warm espresso while I carefully considered my next words, struggling with how to broach the other reason I'd agree to meet her. I didn't want to shut her down after she'd been so open. Like I'd approached her in line earlier, I swung wide first. "What have you been doing since you've returned? Are you working?"

Her expression lightened. "Yes. I've recently been hired at a country club. Not ours. One across town."

I took the small opening and leaned forward, staring at her. "Madison, I have to ask this: You called me out of the blue the same day someone messed with our company. Did you have anything to do with that?"

Her brows drew together. "Cade, I want to be friends with you again. I want things between us to be better— maybe even great. Why would I do that?"

Good question. (I had no idea.) The woman sitting in front of me only physically resembled the Madison I remembered. Everything out of her mouth surprised me.

"I don't know." I didn't have another ready suspect. Hell, I hadn't even let Madison off the hook, but I didn't have proof. Only gut instinct and suspicion.

She nodded. "So will you?"

"Will I what?"

"Will you be friends with me again? We grew up together. We know so much about each other. It seems such a waste to let all that go."

Confused, my expression hardened. My mind warred with the memories of Madison in the past and the person sitting in front of me. Which one was she offering?

I blew out a breath, forcing myself to relax. I didn't have to do shit. I did what I came here to do.

"I don't know, Madison. I don't know what you mean by 'better' or 'great.' To be honest, I'm having a hard time picturing us as friends. And just so you know, I have a girl- friend. If that's where you're going with this, it won't work."

She swallowed hard, unfazed. "I do understand. Please think about it. I wasn't rotten to only you but to a lot of people. I don't have many friends. I'm trying to make new ones. Having you as a friend would mean a lot. You're one of my oldest."

Dammit. Her plea tugged at my heart and it pissed me the fuck off. "I'll think about it. It's all I can promise." I stood from the table. "I need to go." I would've told her it was great seeing her again, but it wasn't.

She nodded. "Thank you for meeting me."

"You're welcome." I left before she decided she needed a hug or some other crazy shit. She'd rattled me enough as it was.

———

WE'D STOPPED at the grocery store for a few last-minute items, then hit the road in my Jeep, heading out to the campground. Hannah kept bouncing and fidgeting, full of nervous energy. Yet every time I took my eyes off the road and glanced at her, she beamed one of her megawatt smiles.

"Excited?" Yeah, I know. Master of the obvious.

She nodded. "Totally. Will we go for a hike? Will there be elk? Do they have different pine trees than in the city?"

I laughed. "We can do whatever you want to do. And I don't know. Guess we'll find out."

A short time into our drive, Hannah finally settled into her seat and gazed out the side window at the passing rural scenery.

"So how did the meeting with Madison go?"

Good question.

I still hadn't figured that shit out. "Weird." My tone dropped, heavy.

She angled her upper body toward me, tilting her head. "Weird how?"

I let out a sigh. "She was humble, apologetic. I don't ever remember her being so...vulnerable. I'm not sure what I'd expected, but it wasn't that."

"Apologetic? Did she admit to making the phone call to the vendor?" Hannah wrapped her hand around the chrome gearshift and looked down, running her thumbnail along the diagram grooves in the top.

I shook my head. "No. She wanted to make amends. She apologized for hurting me. Said she'd been to rehab and therapy. Asked if we could be friends."

"Rehab and therapy for what?" Hannah's tone was neutral, inquisitive.

Warning bells went off inside my head. I hadn't played out how the discussion with Hannah might go—how much I needed to share to remain honest—but I suddenly wished I'd given more thought to it. This couldn't possibly go well.

"Sexual addiction." It's always best to just rip off the Band-Aid, right?

Silence.

I glanced at her.

Her brows were deeply furrowed. "She had a sexual addiction?"

I shrugged. "Apparently. Although, it's news to me."

"Because you didn't have a lot of sex?"

Fuck. In what universe could this ever go well? My jaw clenched. "No, we had sex."

"A lot?"

"A normal amount." There. Safe, and true. But looking back, if I was honest, it was a little wild and desperate most of the time. "But remember, she was cheating on me. And I didn't ask for the details. Didn't want them. Still don't."

Hannah straightened back in her seat, facing forward. "Sooo...she couldn't help it? That's her reason why?"

"That's what she said."

"Do you believe her?"

I snorted. "Hell, I don't know what to believe. That woman had me believing I was in love with her. That I wanted to marry her. And all the while she had a sexual addiction and was sleeping around to scratch her uncontrollable itch. I grew up with Madison. We were kids who all played on the same playground together. She's always been strong, assertive, independent. She's strived to be the best, to win. Never once, in all the years I've known her, has she admitted to having a fault. Or apologized."

"Sounds a lot like you, the strong, assertive part."

"Yeah. We were similar in our personalities. Determined, fearless, driven. Gunning to succeed. We were longtime friends, and our lives were compatible in so many ways. Only I had no clue hers came with a closet full of guys."

"I'm nothing like that." Her voice had dropped low.

I gave her a hard look until she glanced up at me. Reaching over, I grasped her hand. "You are driven to be successful in a creative way, which I love. Everything you are draws me toward you. You're a gorgeous, petite ball of fire who brightens a room the moment you walk in."

She gave me another one of those smiles, then leaned over the console, as far as the seatbelt would allow, and kissed my ear, lingering there for a moment with her lips. "Thank you. You want to know what makes me brighten when I walk into a room?"

"What?"

"You're there."

I let out a slow breath. "Ditto, Maestro."

She settled back onto her seat. "What about the phone call and the order cancellation? You thought it was her, didn't you? Did she admit to it?"

"No. Madison hadn't outright denied it. She'd only questioned why she'd do it. But I'm still not convinced it isn't her." And the woman who'd been sitting at the coffeehouse wasn't the Madison I remembered, so she was tough to gauge. "I was a terrible read of her before—sure as hell fooled me. It's hard to tell if she's doing it again."

Hannah stretched her arms back, clutching her headrest with her hands. "Could it be anyone else? Does anyone else have it out for you? Or Kristen? Someone who would want to hurt your reputations?"

I hadn't a clue. Kristen didn't have any enemies that I was aware of. Then I remembered something. "There might be a woman or two who got upset with me over my casual-sex attitude before you."

"What? I thought you said you were only with women who were on the same page as you—no strings attached."

"Yeah, I did. But right before we became involved, one of those women, Carmen, had a change of heart. Turned out seeing her name on the list of nine didn't go over very well." Looking back, it wasn't the smartest move keeping my fuck buddies' names and numbers on a yellow sticky note, but after Madison had dumped me, my need for detachment had overruled logic.

"Ouch."

"Yeah. Wasn't pretty. But in the end, she knew the score. They all had." And they'd all existed to help me deal with my unexpected breakup with Madison. No matter how cold she'd been when we'd ended it, I'd been invested. My heart had shattered.

But now I had Hannah. The woman who'd healed my heart.

She pulled her travel mug out of the cup holder and took a sip of her coffee. "So are you going to be friends with her?"

I gripped the steering wheel, then relaxed my hands, rolling my shoulders back. "I don't know. She was reaching out to me, saying she didn't have many friends because of how many people she had hurt—*that* I believe. But, if she's being honest, and I was in her shoes, I'd want a second chance. Maybe she really is trying to be a better person. I'd feel like a total dick if I didn't at least try to give her the benefit of the doubt." I swallowed hard, then glanced at Hannah. "What do you think?"

She shook her head. "I don't know her at all, so it's hard for me to give you advice about it."

"For the last hour, since I left the coffeehouse, I've been doing my best to see the good in her. She made the difficult attempt at contacting me and putting herself out there. I figure I could at least acknowledge that maybe she's changed, or is at least trying to be better."

Hannah blew out a hard breath, setting her mug back in the cup holder. "You're a bigger person than I am. If my ex approached me, giving me excuses for why he betrayed me that made me question my ability to trust in myself and others, I'm not sure I'd be able to forgive him."

I gave out a dry laugh. "I'm not sure I'm able to forgive her. Sure as fuck won't forget what she did."

Silence stretched between us for the next mile. I glanced at her. "You okay?"

She gave me a nod, then shrugged. "I don't know. I'm not sure if I like the idea of you and her being around each other. You were intimate with her. Wanted to marry her."

That was the struggle inside my head too. When Madison had dumped me, I couldn't sort out how a woman I thought I was in love with could be so cruel. Then after two years of being emotionally numb, I met Hannah, and none of it mattered. But the Madison I'd meet for coffee sent my emotions and mind back into a tailspin, and I didn't know what to think about her.

I clasped my hand with Hannah's, then brought our

hands to my mouth and kissed her knuckles. "Don't worry. I haven't decided if I want any contact with her. Giving her the benefit of the doubt doesn't mean we have to be friends, or that I want that even if we could."

She squeezed my hand. "Okay, good. Just...please be careful. Women can be manipulative. What if she decides she wants you back? I've just gotten you. I'd like to keep you."

Madison had said she wanted things "better" between us. Then she'd said, "maybe even great" with a hopeful tone. In retrospect, hidden meaning had likely been layered beneath her innocent words. But I wasn't about to tell Hannah that and worry her. And none of it mattered, anyway. "Not gonna happen, Maestro. You have me. And I'm not going anywhere."

"Good."

"Now no more talk about exes. Or the real world. We're camping. The only topics allowed are wilderness and all things related to roughin' it."

5. ROUGHIN' IT

I pounded the last stake into the ground with the end of the folding shovel, satisfied that if gale-force winds decided to wipe Mase's flimsy tent off the face of the earth, Hannah and I would have a fighting chance. Gray clouds hung in the sky to the west, but enormous pines ringing the campsite stretched toward a clear darkening sky above us. I stared up, hoping the stars would be as brilliant out here as I'd heard.

"Are you done with the macho He-Man stuff yet? You're missing it!" she called out from behind me.

"Coming." I chuckled to myself. Well, no one was coming yet. But soon. And often. I dusted my hands off, heading toward the crackling fire we'd started twenty minutes ago.

The moment I caught sight of her, I stopped. She took my breath away.

I watched her as she sat on a log bench crafted either by the campground hosts or some former guest who'd wanted a better place to park their ass than a nearby rock or boulder. Her hair was bound up in a high ponytail, the ends of which she didn't quite pull through, leaving spiky pieces poking in every direction.

Two barbeque forks were perched through her arms, the long wooden handles tucked at her sides, their two-foot shafts extended along her forearms and cradled in her upturned hands. Stuck onto the prongs of the one on the left were two hot dogs, well-done to the point of almost burnt. On the right, two pierced marshmallows, held further away from the flames. Her brows were drawn together in concentration. The glow from the fire cast alternating light and shadow over her face.

When I took another step, a twig snapped, and she glanced up. A carefree smile lit up her face, and in that instant, I knew we'd made a wise decision to ditch every-thing for a couple of days to hang out together.

My gaze dropped to the charred science experiment in progress. "What exactly am I missing?"

"Setting them on fire!" She handed me the double marshmallow fork. The hot dogs also got a reprieve from their barbeque torture when she balanced their spit on the other end of the log bench.

She patted the flat section of wood beside her, and I took a cautious seat, worried about her unadulterated excitement near open flame. She dug her hand into the plastic marsh-mallow bag and speared two more fluffy white victims onto the end of a fresh fork. "When I was a kid, Granpop roasted marshmallows with me. His health didn't allow him to take me camping, so we sat in the kitchen and held them over the gas burners on the stove."

My marshmallows were lightly toasted on both sides, so I held mine back and watched her balance the long fork into the cradle of her arm again. "And you like to set them on fire?"

The multitasking chef extraordinaire grabbed the fork from the other end of the bench and took a large bite off one of the blackened hot dogs, then passed it to me while she chewed. "I did it accidentally the first time. Watched the entire thing as it was engulfed in orange flame. Beautiful, really."

Tearing a gaze away from the questionable hot dogs to glance at her, I snorted. "Pyro."

Ignoring my harassment, she smiled, staring into the flames. "You have to time it just right. Blow it out before it loses shape. C'mon, it's fun. Stick yours in by mine."

Not opposed to sticking anything in by her, I did as she asked, holding my marshmallows next to hers, which had begun to brown like mine.

She stared at the hot dogs I held, then glanced at me, arching a brow. "They won't bite back."

"Yeah, 'cause you killed 'em."

Her shoulders shook with silent laughter. "Try it."

Throwing caution to the wind, I took a bite of the burnt-to-a-crisp meat, figuring she cooked for me most nights and hadn't killed me yet. The initial crunch was alarming but not entirely repulsive. The tough consistency was... interesting.

I chewed. I swallowed. Then I handed the fork back to her. "I'm good."

Laughing, she nudged my shoulder. "Aw, it couldn't have been all that bad."

"You singed the fat right out of it. That's where the taste is. I'm shocked at you, Maestro. Who are you, and what have you done with Hannah?"

"She's gone camping!" She grinned.

I bent down, kissing her temple. "Have I told you lately that I love you?"

She leaned into me, humming her approval. "No. And I'll never tire of hearing it."

When silence followed, I arched my brows. "Do you love me a little too?"

"Nope." She shook her head slowly and looked at me. "I love you immensely."

I grinned, satisfied and happy as fuck we were alone—with only the two of us on our minds—to discover things like Hannah's hidden food-pyro tendencies. With a content sigh, I stared at our toasting marshmallows. "So now what? Do we plunge our forks into the flames in a virgin marshmallow sacrifice ritual?"

Her eyes gleamed. "Nope. We edge them closer, holding them into the heat and away from the flames. The key is to get them to their smoke point and then watch them burst into flames."

I huffed out a laugh, shaking my head. "Woman, you never cease to fascinate me."

And so, safe in our campsite in the middle of the Pocono Mountains, beside the only person in the world I wanted to be with, we watched our poor innocent marshmallows give up tendrils of smoke in surrender right before they burst into flames.

The orange glow consumed the entire surface for a few seconds before Hannah leaned forward. "Now! Blow it out."

Thoroughly intrigued, I did as commanded, resulting in two blackened crisps on the ends of my fork. She continued to blow on hers, and I did the same, but my gaze was locked onto those luscious lips as they puckered with a little hole in the center.

My dick twitched at the incredible image, my mind helplessly guttering. Yeah, I imagined sliding serious wood in there before the night was over. (I'm a guy; we go there. Not gonna feel guilty about it.)

Her fingertips tapped the crisp surface to test its heat. Nodding, she pulled the burnt blob off the end and popped it into her mouth. She moaned as her eyes rolled back.

I sighed, glancing at my unappetizing mess, then back at her. "That good, huh?"

She nodded, moving her jaw around as she mashed it in her closed mouth.

I took a fortifying breath. "Okay, here goes nothing." I plucked one torched lump off of my fork and tossed it whole into my mouth. I lifted my brows, enjoying the surprising flavor before swallowing. It was good in an odd way. "Not bad. *Much* better than burnt hot dog."

Her easy laugh rang out. "There's something about the burnt part that makes all that sickeningly sweet palatable. It's the only way I'll ever eat a marshmallow. Totally hate Peeps." She scrunched her nose and pulled her head back, shaking it.

I snorted. "Got it. No Peeps in the Easter basket."

Our camping had been intended as something fun and intimate, which it was. But I'd never expected all the little things I'd learn about her.

She leaned over to the cooler and flipped up the lid. "Want a beer?"

"Absolutely. Beer goes with everything. Even burnt marshmallow."

She handed me two Fat Tires and a bottle opener.

I glanced beyond her at the grocery bag sitting next to the cooler. "What else you got there?" I popped the last ash-covered marshmallow into my mouth.

Crinkling followed as she leaned over, digging in the bag, then pulled out a package of Double Stuf Oreos.

I raised my arms out. "Of course. We're hitting all the major junk food groups."

She held up the sad excuse for hot dogs. "Protein."

I pointed at her remaining marshmallow. "Fruit."

Tilting her head, she stared at it. "It's a root that grows in the ground. We'll allow it."

"Carb." I nodded to the Oreos.

She snorted. "'Carb' is not a food group. We can call Oreos a grain." She paused. "And veggie. We got it covered."

I coughed. "Wait. What's the veggie?"

"Your beer."

I shook my head. "It's made with hops, Maestro. *That's* a grain."

She scowled. "Close enough."

After a minute of staring into the flames, she leaned far back. "Damn. That fire's getting hot. It's gonna melt the soles of my tennis shoes."

It *was* getting hot. I leaned back too. Her sudden movement caught my eye, and I blinked as Hannah tugged her shirt over her head. "What are you doing?"

Turning my way, she stood, a wicked smile curving her lips as she took careful steps backward. "I'm getting undressed. What does it look like I'm doing?" She pulled the hair tie from her head, sending the ends of her hair down to just above her black-lace-covered breasts.

"Shit!" I jumped up from the log but stood there, unmoving, torn between stalking her down and putting out the blaze we'd created with plenty of firewood. Protective instincts won out (which I hoped to be thoroughly rewarded for), and I rushed over to the small folding shovel, then scooped dirt onto the fire.

"Be right there." I glanced over my shoulder right as

something lacy flew out of the tent opening. My nostrils flared as I imagined all the skin being bared in my absence. "Feel free to start without me."

"Oh, I am..."

I shoveled faster, images of Hannah naked in the wilderness, pleasuring herself, motivating me. I didn't know where the hell the water was, so I dumped the rest of my beer over it to completely douse the flames. At the last second, I grabbed the groceries, threw them into the cooler, and stowed it all into the Jeep.

Charging toward the tent entrance, I tore my shirt over my head, unbuckled my belt, and ripped open the button fly of my jeans. In the darkness, with only a partial moon lighting the night, I barely made out her shape lying on the sleeping bag.

Her legs were spread wide, her lustful gaze tracking me. Dark waves of hair tumbled down her shoulder, curled ends brushing above her peaked nipples.

Fuck.

I swallowed hard as I stepped into the tent, chest heaving as I watched her drag lazy fingers between her breasts.

Perfection.

Mine.

Hours. For what seemed like hours, I buried myself into everything Hannah offered me—her talented mouth, her welcoming body. And the more she gave, the more I wanted.

By the time she'd hit multiple orgasms and I'd had my first, we collapsed onto the sleeping bag, panting, covered in sweat. She exhaled, blowing out a hard breath from between pursed lips. "Wow."

"Exactly."

Nestling into my side, she draped a hand over my chest. "I love camping."

"Best camping trip ever."

A lazy silence followed as our breaths slowed. She threaded her fingers into mine, a perfect calmness surrounding us. "Do you ever wonder what they thought of us?"

Confused, I tipped my head toward her in the darkness. "Who?"

"Our exes."

"Oh, no. No exes here tonight."

"But I'm not really bringing them here. I'm actually talking about us. How to make us better. Like was there something we did, or didn't do, to make the relationships crash?"

I shrugged. "I haven't thought about it in a long time."

She pressed closer, resting her head on my shoulder. "A relationship isn't one person; it's a couple. The failure couldn't have been all their fault."

"Sure as hell is easier to blame them. But there are two sides to every story."

She nodded against me. "With the truth somewhere in the middle."

Intrigued that we could talk about our experiences with our exes in an analytical way after such incredible sex and be calm about it, I nudged my knee against hers. "You've given a lot of thought to this?"

"No. Only in the last few days. If I made mistakes in my only other serious relationship, I don't want to repeat them with you."

I stared up at the tent roof, thinking. "I suppose with mine, I coasted too much. Once we were together, I let the relationship run on autopilot. If there was a lesson I learned from the whole disaster, that would be it. With you, I want to be better. Invest time into us. Never take us for granted."

She tightened her hold on my hand. "Me too. The investing in us part." She paused, then her voice lowered. "Before, I think I didn't invest enough in myself outside of the relationship. Too much revolved around him. But now, things are different. I have my bakery, new friends. The more I have in my life, the more I bring to our relationship."

I pulled her hand up and kissed her forearm. "You're perfect. You bring plenty to our relationship."

She squeezed my hand, then our arms settled back onto my chest. We grew quiet, listening to the chirps of crickets outside. We'd banned talk of our exes on our camping trip, but traveling forward sometimes meant looking back. I hoped we both learned enough from the failure of our previous relationships to make ours succeed.

After a few minutes, she took a deep breath, then let out a long sigh. "I have to pee."

I huffed out a laugh as she broke away, stood, and rummaged through our discarded clothing. "There's a whole forest of 'pee' spots to choose from." I reached over to the corner of the tent, grabbed the new roll of toilet paper we'd brought, and handed it to her. "Want me to stand guard?"

She scowled before tugging my black T-shirt over her head. "While I pee?"

"What if a bear decides your pert little ass looks tasty? He wouldn't be wrong. It is." I snapped my teeth.

"Pffft. What makes you think it's not a girl bear wanting to take a bite?"

I sat up, grabbed my jeans, and pulled them on. "Oh, do you swing that way too?"

She shoved my shoulder, knocking me back down to the sleeping bag.

"Hey, just checking, little miss wild one. I need to learn your boundaries."

Shirtless but ecstatic about it, since my T-shirt was the only clothing she wore besides her socks and tennis shoes, I stood and grabbed the flashlight before following her out. She went downhill a few paces from our tent, heading toward an old-growth pine as I shined the beam of light at her legs.

I sighed, happy as fuck. A man could get spoiled with a woman like Hannah. Best friend turned lover, and becoming so much more. Who would've thought the woman I'd originally labeled an Ice Queen was sexually adventurous? I never would've guessed in a million years.

She faced me, squatted, and stuck her ass out in the opposite direction, pointing downhill. Smart.

A faint splattering sound followed seconds later. She sighed. "I can't believe I'm letting you watch me pee."

I crossed my arms, holding the light just away from directly blinding her. "Hey, I've watched you do all kinds of things. Peeing is a fact of life. I'm only here to protect you."

She lifted her brows. "From bears."

"Exactly." I scanned the darkness but saw no movement and heard no unusual noises.

"Only *male* bears, by the way," she said, her tone absolute. "I *don't* swing the other way."

I glanced back at her and nodded, unsurprised. As time went by, the more I realized we had core beliefs in common. When having sex, we didn't like to share, or get distracted. "Got it. No marshmallow Peeps, and no mama bears."

"I am, however, willing to try honey, caramel, and chocolate sauce…"

I grinned. I'd been teasing her for months about the creative use of condiments. It was good to know she still had them on her mind.

"Of course you are." My lips twisted into a smirk.

6. LIMITS ON INSANITY

"Hey, Daniel."

I nodded my chin toward Hannah's employee before taking a seat on the couch in Sweet Dreams, Hannah's cake and cupcake shop. It'd been two days since we'd returned from camping, and I hadn't seen her since.

She'd been slammed at her bakery, and I respected that she had a life outside of me, but texts and phone calls hadn't cut it. I missed the fuck out of her. Which was why I'd offered to pick her up for the meeting with my sisters.

Daniel gave me a chin up back. "Cade. Good to see you. I'll let Hannah know you're here."

I smirked. *She already knows.* I'd sent her a teasing text the moment I'd parked my motorcycle.

To calm the nervous energy I felt, I fired up my tablet. I was about ten minutes early, which was my OCD norm. And I hadn't checked emails since yesterday. Today I'd finally sketched out a finished backyard with Mase while Ava, our German Shepherd pup ("our" being Hannah's and mine, although Mase was essentially Ava's master and keeper), ran back and forth with a ball, demonstrating a need for grass and better fencing.

There were fourteen emails. Most were standard communications from Invitation Only's vendors, but three were from Kristen. With urgent subject lines, shouted in all caps.

I frowned and pulled out my phone. Had I missed texts from her? I clicked the thing on and then off, verifying I hadn't.

With limited time, and since Hannah and I were heading to Kristen's place anyway, I opened the most recent one entitled "NEVER MIND" to be sure she still didn't need me to call or text right away.

All the email said was:

Never mind. Crisis averted.

Feeling an acute hit of déjà vu, I checked the other emails from Kristen.

The first was a rant about how our florist had screwed up an order for an upcoming wedding vow renewal that Invitation Only had been planning for months. She was pissed as hell to have to deal with the client's disappointment.

The second outlined how she had argued with the florist for over an hour. They insisted Kristen had called and substituted the flowers. She swore to them it never happened—and by swore, she meant she politely but vehemently asserted. But by the time her anger reached my email, she colored it with every four-letter variety known to man, along with a few patented Michaelson creations.

On a scowl, I scanned my brain for who could be

messing with us, and it stopped at the same name it had before: Madison. But "reformed" Madison didn't fit the mold. She'd been right—if she wanted to make amends, it made no sense to screw with me. I pulled up and read again the text she sent a few hours after we met for coffee:

> Thank you for meeting me. It was great to see you again.

Yep. Nothing adversarial about that.

Searching further, I remembered Carmen's anger when she'd stormed out of my house months ago. She'd been happy to be one of my many fuck buddies—until she hadn't been.

My thoughts came up with a big fat zero as to another culprit. Then they gravitated back toward Madison. How vulnerable she'd seemed at the coffeehouse. And how very incongruent that was to everything I'd ever known about her. Of her.

"Sorry I'm late. You okay?"

I glanced up.

Hannah stood in front of me, looking incredible. Dark hair loose around her shoulders. Hazel eyes shining bright green in the late morning light.

I exhaled a slow breath. "Yeah, sorry." I turned my tablet off, shoved it into my messenger bag, and stood. "Trying the figure out what the hell is happening. Kristen emailed about another bizarre screw-up by an Invitation Only vendor."

Concern darkened her expression as she stepped toward me.

I wrapped my arms around her and buried my face into her hair, inhaling her calming scent. "Damn, I've missed you."

When I made no move to let her go, she squeezed me tighter and lifted her face, pressing a kiss to my neck. "Missed you too. Bad. Sorry things have been so busy here."

On a sigh, I bent down and kissed her hard. Then I slowed the pace, savoring her soft sweetness, licking and sucking. With my lips, I nipped her lower one, tugging it as I pulled away. I rested my forehead on hers as I caught my breath. "No. Don't ever apologize for your business being successful. We'll work around the schedule."

She nodded. "Anything I can do to help with the Invitation Only issues?"

"Yeah. Let's get over to Kristen's. It's time for a family meeting at our business meeting."

By the time we stepped into Kristen's living room almost twenty minutes later, I'd pulled apart the puzzle and pieced it together a dozen different ways, but still, nothing fit. Kristen already sat on the far end of the couch, beer in hand with a backup on the table beside her.

Kendall, who was older than me by two years, yet the youngest of my three sisters, shut the fridge. On her way back to her usual spot on the floor, she gave Hannah and me each a chilled Fat Tire. "Tread carefully." She jerked a nod toward Kristen. "She's in rare form tonight."

Kiki popped up from my favorite worn spot on the couch and tugged Hannah away from me, pulling her into a big hug. "Hannah! I've missed you. We need to hang. Get some girl time in again."

I ruffled the top of Kiki's head. "Gee, thanks, sis. Missed you too."

"Pffft. You know I always miss you, Cade. That's a given. There's no one worthy to harass when you're not around." She kissed my cheek, then gave a pointed look toward Kristen, who seemed to be taking a deep breath in between every healthy swallow of beer.

I blinked. Kiki and Kendall not giving me shit? The carefully orchestrated calmness by those two underscored Kendall's warning. Kristen really *was* pissed the fuck off.

Clearly, we were in need of some strategic analysis.

"Okay." I took a seat on my corner of the couch while Kiki dragged Hannah over to a couple of throw pillows on the floor. "The wedding-vow-renewal thing. Tell me what happened with this florist."

Kristen huffed out a breath. "They said I called to replace the same rare orchids Natalie Richards had *on her original wedding day* with white roses. Natalie called me in a meltdown panic when the florist delivered her a beyond-wrong sample bouquet."

"And John, the tent and furniture vendor, said you'd called to outright cancel his order."

"Utter fucking bullshit." She growled in frustration.

"I know, sis. Just bear with me. I've been trying to figure this out. Is there anyone angry with you?"

Kristen polished off her beer and put it on the table before grabbing her backup bottle. "Not that I know of."

"What about the rest of you? It could be anyone trying to hurt any of us. Maybe Kristen seemed easiest to impersonate."

They all shook their heads.

I took a couple swallows of beer as I mulled over the cleanest way to express my suspicion without tainting theirs. "Madison called me out of the blue. The same day the fiasco with John happened."

Kristen's jaw dropped, her expression darkening.

I shook my head. "I'm not sure it's her. It's a long story, but the nuts and bolts of it are that she's back in town, works for a country club, and wants to make amends with those she's hurt. Be a better person, or some shit."

Kiki glanced at Hannah with a concerned expression. But when Hannah didn't even flinch, only watched and nodded to my explanation, Kiki turned toward me. "And you believe her?"

I blew out a hard breath. "Madison's reasoning would negate any motive she'd have to hurt me. But honestly, I'm not sure what to believe."

Kristen gave me a hard look. "What about any other women you've pissed off?"

"Maybe. There's only one I can think of but no obvious connectors yet." I wasn't about to drag my sexual past out into Kristen's living room with my sisters. And definitely not with Hannah. "I'm not excluding any suspects at this point. Neither should any of you. It could be anyone."

Kendall leaned over the coffee table from her spot on the floor and pulled the bowl of tortilla chips closer to her before grabbing a handful. "Might even be competition. What better way to steal our clients than by making us look incompetent?"

Hannah narrowed her eyes. "But how would they do it? I'm sure Kristen doesn't broadcast our plans." Kristen raised her brows and shook her head as Hannah continued. "No one, besides us and our clients, knows which events are scheduled and which vendors we're using."

"Ahhh, but one part of that isn't so hard to figure out." It's what I'd finally realized before we walked in. "The vendors who cater to our caliber of event planning are limited. It wouldn't be that hard for someone trying to fuck with us to call all the higher-end florists pretending to be Kristen, fabricating some excuse to cancel or change our next event. How many party tent and furniture rentals are there in the Greater Philly Area?"

"Not many," Kendall replied. "Maybe a half dozen."

Kiki nodded. "And maybe twice as many florists that are reputable enough to handle the prestigious and large events."

Kristen's expression darkened again, her eyes narrowing. "Whoever the fuck is pretending to be me is twisted."

Kiki groaned. "This is a nightmare. How do we alert our clients that there might be a problem without knowing who is doing this, or when they'll strike next? We can't do that."

"No. We don't want to unnecessarily alarm our clients. Right now, the incidents have been contained. We need to keep it that way until we figure out who's behind this. Before we leave tonight, let's divvy up all the companies we work with. We'll call them to make sure they only change or cancel orders if they've heard from us by our company email."

"And if they ask why?" Kendall arched her brows.

"Let them know someone is messing with our business by changing or canceling orders without our knowledge. Emphasize that if they're contacted in any other way, they are to immediately email us."

Slow exhales sounded out in the room as everyone nodded, ready to play hardball with an unknown enemy. I finished off my beer and got up to grab refreshers.

When I walked back in, Kristen had calmed some. I handed her another bottle first. "Moving on. What's the big event we needed to talk about that couldn't be emailed?" I dropped onto the couch and took a long pull off my fresh beer.

Kristen put hers down onto the table and grabbed her electronic tablet. "A double event. Two bar mitzvahs."

My lungs seized, and I choked, trying to catch my breath. I stared at her like she'd gone insane. "No. No *fucking* way."

"Yes. Yes fucking way." She arched a challenging brow at me. Our pragmatic Kristen was back.

I sighed, irritated I had to state the obvious to make my point. "Are they kids?"

"Well, yes," Kristen admitted.

"Then, no. We unanimously agreed on a 'no kids' rule when we formed Invitation Only."

"They're turning thirteen, and these bar mitzvahs are significant coming-of-age events; they're becoming adults."

Sensing a technicality coming on, I narrowed my eyes. "When, exactly, are they becoming adults?"

Kristen smirked. "Actually, they're turning thirteen midway through the event. Their mom thought it would be special to throw the event during the actual time of their birth."

"How fucking cute." I snarled the words, then downed the rest of my beer. My mood apparently could only handle one topic of bad news at a time. Sabotage *and* kids? There had to be a limit to the level of insanity we had to swallow in one night.

I stared hard at Kristen. "They magically poof into adults halfway through? Fine, we'll throw them half a party." I closed my eyes, willing the madness away. "No. Kids."

"They aren't kids, Cade. They're becoming teenagers— in the Jewish religion, full-fledged adults."

Yep. I knew Kristen would play that angle. "A technicality," I grumbled. "There should be a height requirement."

Kiki snickered, nodding in agreement from the floor.

Goaded on by the encouraging sign of a defiant comrade, I continued. "Like the really crazy roller coaster rides. If you aren't at least forty-eight inches tall, you don't get to climb inside."

"I think it's forty inches on rides," Kristen countered.

Kendall held her phone, typing with one hand while she grabbed another tortilla chip with the other. "Forty-two. Just Googled it."

Kristen rolled her eyes. "Doesn't matter, Cade. Go check the height chart Mom kept. You were well past forty-two inches by the time you were thirteen."

Kiki snorted. "Cade's confusing it with *his* height requirement. Isn't that kinda low for sex bombs on stilettos?"

I glared at Kiki while she tried not to smile. "I thought you were on my side. Traitor. Also Hannah is sitting right next to you. Show some respect."

Kiki nudged Hannah. "Sorry. No offense meant. I'm too used to giving him shit."

Hannah nudged her back. "No biggie."

"Could we *please* change the topic?" Before anyone said another word, I stared hard at Hannah to make sure she was cool.

She smiled, then pursed her lips in an imperceptible kiss. That one action calmed me from twelve feet away. I grinned and winked at her.

Kiki nodded a chin toward Kristen. "Okay, so back to the bar mitzvah."

"Bar mitzvahs," Kristen corrected.

Kendall held her phone up again, flashing the screen toward Kristen, as if she could see it from that distance, let alone read the damn thing. "Technically, it's b'nai mitzvah. That's the plural."

I pinched the bridge of my nose. "Tell me again why it's plural? I missed that detail."

59

Kristen pulled her bottle from her lips. "Twins."

I slumped my shoulders, dropping my chin onto my chest. "*Fuck.*"

"Hey, look at the bright side, Cade. The reason we're doing two is because they've got differences of opinion on the parties they want to throw afterward."

Grabbing one of the chips Kendall had been hoarding, I dipped it into the salsa. "Why is that a bright side for me?"

She smiled. "Because you've got carte blanche on the music."

Narrowing my eyes, I leaned toward her, resting my forearms on my knees. "What's the catch?"

She shrugged but failed to look at me.

"Bullshit. There's a catch. I can smell it. What, is one into AC/DC and the other—"

"Justin Bieber." Kristen tried to hide a smile.

"*Fuck.*"

The sadistic group burst out laughing.

I collapsed back onto the couch. "No. *Fuck* no."

Kendall tossed a chip at me. "You going for a record of most 'fucks' uttered in one sitting?"

"Fuck yes. And fuck no." I groaned. "Not gonna do it."

"Yes, you are." Kristen gave me the classic Michaelson strip-paint-off-a-car glare.

Defiant, I shook my head. "No, I'm not."

"All for one and one for all. That was the deal when we formed the company, Cade." Kristen settled back, her tone low and unyielding. "It's blasphemy to disregard clubhouse code."

I sighed. Of course she had to bring up our sibling pact from childhood, when everything cool was controlled by my three older sisters, and they had the keys to the clubhouse. I was their whipping boy in exchange for an all-access pass—the exception to their "No Boys Allowed" policy.

Still, I couldn't swallow the idea down. Two events at once with teen siblings would be a clusterfuck of epic proportions.

"We said 'no kids.' We have an out." I fell back on my initial argument, grasping at straws.

Kristen glanced at Kendall, then Kiki and Hannah. "You girls with me? You on board with the boys-to-men parties?"

The three all nodded, grinning.

"We're overruling the technicality." Kristen held my gaze, unwavering. "The kids become adults during the event. Think of the publicity this unique dual event would bring. We can't pass this up."

I stared up at the ceiling, trying to find the will to stomach the idea. "Fine. But only because you pulled the clubhouse-code shit. I want it noted that I'm participating under duress. And I'm not in charge."

The corners of Kristen's mouth twitched. "Noted. And *yes*, you are in charge."

I sighed for a hundredth time. "Why? I know nothing about bar mitzvahs or b'nai mitzvah."

"Neither do we, which is why you should lead this one. You want to be a business consultant? What better practice? Study the client's needs, then tell us how we can plan a successful event for them. We have five weeks. Plenty of time for you to learn and educate us." Kristen glanced around the room as the rest of the Michaelson Musketeers nodded, all crossing their arms in solidarity. Even Hannah joined in when prompted by Kiki's nudge.

Hard to argue logic. Or fight the musketeer code.

Dammit.

"Fine. But I am *not* listening to Justin Bieber to make the 'sensitive one' a soundtrack. He can give me a list of favorite songs. I lay the track unheard."

"Done." Kristen nodded.

"Anyone needs me that night? I'll be with the AC/DC kid...uh...adult."

And really, for as much shit as I was giving Kristen and the girls, anything that took my mind off annoying exes and the company sabotage bullshit was worth tolerating.

7. TEA PARTY

Later that week, after I had worked nonstop on both Loading Zone and Invitation Only planning and Hannah had been slammed with the growing orders at her bakery, Kristen dragged us all out for "field research" for our upcoming dual event. Even though this was a sedate lunch at a nearby country club, my guard was up. No suspicious activity had happened since the flower mix-up, but I didn't think for a second our saboteur had given up. Silent often meant scheming in the business world.

A waiter walked by with mint juleps on his tray. *Mint fucking juleps*. Stately columns lined the patio where we sat. Little sandwiches—food no grown man would touch unless nothing else existed—were arranged on a tower of connected silver platters.

And I thought *our* country club screamed pretentious old-money.

When we strolled through the front doors of Lakemont Country Club, we'd been transported straight to the South. On the surface of Mars. In an alternate universe. I blinked at a teenage girl who walked by on the grass beyond the patio, tennis racket resting on her far shoulder, bright-pink streaks in her hair. And not one uptight head on the patio turned.

Toto, we aren't on planet Earth anymore.

"Explain to me why we're here again?" On a hard sigh, I glanced around the table. My sisters and Hannah seemed just fine with tiny cucumber sandwiches. *Cucumber.*

Kristen stirred her mint julep. The drink was a club special or some ridiculous shit. "The client demanded we hold the bar mitzvahs in their club. They're new members. We're doing reconnaissance, plus a tour."

At least Kiki sipped a hot green tea. Daring Kendall had ordered something stronger: iced tea, of the Long Island variety. And thank fuck for Hannah, who'd shown solidarity by ordering the same as me: beer, of the all-is-right-in-the-world variety.

I leaned over to my comrade in normalcy. "Wanna see if they have a supply closet?"

Hannah's shoulders shook in silent laughter at our private joke. (We'd rounded second base for first time in a church supply closet, our mild claustrophobic issues had been trumped by our pent-up sexual frustration.)

She dropped her gaze down to the folded napkin in her lap and blushed spectacularly. I loved putting naughty thoughts into her head, flushing that pink onto her beautiful face.

I nudged her with my shoulder, lightening the mood as I took a pull from my bottle. "You realize you're gonna need to feed me later, right? Those sad little triangles do not qualify as food."

Kiki grabbed another miniature sandwich. It was her fourth; I'd been counting. And still, when you added them all together, it didn't equal a whole sandwich. "Cade, you don't know what you're missing. These are delicious."

I grunted. "Bet they cost north of twenty bucks too."

Kristen smirked, pretending to read the prospectus of the room rental and add-on costs she'd been emailed by the country club. "Twenty-seven."

Shaking my head, I set my nearly empty bottle down. "Captive audience, outrageous rates, and low nutrition. Keep the members brain-dead, and they'll keep spending money."

Kendall drew another sip of her long island through her straw, sucking up the last inch of the potent liquid from the bottom, her cheeks rosy from a healthy buzz. "You could've ordered a salad. Or a burger."

I coughed, swearing under my breath. "Those weren't burgers; they were sliders. Three paltry excuses for burgers, designed to give you more bread and less meat. What do their salads look like? Are they served in a pudding cup?"

The table burst out laughing.

That's right. Tip your event coordinator. He'll be here all week.

And truly, making fun of the über-rich was the only way I knew how to survive being on the grounds without requiring an oxygen tank. And a keg.

Nothing personal against this country club, just the uptight establishment as a whole. Sure, a few members sought to make a difference with the power of their membership and their wealth; however, the majority sadly belonged solely to gossip and jockey for social standing. And I could think of far better places to have lunch for the day, like a sports bar or a backyard barbeque. But the members around us put on easily recognizable airs. And the bullshit made me cynical just being exposed to it longer than necessary—without the distractions of music and an open bar.

An attractive redhead stepped into my line of sight, making eye contact with me as she approached our table. "The Michaelson party?"

I nodded, watching a smile flirt across her face. She held my gaze a few beats longer than necessary before acknowledging the rest of the group. I dropped my head and stared to my right, sending a pointed look at Kristen with an unspoken request, one I knew she heard loud and clear with her imperceptible nod. Hannah was here. And even if she wasn't, I had no interest in any other woman on the planet. We needed to douse Little Miss Redhead's interest with an ice-cold bucket of water.

"I'm Suzanne Bradshaw. I understand you want a tour of the facilities."

Kristen gathered her paperwork into a pile, tapped the stack onto the table, and stood, extending her hand. "I'm Kristen Michaelson. These are my sisters, Kiki and Kendall." She pointed at each of us as she said our names. "This is my brother, Cade, and his girlfriend, Hannah."

We nodded at our introductions except for Kiki, who gave a friendly single-handed wave.

When we began to stand, Suzanne seemed to take the "girlfriend" clue to heart, gravitating toward Kristen, who'd agreed to pilot this meeting. I'd promised to coordinate the actual event. But a frou-frou luncheon with a boring tour? All hers.

I stood and pulled Hannah's chair away as my sisters followed Suzanne. I tugged Hannah's elbow, holding her back, until we had a good fifteen-foot gap between us and the tour caravan. "I'll keep on the lookout for potential closets. You scope out promising dark corners."

She'd brought along her half-full beer, and I took the

bottle from her, shifting it to my other hand as I wrapped an arm around her shoulder.

"You're incorrigible." Shaking her head, she looked left, then leaned back to look beyond me after we entered the main building through open French doors. "So how dark is dark enough?"

I choked out a laugh. "Really? Your hard limits don't include exhibitionism?"

"I don't know. Maybe we should find out."

As the rest of the group rounded the corner, I crowded her up against the nearest wall, in plain view of the dining patio guests twenty feet away. "Here? Now?"

She gasped as I pressed my mouth to her neck. Sliding a hand up a bare thigh, I lifted her short hem inches at a time. Thank fuck she'd decided to wear a sundress. She moaned her reply.

Yeah, we played a seductive game of chicken. Lust tried to overrule my brain, sending us full speed ahead. Yet there was only so far we could take indecency before a club member had us kicked out. A restraining order would make it impossible for us to hold the event here and cause us to lose a well-paying client.

Fuck. If only we'd crashed a random country club. Then I'd be down for all kinds of rule breaking and testing Hannah's limits.

I sighed, dropping my forehead to hers. Her breathless pants matched mine until oxygen filtered back into our brains. "We are *so* scouting out a country club we never plan on doing business with."

Confusion wrinkled her face. "What?"

"Are you two coming?" Kendall popped her head around the corner.

No. But we'd like to be.

Like good little event-planning teammates, we caught up and followed along with the group, feigning interest in the architectural details and coveted pieces of art as Suzanne pointed them out.

Yada. Yada. We know, Pilgrims on the Mayflower. Provenance back to Ben Franklin.

We get it. You're important.

After the nickel tour of priceless artifacts ended, we finally got down to the nitty-gritty. Kristen flipped open her manila file folder, bending the cover back behind a yellow lined notepad. "When we spoke over the phone about room possibilities, you said we had a couple of options."

Suzanne nodded, stepping down the hall. "You said you had two parties for a set of twins. We could do both in one room. This is our largest available that evening." She opened double doors into a sizable space.

Scowling, I glanced at Kristen. "You want a battle of the bands? Heavy rock versus teen pop?"

Kristen shook her head at Suzanne. "No. What's the other option?"

It had better be doable. From what Kristen had explained, the client wanted the event here. On that day and on their perfect time schedule.

"This way. We have neighboring rooms, both equal in size."

Perfect.

After a quick check of each of the rooms, Kristen glanced at me, deferring to my judgment before agreeing. I gave her a nod, then shoved my hands into my front pockets and turned to leave. My work for the afternoon was essentially done.

The place would do. Although stuffier than most country

clubs, my family's club was only more tolerable by a matter of degree. They were all archaic establishments. But for the sake of serving as museums of times gone by, overflowing with fancy historical accessories to prove it, I supposed they served their purpose. Time capsules with ridiculous little sandwiches.

Plus, many events the bored wealthy members held were charitable functions to benefit the less fortunate. And I fully supported the means to that end.

Barbra Streisand once said at a concert I saw on TV, "Money is like manure; it's not worth a thing unless you spread it around..." When I repeated the phrase later to my charitable mother, she'd informed me that Streisand first said the line in the musical *Hello, Dolly!*

I did not confirm that fact. The only musicals I agreed to tolerate were the future ones Hannah had committed me to. And said rare event would only take place because Hannah suggested we might have sex there. Damn. My mind kept guttering.

"Feel like attending any musicals in the near future?" I wondered if she remembered our discussion at my mom's charity event all those months ago.

Her eyes glittered with amusement. "Sure. Why don't I pick out the musical, and you can pick out the seats. Something in a dark corner, I'm guessing."

Chasing her out into the hall, I wrapped my arms around her, growling low against her neck. "Have I told you lately how much I love you?"

She glanced at the ceiling as we walked along, pretending to think. "Nope. Not since right before lunch."

"Well, I do. I fucking love you."

The ostentatious airs of our surroundings must've affected her brain, because she lifted her nose a little into the air, pulling away from me. "Well, I should certainly hope so. I won't ride just anybody during live musicals."

I halted abruptly. "*Fuck*."

Hannah broke away and turned, staring at me with a sly expression. Damned woman thoroughly enjoyed throwing me off-balance.

My sisters' voices grew louder as they stepped into the hallway, scattering our naughty vibe into the stale air.

Something pricked at the back of my neck. I couldn't put a definable reason to the change, but it had nothing to do with losing our moment of fun.

A woman rushed down the hall and entered a far door we hadn't gone through. Then an older woman followed the first, scanning down a clipboard in her left hand as she stood in the entry to the unseen room. "Maddie, the mayor will be here at four."

I frowned and stared toward the doorway. *It couldn't be.* I shook my head, feeling like a paranoid idiot.

Fate wouldn't be that twisted.

Hannah clasped my hand, and I stared into her joy-filled eyes.

In my peripheral vision, movement caught my attention, and I glanced back down the hall.

Out of the doorway walked the only "Maddie" I'd ever known: Madison Kensington.

Another coincidence? They were beginning to stack up.

8. GHOST OF VALENTINE'S PAST

In the wide hallway, the walls started to close in on me. I blew out the breath I'd been holding. *Holy shit.* When Madison said she worked at a country club, I should've asked *which* country club. How the fuck did I miss that detail? Oh, now I remember. Sex addiction. That's where I'd gotten thrown.

Madison shifted her attention, making eye contact with me, and stopped in her tracks. She held my gaze while speaking with her two companions. A moment later, they rushed down the hall in the opposite direction.

Suspicious, I narrowed my eyes. The situation felt like a showdown at the high-society corral. I'd be fucked if I made contact and fucked if I didn't. Ingrained mistrust for the blonde staring at me, waiting for me to make a move, tanked the high I had from the last few minutes.

"Cade, is everything okay? Who is that?" Hannah put a gentle hand on my back.

Not daring to take Madison out of my sight, I snarled, "That, Maestro, is my ex."

"Seriously?"

"I had no clue she worked at *this* country club. I need to find out what's going on." And yet, I remained rooted in place, needing to get my bearings.

Actually, maybe our meeting by chance was a good thing. I could get a more defined feel on my suspicions. But I didn't like being blindsided by her presence. And I sure as shit didn't like Madison and Hannah under the same roof. Things felt out of control. Volatile.

Hannah stood proudly by my side, resilient. She crossed her arms, chin up, shoulders back, her body loose but confident.

I glanced at my sisters, who remained a few feet away. They faced us with relaxed stances, but their easygoing demeanor was a front. I'd caught the suspicious narrowing of their eyes. I centered my gaze on Kristen. With an imperceptible nod, Kristen signaled me; she had my back.

A smile appeared on Kristen's face, one I'd seen a thousand times when she geared up to ask our parents for permission to do something she knew they wouldn't ordinarily approve of. "Hannah, why don't you join us? Suzanne's about to show us the salon and spa area."

Suzanne nodded with a cheerful grin, oblivious to the thickening tension in the hallway. "I can even get each of you complimentary treatments for the morning of the event, if you'd like."

Hannah glanced up at me. Everything was there in her eyes: pride, worry, confusion, love. I focused on the last. Her love—all that mattered.

Sudden fierceness flared in her eyes, and she leaned in, whispering, "I'm right there with you, Cade. If she's reformed, fine. But if she's Selfish Bitch, I *will* knock her on her ass."

I barked out an unexpected laugh at the reminder of the

mocking nickname. "Thanks, Maestro. Thank you for knowing exactly what I need." I bent down and brushed my lips across hers. "Go. Find out what kind of spa these mint-julep drinkers run."

She smiled and turned as I playfully swatted her ass. While I took a steadying breath, she got swallowed up into the protective embraces of my sisters. They all laughed seconds later. *Good.* I counted on my crew to keep my girl smiling.

After they rounded the corner, I turned around to face Madison again.

She stood there in all her shellacked glory, proud and immovable. In her element, she resembled the old Madison. Confident. Not in any way the vulnerable coffeehouse version.

I strolled down the hall, assessing her as best I could with a fresh perspective. Common sense told me she held an obvious managerial role, but warning sirens blared in my head that her being in the hallway at the exact moment of our tour couldn't possibly be a coincidence.

I had no illusions about the situation. Lakemont Country Club was clearly her territory, and she was in a position of power with whatever knowledge she held and I didn't.

"Madison." I stopped three feet away, dropping my hands in my pockets. I had no desire to touch her, and she needed to understand that fact with no room for misinterpretation.

The artificial smile that had been curved onto her face faltered. "No 'hello'? Are we not able to be friends yet?"

I sighed. Did I really need to go through the motions of something I didn't feel? "Not yet. I'm still trying to figure out how we're standing in the same hallway."

Her mouth tightened, spreading into a thin line. "It's good to see you too, Cade. You look great."

My jaw tensed, but I worked it loose, forcing myself to relax. "You're here, I'm here. How do you *propose* we coexist in the same space professionally? That's all I'm interested in."

Her gaze swept down my body and back up. Her lips twisted into a smirk. "I don't know, Cade. You tell me?"

The question was rhetorical, laced with heavy sexual undertones. Which pissed me the fuck off. Yet in this game, I didn't hold the cards, she did. Until there was no reason not to, I would play nice. Even though my gut told me she wanted to do everything besides, regardless of her request to be friends. "What's your position here?" I needed to know what kind of minefield I had to navigate.

"General Manager."

Fuck.

Impressive, and shocking. Either she'd fast-tracked her education and experience in the two years she'd been away, or she'd taken advantage of more efficient ways of advancement. The latter thought may have been callous, but I had no misconception about what she was capable of. And using her body to climb to the top wouldn't have surprised me, sexual addiction or not.

Her official position, however, meant she would be as involved in our event at her club as she wanted to be, and likely already had been.

"Did you know I would be here today?"

She gave a slight nod as she crossed her arms. "I did."

"But you had Suzanne give us the tour."

The fingers of her right hand drummed onto her left bicep. "There was no need for me to parade you around the grounds. It's Suzanne's job."

"Which is?"

Something electronic chimed, and it wasn't my cell phone. Madison ignored the sound without so much as a muscle twitch. "Private event coordinator."

"And who will we be working with on this event?"

Her brows raised slightly. "Who would you like to be working with?"

"I'm good with Suzanne." The words were flat, not from force but by my lack of emotion in this negotiation. In her. Everything about her being here without my knowing didn't sit right with me.

Disappointment flickered across her face before she took a deep breath. Then her eyes narrowed imperceptibly, like she was trying to read me. Her head tilted slightly. "Who was the girl?"

"What girl?"

"I know your sisters. The other girl, the pretty waif."

I smiled. A genuine actual fucking smile lit my face from the inside out, both in thinking about Hannah and in knowing how badly Hannah's presence likely bothered Madison.

"That's Hannah. She's my girlfriend, and our baker."

Madison countered in a matter-of-fact tone, "We have a baker."

Transparent. But not unexpected. "She is *our* baker. The client hired Invitation Only, and we only work with Hannah. It's a done deal; the ink is already dry on the contract."

She gave a slight headshake. "Nothing happens here without my approval."

Ah, power. There were the old Madison I remembered. She loved it, clearly got off on it. But power was a perception. And fleeting.

"Well, tell that to your member, *our client*. If they want

the event in your country club and you don't 'approve' of us running our show exactly as we want, you can tell them they need to find another event company. Good luck with that."

I turned away to leave.

A heavy sigh huffed out behind me. "I suppose I could make an allowance."

When I glanced over my shoulder, her arms had dropped, hands fisting at her sides. The concession was killing her. Good. A little pain would be healthy to someone who inflicted it so easily.

I stared hard at her, unblinking. Invitation Only's business was at stake here, and I needed to define all the boundaries. "Remember, we work with Suzanne, and only Suzanne. We have free reign over everything regarding the event. It's the only way we work. And no interference. If I even catch wind that you've had a hand in anything that goes wrong, I'll hold you personally accountable. Oh, and our mutual client will be fully informed of our history."

Her eyes narrowed. "You're planning to tell the client about us?"

A wry smile twisted my lips. "I believe in full disclosure, Madison. Clients don't like surprises. Neither do I."

For an instant, her expression flashed mild amusement before hardening once again. Like none of my conditions fazed her. Like the obstacles were nothing more than a challenge, a game.

Yeah? Well, game on.

Unimpressed with her as a threat, I turned without another word and strode down the hall. I looked forward to the upcoming dual event going smoothly. In spite of the unpredictable five-foot-eight blonde.

As I rounded the corner, I sensed Madison still stood down the hall. No need to glance at her to know she fumed, wishing she had more control of the situation—control over me.

But she didn't.

I was happy. In love with a real woman who knew what love meant. And Hannah and I were invincible together.

My step lightened along with my mood. Nothing could touch that. Not the outside world, not fate, and certainly not one Madison Kensington.

The best revenge is living well.

9. CREATIVE THERAPY

After searching the front lobby of the country club for any clues of where the spa area might be, I spotted the girls through the glass doors that led onto the patio.

All of them were laughing, Kristen shaking her head and Kiki clapping Kendall on the back. But my gutter mind suspected Kendall had lost her filter with her potent long island iced tea and voiced a naughty thought they shared, because every one of them held a guilty expression.

I'd been outnumbered by women enough to know when girl talk went wild by casual observation. My gaze trained on Hannah, however, the one girl I hadn't been around long enough to read all her little nuances. After the Madison encounter in the hall, I wanted to be sure Hannah was okay.

It didn't take rocket science, however, to know she wasn't her comfortable free-spirited self. A subtle sign was in the smile that failed to hold true. But the moment she saw me approach, she tilted her head and her concerned expression changed into a reassuring smile.

"How did it go? Are you okay? Do I need to knock Selfish Bitch on her ass?" Hannah's eyebrows raised in hope.

I wrapped an arm around her shoulder. "What I wouldn't pay to see that happen. And yeah, I'm good. Madison may be trying to change, but I saw glimpses of her old self shining through."

"Selfish Bitch?" Kendall snorted. "That shit's hilarious."

Kiki blinked. "Am I missing something? We know you guys broke up. But do we need details? Should I deck Selfish Bitch too?"

I shook my head, needing to diffuse the situation. This wasn't the time or place. "Someday, I'll fill you guys in. Let's just say, it's a bitch of a story. That's why I've never shared it."

Hannah asked, "What's she even doing here?"

I cleared my throat. "We have the luck of Madison being GM of the club."

Kendall shook her head. "How is that even possible? Wouldn't the club want years of experience in a GM?"

I shrugged, not wanting to give more brain cells to the matter than necessary. "We were all born with country club silver spoons in our mouths, raised in a place like this. That's a qualification right there. When we dated, she took a handful of undergrad courses in hotel and restaurant management. Maybe she got a degree in Europe. The place seems to run smoothly, so she hasn't botched things up yet."

Kristen crossed her arms as understanding washed across her expression. Of all my sisters, she likely suspected how bad my breakup with Madison had been. She glanced at Hannah, then looked pointedly at me. "Cade, what's your gut tell you? Is she the one behind the games?"

I exhaled a slow breath, thinking about it again. "Madison is plugged in to the industry. Our suppliers are likely the same as hers. With her connections, she could probably draw our network map in the span of a lunch hour."

I glanced at them all. "It's possible. Can't rule it out. But we also can't do or say anything about it without proof, so keep your eyes and ears open. If it's her, and there's an opportunity for us to catch her, we need to jump on it."

Kristen pursed her lips, staring hard at me. "You still good with running point on this?"

"Yeah." I nodded, giving Hannah a tight squeeze of reassurance. "If Madison decides to meddle, we've got her. And if she catches wind that I'm running the show, she might be more inclined to toss a wrench in the gears. Besides, you've got too many other things on your plate to take this on too." Plus, the business side of me railed at the thought of stepping aside because of Madison.

"Madison attempted to flex her authority already. She tried to dictate how a detail was going to go down. But I snapped back full force, reminding her who her client was and that we didn't operate from under anyone's thumb. She either gave us unrestricted authority to serve the client who hired us, or we didn't play ball at all. Still, I'm willing and able to handle the project in spite of her being a nuisance. I'm more motivated than anyone else because of it."

"Good. Let's get out of here." Kristen nodded, then turned, leading us out through the lobby.

Kiki pulled on the door heading out the front of the club, but then paused, glancing back. "What detail did she try to dictate?"

"We use her baker, not Hannah."

"Fuck that!" Kiki scowled, whirling around.

Kendall's and Kristen's mouths dropped opened.

Hannah simply shook her head and huffed out a laugh.

Kristen's deepening scowl was epic. "We're in this together. Period."

I grinned. "Damn straight." I gave Hannah another tight

squeeze as I guided her through the door. I squinted in the midafternoon sun, then unclipped my sunglasses from my T-shirt and slid them on.

Did I feel bad about my sisters and Hannah calling her Selfish Bitch? Fuck no. I didn't like being surprised in the hallway earlier. Madison should've known that would set me off. And besides, she'd put me through the ringer years ago. Madison had earned the nickname. The vulnerable side she'd shown at the coffeehouse last week was too new —foreign.

It would take a lot more than that for me to trust she could be different.

THE RIDE back to my place was quiet with the wind tunnel around my bike and helmets on our heads, which gave us both mental space to process what had happened at the country club. Hannah didn't say much during dinner prep or the main course, but I didn't want to have a heavy conversation in front of the guys. Yet, even with Ben and Mase being in rare comedic form, her difference escaped no one's notice.

I began to worry, and was about to say something, when Mase spoke up.

"Hannah, you okay? You're poking that fish like you expect it to swim away at some point." Mase slipped a scrap under the table to a whining Ava. The sounds of chomping quickly followed.

Hannah glanced at me like I understood.

And I thought I did, if being unsettled was the source of her hardened expression and quiet demeanor. Sure as fuck was for me.

She shifted her gaze to Mase. "Yeah. Just got to see the notorious Selfish Bitch from afar."

Ben choked on the wine he'd been swallowing. "What? Who's 'Selfish Bitch?'"

"Madison," I muttered as I scowled at my empty plate.

The guys stared hard at Hannah. Ben put his wineglass down. "Hannah, that 'Selfish Bitch' could only *hope* to be anything remotely close to you."

Mase gave a single hard nod. "Never liked her. Cold. Calculating."

I agreed with Mase and Ben. "Is that what's wrong? They speak the truth, babe. You are amazing."

She let out a hard sigh and pushed back from the table, straightening. "No, it's not like that. I'm just pissed. I'm mad that she may be trying to hurt Cade. The business. What we're all working so hard to create."

"Madison can't hurt me. She can't hurt us."

Hannah's gaze dropped down to her plate, frowning.

Frustrated at seeing her unfazed by our words, I scraped my chair back and stood. "That's it." I scooped Ava up into my arms. "My room. Now."

I towered beside her, pointing in the direction of the hall. When all Hannah did was glance up at me, raising her eyebrows with a challenging expression, I plopped Ava into her lap, yanked her chair back, and lifted Hannah out of it, puppy and all.

Hannah squealed, then laughed as Ava drowned her face in puppy-bath licks on our way down the hall. I shouldered through my half-open bedroom door, kicked it shut, and leaned over the bed, carefully depositing my cargo on it. Ava raced around on the comforter, tail wagging on her fuzzy little body as she vibrated with excitement.

83

Hannah grinned. "What was that all about, Neanderthal?"

"Sudden puppy-love therapy. I've heard it's effective." I crossed my arms.

Hannah straightened out, reclining on the bed as she extended a welcoming arm toward me. I took her hand and stretched alongside her, kissing her softly. Ava, however, wriggled her cute little ass in between our chests. Then, once she got situated, she collapsed from her effort with a soft chuff.

Ava's eyes drifted shut while Hannah stroked a soft ear before kissing it.

Not wanting our sudden happiness to subside, I lifted Hannah's fingers and kissed the back of her knuckles. "I meant what I said. You are amazing. You are everything to me."

"You are my world too. I'm just frustrated. On how to protect you from her. It doesn't matter to me what she said to you at the coffeehouse. About her having changed. The stunt she pulled at the country club doesn't show it. I don't trust her."

When she exhaled on a heavy sigh, I tucked a finger under her chin, forcing her gaze to mine. "You don't have to trust her. Hell, I don't. Just trust me. Believe in my ability to protect us—to handle everything." I leaned forward, careful not to disturb Ava, and kissed Hannah, long and slow.

When I pulled away, she said, "I'm sorry little things keep throwing me. Especially surprises from our past."

Irritated that any shit from my past was affecting Hannah, I took a deep breath, then exhaled slowly. I had to stay calm, bolster her. Not get sucked under by it. Because the damned surprises were throwing me too. "No, Hannah.

Don't apologize." I shook my head. "Pissed and frustrated, but staying here to fight with me—that's being strong."

She lifted a corner of her mouth in an attempt to smile but it fell. "I hate that you have to see her. I don't like *any* authority she has over us."

"She doesn't have authority over us. Not real power."

"Okay, but I can't promise that I won't get frustrated. Or angry, if she keeps pulling stunts like she did today. Or want to knock Madison on her ass." She gave out a dry laugh. "I may need more puppy therapy."

With care not to wake Ava, I lifted her limp body and tucked her into a far corner of the bed, up against the pillows. Then I sidled next to Hannah. "Actually, if we have this discussion again, we need to ramp up the method of therapy."

She smiled, then bit her lip. Her gaze dropped to my mouth, then lifted to my eyes. "Oh? And what's the next step above puppy therapy?"

I leaned forward, giving her a hard kiss.

Hannah moaned.

The kiss wasn't an answer in and of itself, but I needed the contact.

I pulled back and sucked on her lower lip before releasing it. "I'm thinking the next step above puppy therapy is kitchen-island-condiment therapy." When I'd first teased her about it, I'd imagined her on her kitchen island. And had told her so.

Her body shuddered. Had she pictured herself naked, exactly as I'd described? I hoped so. I imagined her shivering for my touch, waiting for me to cover her with various condiments before slowly licking her body clean.

I sucked in a breath, the fantasy affecting me.

A seductive smile curved her lips. "And if that doesn't work?"

I barked out a laugh. "If I can't make you forget the chaos in the middle of it, then I'm ditching the rest of the world, kidnapping your sexy ass, and we're doing private-island therapy."

"Mmm..." She nestled close, pressing her lips into my neck. "*Love* that idea. Let's go now."

I chuckled. "So tempting."

She wanted to chuck the rest of the world and have life as we knew it be about only her and me. I did too. But not yet.

I wasn't about to fly off to a private island on our first vacation because either of us needed therapy. We had events to plan, businesses to run, in spite of a potential nuisance. Then we would make time for play.

LATER THAT NIGHT, after I'd dropped Hannah off at her place, I stretched out in bed listening to "Hurricane" by Thirty Seconds to Mars. Sure as fuck felt appropriate. Chaos. Emotion.

I sighed heavily, staring at my ceiling. I never expected life to be easy. But Hannah and I were due for some kind of an easy stretch after the struggles we'd had. Hers. Mine. Ours.

My phone vibrated, and my heart jumped. I smiled, thinking Hannah wanted to wish me a good night. Would the text have three naughty little dots? Our secret code always made me smile.

Fuck.

Not Hannah. Madison.

"Really?" I grumbled into the darkness as the song ended, leaving me in silence. "Is all this shit some kind of test? Because I didn't sign on for this."

I wanted to be with Hannah. Only Hannah. Yet all this garbage threatened to taint our new relationship.

Frustrated, I clicked into my phone to read the text.

> Hey, Cade. Sorry about today. You were angry. I should have told you.

Fuck yeah, you should have. I slammed the phone back down on my nightstand. For a moment, I considered not replying. But when all I did was get more pissed, I grabbed the damned thing and fired off a reply.

> You're right. You said you've changed. Prove it with actions. No more surprises.

I hit SEND and was about to put the phone down when a reply came through.

> Could we meet for coffee again?

I sighed, struggling with my thoughts. I'd grown up with Madison. In hindsight, she burned through guy after guy as we grew up. Then she turned to me to figure out what went wrong. Once we'd crossed the friend line in college and our relationship grew into long term, I felt lucky being the guy she chose—at least I'd thought I was. I had planned on spending my life with her. There *was* good in her. Back then, I'd fallen in love with that part of her.

But what I didn't know then was that need can change a person from the inside out—addiction can be a bitch.

Convinced clear boundaries were needed, I replied.

> No. I have a girlfriend. Meeting privately is
> off the table.

Wide awake, I waited. No way I'd be able to sleep until I knew she understood. Her reply came through.

> Coffee isn't meeting privately. It's public.
> Drinks and talking. But I understand. We
> need to meet for business soon anyway. It
> will have to do. I'll email details.

Did she understand? With all the mixed signals between vulnerable Madison and business Madison, I sure as hell didn't.

10. BATTLE PREPARATIONS

Another week later, we all sat at Kristen's dining room table, planning for Invitation Only. I pinched my nose, grumpy as hell. Thank fuck, other than one business email, I hadn't heard from Madison again. I also hadn't seen much of Hannah either. With my covering for vacationing bartenders at Loading Zone, and Hannah's bakery exploding with orders, we'd had to cancel all of our nightly dinners, and we'd only been able to get together once.

Then tonight, after an hour had been wasted at Kristen's, we hadn't gotten shit done. I needed to get the calendar straight. In a week, we had the one-year anniversary of Loading Zone, the following weekend was Mom and Dad's Fourth of July party at their country estate, and the weekend after, the double bar mitzvah.

"Focus, people." I glared at Hannah and my sisters, who chattered away about nonessential things. "Kiki, you said invitations went out for Loading Zone's party?"

She nodded while she stirred her root beer float. "Three weeks ago. But you said you wanted to fill the place to capacity. We were two hundred RSVPs short with Loading

Zone's contacts and your filtered country club member list, so I went to your website and installed a banner to advertise."

I sighed. Exclusive meant picking and choosing guests. But the event was to benefit charity, and anyone who wanted to pay two hundred and fifty dollars a head to help those in need would be welcomed.

"Hannah, you got the cake covered? Nothing fancy like the last charity event, more fun and casual." I glanced at her.

She gave me a warm smile. "Got it covered."

Tight deadlines sucked ass. Fitting into calendars of the social elite was difficult enough without short notice. When Kristen had initially said five weeks out for the dual event, the time to plan seemed like forever. However, Ben asked me last week to take over some of the details for the bar event, which had sent me scrambling. Then, to add fuel to the fire, Mom and Dad sprung their summer party on us.

Suddenly the "forever" deadline of the bar mitzvahs loomed on our doorstep. We had a million things to do and not enough people to carry them out without meticulous planning.

"Loading Zone's DJ, Darren, can handle the playlist for the anniversary event. In fact, I may bring Darren to the bar mitzvahs."

Kristen shook her head. "Are you kidding? A DJ in one room and not the other? The kid left without will be jealous. Then we'll have a livid mom on our hands."

"Right. Either no live DJ, or we have two." I nodded.

Then I shot off a quick email to Darren:

Hey, man. Need you to run soundtrack or hire DJs for two parties. One theme is AC/DC. The other, Justin Bieber. No, you

read right. I'll owe you one. And make sure things are tight for
next weekend at LZ.

I clicked back to my master to-do list. "Next. Almost nothing's been done for Mom and Dad's gig."

Kristen shouted from the kitchen as she retrieved another round of beers from the fridge. "What do they want?" Seconds later she returned, sliding the bottles across the dining table. Then she went over to the couch, plopped down, sprawled out, and closed her eyes.

Mom hadn't called Kristen to ask us to run her party— she'd called me. (Anything business related, mom always called me.) "The usual. Dress code: pool party. Which means waiters wearing tuxes in the sweltering heat while they serve bonbons to a star-studded cast lounging in the sun. She instructed me to have fireworks 'shooting shimmering colors over the water.' Sure, no problem, Mom. Piece of cake. Oh, and she wants it on Saturday, even though the Fourth is on a Friday."

Kendall asked, "You can do fireworks in two weeks?"

"That part I've already secured. Fireworks, furniture, and the bar are all set. The rest of it needs to be scheduled: food, serving staff, and entertainment."

Kristen laughed. "I'll talk to her. There's no way we'll put waiters in tuxes for a pool party. She forgets we've got our own style, and she needs to trust our judgment. Besides, we aren't torturing the help."

"So what's the alternative?" I glanced up, a smirk curling my lips. "Shirtless cabana boys?"

Kiki and Kendall burst out laughing. Kristen snorted. "Yeah, good luck with that."

Hannah leaned forward. "No, wait a minute. That's a great idea."

Everyone quieted, staring at her.

She continued, "Think about it. Shirtless men with tousled hair and ripped abs, wearing board shorts and flip flops."

Kristen coughed, sputtering out her beer. "Flip flops? Have you met my mother? There's no way she'll let her society friends see the serving staff's hairy toes."

Kiki choked out a laugh.

Hannah slowly shook her head. "I guarantee you: no woman will be looking at their feet. They won't make it past the sexy V of their obliques slipping into their waistbands."

Under the table, Hannah suddenly trailed a finger along my waistband, then slid it below the edge of my jeans. I swallowed hard at the unexpected action, and for several seconds, forgot what she'd been talking about.

My sisters stared at Hannah, not for her left-field suggestion, but because they were actually considering it.

Kudos to Hannah for her ballsy creativity. Made perfect sense. The one to shake things up when we got stuck in our high-society mold would be the one who hadn't been tarnished by it.

One by one, the girls all smiled.

"And who would be finding these oblique-sporting men?" Kiki's eyes lit up.

Hannah grinned. "We would, of course. Feel like a slumber party tomorrow night at my place?"

Kristen arched a brow. "And Cade is cool with you sorting through man-candy?"

Yeah. Don't forget about your *oblique-sporting man.*

Hannah glanced at me and winked. Then she swept her gaze toward the three of them. "Sure. I had to watch him pick out models as bunnies for Dwight's Easter debauchery. I was quite the good sport about it, if I remember correctly."

I narrowed my eyes at her. "You've planned this all along, haven't you?"

She nudged my shoulder. "No. But it sure helps my case, doesn't it?"

Kristen nodded once, then sat up on the couch and slapped her bare knees. "I'm in. And I'll make sure Mom is prepared. I just need to convince her that the female guests will be happy to be surrounded by their fantasies come to life."

"Plus, Cade can help us." Hannah planted a chaste kiss on my cheek.

"Excuse me?" I blinked, certain I'd misheard.

"You have a knack for picking the best people. You don't want us distracted by good looks alone, do you?"

I grumbled a string of obscenities under my breath. "I think I'm gonna be busy. I'm planning a guys' night in my head as we speak."

Kiki groaned. "*Caaade*. We need your help."

I leaned back and crossed my arms. "I'm confident your combined logic will trump your collective libidos."

Kristen put her beer on the table. "Any tips? Or are you gonna let us fly blind here?"

"Call the modeling agencies. Have them email you their portfolio of sports models. Tell them what qualifications you're looking for, and they'll filter on their end first."

Kendall grabbed her pen and jotted down a note. "I'll do that. How many will we need?"

I scanned the email to confirm the headcount. "Mom's invited two hundred guests. Twelve should cover it, but we should hire fifteen to be safe."

The last unresolved issue glared at me, the cursor blinking in front of it like a ticking time bomb. "Last item: Madison emailed this morning." Even though she knew damn well I didn't want to work with her directly. "She mandated we meet this week at her club for a sampling of the menu, linen, and setting choices, among other things." The tone in the email had been hard-edged Madison. She was becoming an ex-girlfriend version of "Jekyll & Hyde."

Kristen tilted her head at my dread-filled monotone. "There's nothing unusual about that. It's done all the time in the industry."

I clenched my jaw. "She made the stipulation that I come alone."

Hannah tightened her grip on my thigh, but a split second later relaxed her hold.

Kiki scowled. "Sounds more like a hostage exchange than a highbrow tasting."

I shrugged. "Doesn't matter. I replied, instructing her that I don't work alone. And that Hannah is more than our resident baker, she's involved in anything we do with food. So we both go. Or no one goes."

"Good." Kendall shot a venomous glare at my laptop, as if she was sending her irritation through the Internet back to Madison.

I glanced at Hannah. "That's not all. There's no way I'm going into a room with Madison, with only me and Hannah there. Who else wants to go to the taste testing?"

Kiki's arm shot up. "I'm *so* there."

Kendall nodded. "Count me in."

"Wouldn't miss being there for the world. We'll all go together." Kristen's eyes narrowed. "Speaking of our suspect. Any new surprises?"

Kiki shook her head. Kendall did too.

Hannah frowned. "You know, I hadn't put it together until now, but I had a large weekly supply order not show. When I called, they said the delivery had been deleted. He apologized, wrote it off as a computer glitch, and delivered my shipment the following morning."

I glanced at her. "You need to do the same with your vendors that we did with Invitation Only's. Let's not leave anything to chance."

Her expression hardened. "I have a great relationship with the sales reps of all my vendors. I'll ask that if anyone contacts them on my behalf, to try and find out who it is. If it is Madison, and she's messing with my livelihood, this 'baker' is going to pull the rug out from under her country club ass."

I grinned, so damned proud of her. "Agreed. Proof first. Then karma can have at her."

11. ALL ABOUT THE GUYS

> Think you can handle another night
> without me?

Another night without Hannah? *No.* I read her text as Ben and Kristen's husband, Jason, taunted each other at the pool table in my basement.

> Having serious withdrawals.

Balls clacked together and two were dropped into pockets as Mase shouted, "Oh, you dog!"

> Addicted, huh? Need a fix?

I blew out a slow breath.

> Always.

"Cade. C'mon. You're up man."

> Always addicted or always needing a fix?

I smiled.

> Both.

My phone was snatched out of my hand. Mase got up in my face. "Guys night. No girls. Say good-bye to Hannah." He held my phone in front of me, not moving. I shoved him back a step and grabbed it.

> Gotta go. Guys are calling party foul on the phone use. Enjoy your slumber party.

A muffled knock sounded out above, and Ben jogged toward the stairs. "Pizza's here!"

Starving, because I'd worked straight through lunch without realizing it, I laid my phone on the bar and followed Ben upstairs. I grabbed four plates and napkins while Ben paid the delivery guy.

As we headed back down into the basement, Ben glanced over his shoulder at me. "The other night Hannah mentioned Madison was trying to mess with you. Everything cool there?"

I shrugged. "Who the hell knows? No major catastrophe yet, but we had three separate vendors who thought we'd canceled or changed orders: two with Invitation Only and one with Hannah's bakery."

Ben set the two pizza boxes onto the bar and opened them. The moment I put down the plates and napkins, Mase and Jason crowded in.

Jason grabbed a plate, then slid a third of the pepperoni pizza straight onto it. "Yeah, what's up with that? Kristen ranted about the flower mix-up over the phone to me when

I was out of town."

Mase grabbed beers from the fridge and lined them up on the bar. "How do you know it's your ex?"

"We don't. But she's the prime suspect. Too coincidental for her to show up within days of the mishaps starting." I grabbed an olive and mushroom slice, then shoved a third of it into my mouth.

Ben took a seat on a barstool, taking a piece from each box. "How's Hannah with this? She seemed pissed as hell the other night."

I snorted, then swallowed down my food. "She wants to deck her."

"What's Madison's deal?" Jason leaned an elbow onto the bar counter and folded a large slice with both hands. He glanced up at me. "You guys broke up two years ago, right?"

"Fuck if I know." I shook my head. "When we broke up, I learned more about her in a few minutes than I had our entire time together. I don't say this lightly—she's a bitch. And I wouldn't put anything past her." I didn't mention the new "vulnerable" side of Madison. Or the sex addiction. Because that would lead to talking about my struggle with it. Or the guys giving me shit. Probably both. And I wasn't in the mood for either.

Ben nodded. "Well, good luck, man. Anything you need, let us know."

"Actually, yeah. We need to make sure all of Loading Zone's vendors are tight. Since the issues have gone beyond Invitation Only to Hannah's bakery, the bar may be targeted too. Let's send them all emails that any order changes are to be confirmed by our company email. And to give us a heads up if anything suspicious goes down."

"Done. I'll do it first thing in the morning."

As I began to down a second piece of pizza, I

thought about Madison. If she was the one behind all this, she'd only been a nuisance so far. But I needed to stay one step ahead of her. To this point, all the glitches had been business related. Shit better not become personal.

My phone began vibrating again, moving it across the granite counter. I leaned forward to see the screen.

Mase intercepted me, shoving me toward the pool table. "You're up next. We've got a game to play. Then you can check the messages to make sure Hannah's house isn't burning down."

I clapped my hands, then rubbed them together. "I'm good. Rack the balls."

Mase and I played a game. Then Ben and Jason played while we watched. I crossed my arms, glancing at Jason. "You in town for a bit?"

He nodded as he lined up his shot. "Yeah. For the next few weeks."

"So you're coming to Loading Zone's anniversary and up to the parents' house, then?"

Before answering, he sank the striped twelve ball. "Yep. Looking forward to it. Work's been crazy with more traveling than usual the last few months. Kristen's happy to have me around for a while."

After Jason dropped his last stripe and the eight ball, Mase walked over to the foosball table. "Get your ass over here, Ben. Best two out of three." He spun one of the chrome rods.

Jason and I walked over to the bar, and I finally picked up my phone.

The alerts showed one missed call, a voicemail, and seven texts. I went into my text box to see a line of pictures with a comment under each. I clicked on the first picture sent from Hannah, which was a glass filled with frothy pink shit. The text connected to it said:

> Specialty drink of the night: strawberry daiquiris!

Another text from Hannah had a picture of a model on her laptop screen.

> Missing you. But the girls and I are having a blast.

The third picture and comment was from Kiki.

> He's cut. I want him.

Two separate texts without pics followed.

> Dammit. CUTE!

> Well, and cut. I'm so buzzed. :)

The fourth picture, from Kristen's phone, was of a guy with shaggy black hair, a nose ring, and tattoos covering his arms and chest.

> Think he's edgy enough to rock Mom's party?

The last picture was sent by Hannah. Three condiments were lined up on her kitchen island: chocolate sauce, honey, and caramel sauce.

Fuck.

Her comment said:

> Toppings for the only man-candy that matters to me.

I checked my voicemail. Hannah's low voice came over the line, a bit slurred.

Hey, baby. Sorry we keep buggin' you. Miss you. The girls are sleepin' here tonight. Overdid the daiquiris. No drivin'.

My chest was heavy. I missed her too. I debated calling her back as Ben and Mase battled it out at the foosball table.

Jason nodded at me. "How are the girls? I got a text from Kristen. Some half-naked guy covered in tats." He shook his head.

"They're blitzed. And not going anywhere, so she's good. Hannah and Kiki sent me texts too. Like twisted postcards."

"What about Kendall?" Jason pulled his keys out of his pocket.

I shrugged. "I could've gone without the model pics— not about to wonder why Kendall didn't send one."

He grinned. "I gotta head out, man. Ben's had a few. If he's ready, I'll drive him home."

I nodded. "Thanks."

Ben roared suddenly, lifting his arms above his head in a victory stance. "Ha! *Score*, loser."

Mase scowled at him. "Next time you're here, I want a rematch."

I said my good-byes to everyone as they headed up the stairs while I cleaned up our mess, bagging the trash. Then I grabbed my phone and turned out the lights before heading up to my room.

Pulling up Hannah's number, I almost pressed CALL. But then I had an idea.

12. PRIVATE PARTY

I dialed Hannah. It rang twice before she answered.

"Cade?" Her voice sounded sleepy.

"Did I wake you?"

"No. Maybe." She yawned.

"Where are you?"

She huffed out soft laugh. "My bed."

"Where are my sisters?"

"Kiki stumbled into the living room and passed out on the couch. Kendall and Kristen are sound asleep on the other side of my bed."

"Want to see me?"

Her sexy whimper turned into a purr. "Yeah, but I can't drive."

"Don't need to."

Her voice lowered to a whisper. "Where are you?"

"Out back. Look for the guy in the tent."

I heard a short gasp. Then the line went dead.

Her back door opened and closed. Seconds later, a flashlight beam scanned the backyard.

She appeared in the tent opening, blinking. "When... how?"

I grinned. "As soon as the guys left, I grabbed Mase's tent. Looks great in your backyard, don't you think?"

A seductive smile curved her lips. "*You* look great in my backyard."

Her long dark hair was messy, wild. She wore a little black nightie that hinted at her delicious curves beneath.

The breeze caught a corner of the gauzy fabric, whipping it up to her hip. Her thigh was exposed all the way to a tiny lace thong strap.

"When did you buy that outfit?" My voice came out hoarse.

I'd seen her in two states: clothed and naked. Never this in-between phase that made me want to watch her almost as badly as I wanted to touch her. *Almost.*

She shifted her weight and rubbed the fingers of one hand absently up her other arm. "Shortly after our first date."

I tried to remember. "Which first date?"

Her pink tongue flicked out, licking her lips. She pulled her lower lip in with her teeth, biting one side of it, holding it there.

Fuck. I wanted to suck her lip back out. My mouth watered.

When she released it, the skin glistened, plump. "The very first one. Remember? I imagined you naked, in my cupcake meadow."

I chuckled. "And you imagined yourself in *that* outfit?"

A slight headshake sent her hair tumbling over her shoulder, baring the upper curves of her breasts. "No, I imagined myself naked with you, both of us covered in frosting. I licked some off of you, you licked some off of me..."

"*Fuck me.*"

A sexy smirk curled her lips. "That *is* the idea."

I tried to remain calm. My impatient primal side wanted to order her over to me. Demand. Show her everything I craved to do to her, needed her to give to me, repeatedly. But I didn't. Not yet. The lazy foreplay unfolding between us was unlike any other. And she seemed content on standing right where she was—teasing me.

"We need to add frosting to the list, Maestro. Right beside honey, chocolate sauce, caramel sauce, and whipped cream."

Her brows drew together. "Wait. Was there whipped cream?"

I grumbled, "If there wasn't, I'm adding it."

She smiled. "Okay. And now frosting. You know we'll have to make it fresh. Half the fun will be making it and deciding on the colors."

"The other half will be licking it off." I frowned. "Wait. That's not right."

Confused, she shook her head. "What isn't right?"

"That the 'licking off' part would only be *half* the fun. More like three-quarters."

Her shoulders shook with silent laughter—which did this amazing bouncing thing to her breasts hidden by that black nightie, the subject of our discussion. "So where exactly did you buy that?" I gestured my finger to the outfit.

She tilted her head. I had no idea whether she was aware of her actions, but her hand had abandoned her arm. She now rubbed it back and forth in barely perceptible movements, just underneath the curve of her breast. "It's a baby-doll. And why do you want to know?"

My gaze got stuck on that tantalizing movement. I swallowed hard. "Oh, I don't know. To buy you presents, send them a thank-you card, buy stock in their company..."

There went her lower lip again, sucked into her mouth, before she slowly released it again. Her talented mouth had teased and sucked other things so well, my mind blew, thoughts scattering.

Her hand shifted from the gentle stroking below her breast and smoothed up over it. She hissed in a breath when her fingers drifted over the center. I couldn't see her nipples, but I imagined them hard, aching for my lips, my teeth.

She took a step closer. "I bought it at Nordstrom, but it's made by Agent Provocateur."

"I like this Agent Provocateur. Why did you buy a baby-doll over anything else?"

She smirked. "Because they don't sell burlap bags."

"Fuck burlap bags. New rule: baby-dolls are the new burlap bag."

She pursed her lips together as her gaze drifted over me. "Watcha got under there, Cade?"

I looked down. My bare legs had tangled in the sheet. One was exposed all the way to my hip with the sheet covering only part of my waist and groin. I leaned back, crossing my hands behind my head on the pillow. "Why don't you come over here and find out?"

She sucked her lip in for a third time, capturing it between her teeth.

"You know that drives me crazy, right?" Part of me wondered if she knew she pushed my buttons, but the other part hoped it was coincidence—like everything she did, and all that she was, had been made just for me.

"What?" She stepped closer and pressed her breasts together. One of the little lace straps fell off her shoulder.

I swallowed when her teeth released what she'd bitten.

"Your lip. When you pull it into your mouth. Jealousy has me torn between wanting to be the one to bite it and needing you to put that pretty mouth all over me."

She gave me a slow smile as the other strap fell off her shoulder. My gaze drifted down to her breasts. When she pulled her arms away, the gauzy fabric clung to her body only by her curves. "On or off?"

"Off." My voice sounded gruff. The time for talking had passed. I wanted Hannah naked, on me. I needed to be in her.

Fabric fluttered to the ground.

My breath caught at her beauty, every dip and curve, delicate skin over deceptive strength. *Exquisite.*

Mine.

She'd left her thong on. But as she knelt down and crawled over me, the tiny scrap of lace between us ceased to matter.

"Cade?" She pulled the sheet away, and my erection sprang free, hot and pulsing. I sucked in a sharp breath, hoping her warm mouth might soothe it, those plump lips and teeth finally finding a better use than chewing on her lower lip. Then I exhaled slowly, my cock twitching, as I imagined sinking deep into her.

"Mmm?" I blinked, focusing on her face.

She hadn't touched me yet. Only stared at me, reading me.

When she opened her mouth, I leaned up and captured it in a hard kiss, silencing her. Then I pulled away, eyes narrowing. "Not *words* from your mouth. *Actions* by your mouth."

"So bossy." She shoved hard on one shoulder, and I relaxed, letting her push me back down onto the pillow.

She gave me a mischievous grin as she crawled down my

body. Then she pulled her damned lip inside her mouth again. "No. No more lip biting. Cock sucking."

She released her lip, hovering her mouth over me. Hot air fogged across my skin, and my breath caught while she watched me. A deep ache fired through my cock, and I clenched my fists in the sheets to hold still. My brows furrowed as my chest rose and fell in shallow breaths.

"Yes, sir."

Her lips pressed against my tip. Then she sucked—hard. Sweet. Hot. *Excruciating.* Her smirk was the last thing I remembered as my head fell back on a sharp inhale.

I'd missed the fuck out of her.

When we came together, nothing else existed. I needed what she provided: grounding, understanding, comfort. To be lost and found—with her.

I let out a ragged groan as Hannah showed me I had nothing to be jealous of with her abused lower lip. She'd been saving all of the talented things her mouth did for me.

13. TASTE AND A TEST

The day had come for our scheduled sample run at Madison's country club. As we stepped into the ballroom Suzanne led us to, an understanding about one thing hit me with clarity: Madison had no intention of making anything easy for us.

In the past week, she'd completely disregarded my demand to deal with her private event coordinator, Suzanne, directly. Every email I sent to Suzanne, Madison replied to it. When I redirected my response to Suzanne, Madison replied again.

Putting an end to her game, I decided to pick my battles. I began to send the damn emails to both of them. Let them sort out their shit.

My sisters, Hannah, and I stood in the ballroom set with various examples of how Madison's team envisioned the event, complete with ridiculous floral centerpieces, fine bone china, and thousand-plus thread count table linens.

No need to guess whether or not Madison would show her new kinder-gentler side. She stood on the far side of the room, arms crossed, glacial expression.

Message received. Her territory? No chance in hell she'd show vulnerability.

Worked for me. This whole ordeal put me in a piss-poor mood, and my sadistic side clamored to butt heads with her.

I blinked. "You're kidding, right? What part of bar mitzvah did you not understand?" I gave Madison a weary stare. "It looks like a fucking spring garden explosion in here."

Ivory tablecloths, green linen napkins, frilly center-pieces with pink, purple, and yellow flowers arching out of small vases made every male cell in my body twitch to dump the tables in rebellion. The other two tables were worse. One actually had gold-rimmed crystal goblets. The other... "Are those *pink* napkins?"

Blinking in confusion, I lifted the offending color up toward the overhead lights, thinking I had to have gone colorblind from the bright sunlight outside.

Madison smirked. "It's salmon. More coral than pink."

Hannah coughed next to me. "*Selfish Bitch.*"

I snorted but inhaled a deep breath, forcing myself to relax. My words came out calm. Smooth. With no margin for misunderstanding whatsoever.

"I don't give a good goddamn what you call it. They're bringing their boys into the world, transforming them into men. We're not ousting them out of the closet. If they want to throw that kind of party, I have no issues with it. But you aren't making that poor-taste call.

"And you're sure as fuck not deciding colors. I am. Keep the colors primary, the shades with names from the basic Crayola box. Black and green" —I lifted her idea of a green napkin off the table— "not this *chartreuse* shit. The other room can be in blue, as in 'lake blue,' not *peacock*. And if you want to go wild with a third color in either room, go with silver or white. That's it. No other colors."

Madison had the audacity to look bored. "Fine. What else?"

I sat my ass in the nearest chair. "Why don't you bring around the food samples? Let's hope your chef realized there will be teenagers at the party and opted for appetizers over hors d'oeuvres or, God forbid, an *amuse-bouche*."

Yeah, I openly mocked her. But she started it. With her home-field advantage at *her* club, she boldly fucked with *our* event to our faces. I planned to end this bullshit waste of time.

We began to take seats at the first (least offensive) table, chairs enough for only the five of us. Madison and Suzanne stood a few feet off, hawking around, watching and waiting. I ignored them.

Finding some good in the middle of it all, I plucked one of the flower stems from the vase and handed it to Hannah. "For you." I winked.

She smiled. Up the tall stem spiraled bright yellow snap-dragon blooms. In one fell swoop Madison had given us something of value without realizing it, diffusing my anger with a good memory. The distraction grounded me a bit and seemed to bring joy to Hannah too. Secrets had that magical effect.

Hannah leaned closer to me. "So far she hasn't sprouted horns or breathed fire. I'm waiting for the other shoe to drop. Sure you're okay tasting without Madison and Suzanne participating?"

My lips twitched. "You think she'll poison us?"

She shrugged. "I'm just saying, prepare yourself."

I gave Hannah a quick nod, then tapped my leaded

crystal water glass. "What do you think of the stemware, Kristen?"

"It's too formal, completely wrong. We need simple glasses, basic plates." Kristen stood and surveyed the options at the other tables. "These glasses." She held a glass up until Suzanne typed a note into her electronic tablet. Kristen then tapped on a plain white dinner plate on the third table. "This place setting."

Two waiters brought out trays of food. We proceeded to taste everything they supplied. Each item was introduced as they served, from tiny quiches to crab cakes to pigs in a blanket. The current waiter served the next item. "These are vegetable pot stickers with an apricot-mango spicy dipping sauce."

I nodded, satisfied. "All of it will work, except for the pigs-in-the-blanket and crab cakes."

"What? One too gauche, the other too highbrow?" Madison crossed her arms but nodded to Suzanne who took notes.

"No, Einstein. They're Jewish. They don't eat pork or shellfish. Even if some would, I'm not risking it."

"We could serve beef hot dogs instead of pork," she countered.

"No. I don't want guests concerned, whether or not it's warranted."

"Fine. Any other requests?" Her lips pressed into a firm line as she stared at me, jaw clenching.

Yeah, well, she had only herself to blame for being the brunt of my fury. With at least half of this shit, she should've known better. Either she was incompetent in her role, or she was goading me.

"I'll send over a list of additional requests for each room. We want wood flooring in the centers for dancing, tables along the perimeter. We'll determine table count and seating and send those over by the weekend. Do you have access to two popcorn machines?"

Madison glanced at Suzanne, who then confirmed, "We have one. I can rent another."

"And photo booths." Kiki twisted in her chair to face them. "Rent a photo booth for each room too."

We all nodded in agreement.

Suzanne gave a short nod. "Done. If you think of anything else, email me by Friday. That'll give us a week to arrange for any last-minute details." She stepped away from Madison toward me. "Cade, could I borrow you for a few minutes? I've got some paperwork in my office for you to sign."

"Sure." I stood while giving Hannah's shoulder a gentle squeeze. "I'll be back in a few."

I was done with this meeting. We'd accomplished what we'd come for on the surface, and Madison hadn't shown her hand regarding our suspicions. "Meanwhile, if *you* have any questions" —I looked pointedly at Suzanne— "or clarifications let me know. These events need to go off without a hitch, which will make the client happy. Then we're all happy. Right, Madison?"

Her eyes narrowed imperceptibly, but I caught her irritation. *Good.* Enough dicking around. We were here to conduct business, not a pissing match.

I suspected this stupid setup was all an elaborate test to see how far she could push us.

The answer? Not at all.

I followed Suzanne out of the ballroom, down hall, and around the corner to her office, the first door on the left. Normally efficient, Suzanne suddenly appeared to be disorganized as she rifled through one file after another on her desk. She frowned, then moved over to a file cabinet and opened the top drawer. "Sorry. I thought I left the file in the center of my desk."

"Is it something you can email? Can it be digitally signed?"

She shook her head. "Give me just a minute. It has to be here somewhere."

I remained in the doorway while she searched.

"Madison gave me a few new files this morning." She moved back to her desk, then moved files one by one off a stack on the corner. "Here is yours."

I stepped closer as she slid the bottom file out and opened it on her desk. From it, she grabbed two sets of standard agreements. After signing the obligatory liability releases, I handed her back the pen and one signed set. "Thanks for your help with the events. I'll keep in touch through the week."

Eager to return back to my sisters and Hannah, I left Suzanne's office. Suddenly, I came to a jarring halt, nearly colliding with Madison, who stood right outside Suzanne's office.

Fuck. The hairs on the back of my neck raised. The instant adrenaline spike forced me to take a deep breath. "What do you want, Madison?"

"Isn't it obvious?"

I dropped her a deadpan look. "No. Enlighten me."

She stepped closer. Too close.

I refused to back down from her and held my ground.

"I want you." Her fingers touched my forearm, and it took every ounce of restraint I had not to flinch. Her head tilted. "I only didn't want to get tied down before..."

Before fucking your way through Europe?

She opened her mouth, but I spoke first. "Not gonna

happen, Madison. Accept it. Then we can all get these events done with minimal stress."

"Why? Because you're with Hannah now? Don't you remember how good it was?"

"Yes, I do." I lowered my voice to a near growl. "Right up to the point you told me what a slut you were."

"I explained why. I'm better now. I'm done with all that. But I'm not done with you."

I gave her a tired sigh, shaking my head. "What's it gonna take to convince you I *am* done?"

Her lips twisted into a smirk. "Let me give you a taste. You know I'll be better than the flavor of the month you're hanging with right now." She licked her lips suggestively.

I almost puked in my mouth. Then I shook my head. "Take care, Madison."

It was an unreal struggle to remain professional (yeah, I got the irony of that after what an asshole I was at that ridiculous tasting), but I didn't want to get dragged down any further by her tactics. I sidestepped around her to continue toward the end of the hall.

When I rounded the corner, my sisters came out of the ballroom. Kiki was in the lead with her cheeks puffed full, a napkin on her hand holding a pyramid of pigs in a blanket.

I stared in amusement.

She shrugged, mumbling around her mouthful, "What? *I'm* not Jewish."

"Where's Hannah?"

"She just went into the ladies' room. We told her we'd meet her in the lobby."

"Why don't you guys head out? I'll take her home." Hannah appeared by my side before I finished my sentence. I wrapped an arm around her and gave her a gentle squeeze. "I'll email last-minute items later tonight for Loading Zone's event." Although everything was lined up for the anniversary, I needed to triple check to be able to sleep at night.

Kristen nodded. "We're set. Fire away when ready." She waved, then joined my other two sisters, who were already involved in an unrelated conversation and didn't bother to look up.

Once we were alone, Hannah nudged her hip into me. "You were gone awhile. Everything okay?"

I glanced down at her and gave a short nod. "Yeah. Suzanne had a problem finding our file."

"Madison left the ballroom about a minute after you and Suzanne did." Her tone dropped, heavy.

"Really?" My mind raced, wondering what might've happened.

Hannah pulled away and stared at me.

I frowned. "Nothing happened in the ballroom after I left, did it?"

Her brows drew together for a beat. "No."

"Were you okay in there with Madison today? Did you feel like knocking Selfish Bitch on her ass at any point?"

She sighed. "I feel like knocking her down now."

"I feel the same. C'mon. Let's go find a way to work through our frustration." I tugged her hand and led her out the back patio doors.

The moment we stepped outside, she jolted to a stop, tugging her hand out from my grasp. "I overheard you and Madison talking in the hallway."

"Which part?"

Her eyes narrowed. "Does it matter? Why didn't you tell me?"

I had no easy answer. Instinct? Protecting her? Self-preservation? I hadn't a clue. "Not sure. Everything she says keeps pushing me further away from believing her. It's actually pissing me off. Didn't seem worth mentioning to piss you off too."

She put her hands on her hips. "What affects you, affects me too. Of all the people needing to believe and trust each other, it's you and me. A few months ago, you wanted to help me with Dumbfuck. Now you have to keep me in the loop to help you with Selfish Bitch. That's how this relationship thing works. We support each other. Don't cut me off so I'm not able to do that."

I stood there a moment, absorbing her words. Then I gave her a hard nod. "You're right. We're a team in this. Sorry that I'm keeping too much shit to myself." Stepping closer to her, I pulled her into my arms. "I've kept this whole thing with Madison a secret for so long, I'm just used to working through it on my own. Please be patient with me. I'll work on it."

She nodded, wrapping her arms around my waist. "That's all I'm asking. Include me."

"Deal." I exhaled a relieved breath, then gave her a soft kiss. Pent-up energy pulsed through me, reminding me why I'd pulled her out here in the first place. "Where's that spa area you visited the other day?"

"In a separate building, toward the back, why?" She glanced at me.

My guttered thoughts must've reflected in my eyes, because hers narrowed at me.

"Because I need to defile these grounds. And I need you." I tilted my head with a smirk, eyes devouring her curves before meeting her gaze again. "Find me a dark corner."

She hesitated, concern crossing over her face.

Determined, I tugged her forward again and finally broke through her subtle resistance.

I leaned down and pressed my lips against her neck. "Do they have a sauna?" I murmured as we crept into the spa's unmanned lobby area.

She nodded and led me around the front corner. At the end of a long corridor, a door with a cedar frame and glass insert appeared. She yanked it open and steam poured out. I grabbed an armful of towels off the shelf and followed her inside. She turned around, then bit her lip.

I blew out a slow breath. She looked sexy as fuck.

I had an undeniable urge to mark my territory. Primal. Couldn't explain it if I tried. Thank God I didn't need to— Hannah had a sudden wild look in her eyes, totally onboard with it.

"Come here, Maestro." I crooked my finger at her.

With a smile, she grabbed one of the thick towels, tossed it onto the floor, and dropped to her knees. "You first." She pulled her top off and unfastened her bra before tossing both aside. Then she unbuckled my belt and ripped open the button fly on my jeans.

During a last flash of rational thought, I wondered if we should've gotten naked before the steam soaked our clothes. Then her lips surrounded me, and I groaned as coherent thoughts scattered.

She expertly worked away my stress and anxiety. I didn't have to ask. She sensed what I needed, knew before I did.

And with a shaky exhale, I let sensations overtake me.

14. SHABBY CHIC

To say that Philly's Society Elite and the Fifth Avenue Contingent were slumming it tonight was an understatement, but as far as I was concerned, they'd never looked better. Furs and jewels had been abandoned in favor of fair-trade garments and accessories. Hair normally pinned up had tumbled free into loose waves. And noses typically high in the air had come down tonight. All who attended our function embraced one another—and those in need—with the spirit of support.

Standing in a quiet corner in the shadows toward the back, my father, Ben, and I surveyed a scene that through our innovation, belief, and financial commitment had transformed Loading Zone from a rough idea scrawled on paper one night in my economics class into a successful reality.

We watched guests continue to file in as our few minutes of private celebration wound down before the public party revved up. My dad, dressed in fair-trade black linen pants and white embroidered dress shirt, raised his beer. "Gentlemen, we did a fine job. Smart decisions, great marketing, and imaginative operating practices have turned this place into something to be proud of. Congratulations, sons."

We clinked bottle necks before I took a long pull from my Fat Tire, enjoying praise from a man who didn't shell it out often.

Needing to find calm in the growing buzz of energy of the room, my gaze drifted over to Hannah. She stood near the end of the bar. Her and Daniel maneuvered her cake a safe distance away from the bar edge.

Hannah looked beautiful tonight. Her slim black dress had a high hemline, exposing the olive skin of her toned thighs. The material was cinched by a belt resting just below her breasts, then rose up over them, covering her curves only as far as was publicly decent.

My thoughts were anything but.

However I remained a patient man. Tonight's focus was on others: the charity, the guests, the employees. There'd be plenty of time later to show Hannah how much I loved her dress.

I checked my watch and confirmed we were twenty minutes from the event start time. "You two ready? We've got a party to run."

"Let's do this." Ben finished his beer, placed it on the tray of a passing waitress, and stepped onto the dance floor, mingling his way through the crowd.

Before I immersed myself in host obligations, I veered off and pressed behind Hannah, gently gripping her hips as I pulled her back into me. Dropping my face against the side of her neck, I growled low, "You look delicious tonight. I love it when you wear your hair wild. Reminds me of how sexy you look after hours of bed play."

She laughed softly and shivered. With a slight turn of

her head, she glanced up at me with a warm smile. "You look incredible yourself. I've never seen you in linen."

"Don't get used to it. I'm more of a jeans and T-shirt guy."

She turned fully in my arms and stared up at me. In slow motion, she drew a finger along the muscle in my forearm, then bit her lip when she tucked the tip of it under the rolled cuff below my elbow. "It's not the attire, but the man underneath I see and want."

I smacked her ass, then kissed her deep and slow. "When the public party ends, our private party will begin." With a sigh, I planted my hands on her shoulders and separated her body from mine before we got carried away. *Others first.* "The cake looks perfect, Maestro. Thank you."

While we lingered for our last private seconds, I paid closer attention to the cake's details. A likeness of our club—in all its rust-and-chrome, shabby-chic glory—stood on one end. On the other side, she'd depicted dark inner-city alleys, complete with towering buildings with graffiti painted on the walls. But both ends were barren of people. The closer your gaze drew to the center, the more people populated the scene. The middle featured a park, full of life from the green grass, trees, and geese floating on the lake to the people engaged in various park activities, like Frisbee, a softball game, and a picnic.

"This truly is a masterpiece, Hannah."

A member of the press we'd invited stepped into view, edging behind the bar. "Mind if I start taking photos?"

For the next few minutes we posed for some of the night's publicity shots. The party hadn't officially started, but we were close. I took a deep breath and relaxed as much as possible for the short time with Hannah before I needed to migrate over to the DJ booth.

Guest headcount had almost reached capacity, but people sat at tables or stood on the dance floor, waiting. The low-volume soundtrack streaming through the speakers kept them all tame, and the waitresses hustled, making sure everyone had a drink in hand.

Once the obligatory photos were done, I glanced around and spotted Kristen waving us over. I put a hand at Hannah's back and urged her toward my family and our friends who'd gathered up in the larger VIP section. "C'mon, Maestro. Showtime."

Darren manned the DJ booth in the far corner of the room, and I wound through the crowd on the dance floor as quickly as possible to join him. At my nod, he faded the music down, then gave me the microphone.

I scanned the crowd, which hushed as the lights dimmed over them and brightened on me. I tapped the mic once to verify the thing worked before speaking. "We all want to thank you for coming here tonight. This weekend is special for us as we pass a milestone. One year ago today, Loading Zone opened its doors, marking the transformation from a decrepit, abandoned warehouse into a successful business.

"Not only did we provide valuable jobs—thumbing our nose at the local down economy—but we included each employee in a portion of the profits, making them a part of our family. And we've all worked hard to make every guest who comes here feel at home."

A rolling wave of cheers and applause thundered through the room.

"But tonight is about more than Loading Zone. And the celebration serves as more than tonight's good time. On the invitation, you were encouraged to wear fair-trade attire, from your clothes and jewelry to your handbags and shoes.

For some, you only had to go to your closets. For many, you had to shop for the very first time from merchants who support fair wages and living conditions.

"What you may not know is that we make every effort possible to do the same in the running of our business: where we buy our alcohol, what decorated the bar you're standing in, the cutting-edge bathrooms my sister Kiki designed. We even scrutinize what goes inside them, down to the toilet paper that wipes your ass."

Laughter erupted. I grinned, then shrugged unapologetically.

"I want you all to think about where you buy your goods from, not just tonight, but every day. Every one of your purchasing decisions can make a difference in someone's life halfway around the world."

I glanced at my mom, nodding to her. "My mother, Victoria Michaelson heads a charity that supports fair trade as one element of its cause. One hundred percent of your two hundred and fifty dollar entrance ticket goes toward her foundation."

Kristen approached the DJ booth, and I leaned down while she stretched up and whispered into my ear. My eyes widened in surprise, but she nodded. I whispered back a question, to which she nodded again.

"Ladies and gentlemen, Kristen's just informed me that not only have the ticket sales raised half a million dollars. But through additional private donations of guests tonight, and through our website, we've topped one million dollars in total donations. And I've confirmed that the donation banner will remain active on both Loading Zone's and Invitation Only's websites for you to contribute on an ongoing basis."

Still astounded, I blinked. "Wow. Tonight has turned

into more than any of us had hoped for. Your generosity never ceases to amaze me. Oh, one more thing before we knock this party off the hook. Please take a moment to appreciate the cake designed and created for tonight's event by Invitation Only's very own Hannah Martin.

"She illustrated perfectly what's transpiring here tonight and what all of us can do afterward: leave our comfort zones and step *toward* one another. Life isn't about business. It isn't about buildings, neighborhoods you were raised in, or the social class you think you 'belong to.' No" —I shook my head, scanning the crowd of people who nodded in agreement— "life is about the people you choose to include, showing them what kindness means."

I paused, pegging a hard stare out to the crowd. "Life is about love."

Whistles and cheers erupted louder than before. Those who'd been seated stood and clapped.

I tilted my head as I glanced at Darren.

He nodded.

"Darren, drop our guests a heavy beat."

Thumping bass pounded a rhythm over the cheers, and the guests began to dance. Even those seated in the booths and at the tables stood, joining in.

My gaze scanned the room until it landed squarely on Hannah. Up in the elevated VIP section, where my parents, sisters, Jason, Mase, Ben and their girls were, one stood out among the rest—my girl.

As her eyes met mine, she smiled. My heart thudded at how happy she looked.

I began to make my way through the thirty feet of crowd toward her until I was waylaid by a guest. After a short conversation, another detained me.

"Congratulations, man. Such a great event." Walter Simmons held his hand out.

I clasped it in a firm shake. "Thanks, Walt." I looked beyond him, searching for his wife. "Where's Cindy?"

He chuckled low as he shook his salt-and-peppered head. "You've created a monster. She's showing off her new fair-trade 'pashmina' that matches her skirt. All the girls are taking notes."

I clapped him on the shoulder. "Responsible shoppers? I'm down with that."

When I glanced back up at Hannah with helpless raised brows, she laughed, waving me off with the back of her hand to take my time. Kiki leaned toward her before they both glanced toward Darren.

Walt leaned in, a hand on my shoulder. "Let me know what else I can do. With no kids and a growing portfolio, Cindy and I are looking for charities to add into our estate planning."

"You have my mom's number, right?"

He nodded.

"Give her a call. She's got the paperwork to provide to your attorneys."

"Will do."

Turned loose into the crowd again, I got several more congratulations and pats on the back before I made it up to the VIP section. The girls huddled together with Hannah on one end of the couch, Ben, Mase, and Jason sprawled out a few feet over. Mase had his arms stretched wide on the back cushions, feet kicked out.

My dad greeted me with a nod, but Mom nearly tackled me over in a hug.

"Unbelievable turnout. And those donations?" Her eyes brimmed with tears.

At her speechlessness, I drew her into a hug. "I know, Mom. We've got great friends backing us and the cause."

Jillian, our VIP waitress for the night, walked into my line of sight holding a tray filled with opened beers, one of them my Fat Tire. I broke away from Mom, scooting her toward Dad who actually bounced to the beat. I whispered in Mom's ear as I gently nudged her. "Go show Dad your moves. We don't want him hurting anyone."

She laughed and kissed my cheek before stepping into his arms.

"Thanks, Jillian." I lifted my bottle off her tray and headed toward the crowd on the couch.

Kristen shifted onto Jason's lap and muttered something. He laughed. "Your sis seems to think you're king tonight."

Hannah stalked over to me, pressing her body into my side. "He is king. He took a random thought, saw possibilities in a forgotten, rundown warehouse, and transformed it into an empire. Even his subjects are loyal and grateful."

Shaking my head, I ushered Hannah to the couch and sat beside Jason, pulling Hannah onto my lap. "You're all high. And if I'm king, so is Ben. We're co-kings."

Ben raised his beer. "To royalty. And sharing the spoils with everyone."

"Cheers to that." I lifted mine along with the rest of the group.

My gaze drifted beyond my parents. The entire dance floor bounced to a rhythmic beat—all except one. One leggy, blonde-haired, blue-eyed nightmare from my past stood motionless and stared straight at me.

"What the *fuck* is she doing here?" My mood tanked, bottoming into the pit of my stomach.

15. PARTY CRASHED

A ll those within earshot of the couch turned to see what made me snarl in rage.

Of course. Madison must've bought a ticket through our website. The thought never occurred to me I'd have to blacklist someone from the party. Was she good Madison or bad Madison tonight? Guess we'd find out.

Head held high and shoulders back, she wore a confident smile and strode through the crowd escorted by Vivienne, a longtime family friend and co-organizer of my Mom's charity.

Mark, our VIP security for the night, grabbed the rope at the base of the steps but glanced my way for guidance. *King indeed.*

I nodded at Mark, even though I wanted Madison as far away as possible from my family and friends. This was our night. Our celebration. But Madison being led our way by Vivienne perplexed me.

Kristen leaned toward me. "This could be interesting."

Madison gave us all a warm smile as Vivienne brought her toward my parents. Curious, and needing to make sure everything was cool, I gently moved Hannah off my lap. "Be right back."

Vivienne gestured between my parents and Madison in what looked to be an introduction.

As I approached within earshot, Madison laughed. "We've already met. I wanted to congratulate you. I believe strongly in your charity and donated an additional five thousand dollars."

Mom's eyes widened. "That's very generous of you, Madison."

My loyal mother shook Madison's hand, but made no move to go closer. They all knew bad shit had gone down between me and Madison, even though most of them had only sketchy details. But they had witnessed the self-centered angry mess I'd become in the wake of the breakup.

Only Hannah knew the entire painful story, including the memory trash pile loaded onto my driveway, the reason for the meaningless string of women, and the final bonfire ritual in Hannah's backyard.

An awkward silence followed, no one making any further welcoming move. I sensed they all waited on me.

Vivienne turned, smiling. "I'll see if I can find any more generous guests."

"Thank you, Vivienne," Mom replied.

Madison gave a single nod. "I didn't mean to interrupt. Enjoy your evening. I'll go mingle in the crowd and get a refill." She shook her empty glass, clinking the ice cubes.

Mom sent me a pointed stare, and I inwardly groaned. Yeah, even kings granted mercy. And I would have to deal with Mom's wrath if I didn't show gratitude for Madison's donation. It's what those in high society did every day. Smile at your enemies and invite them in.

I sighed. "No, stay. Jillian can get you whatever you need.

Thank you for the donation." I lifted a finger to get our waitress's attention.

Within seconds, Mom engaged Madison into an animated conversation.

But it hadn't escaped my notice that Hannah had flinched when I'd spoken.

I crossed back to the couch, sat down, and pulled Hannah back onto my lap before whispering, "I'm doing this for Mom."

She gave me an understanding nod and spoke low, "Plus Kristen made a good point while you were talking with them. Maybe they can find out if she's involved in all the problems we've been having."

"They?"

"Yeah." She gave me a half smile. "I'll let your sisters take care of that investigation. It would look bad at your anniversary party if Madison got a black eye from your girlfriend."

I grinned. "Damn."

Satisfied my sisters had this covered, I gave a quick glance around, aware of time ticking by. Ben, Dad, and I had holed ourselves up here, away from our guests. We had obligatory mingling to carry out.

I side-eyed Madison as she left my Mom and approached us. She settled herself onto the other end of the couch. Kiki sat on the edge of the cushion, leaning forward as she drew in the girls with one of her stories. Madison listened right alongside them.

I tightened my hand on Hannah's hip. "You gonna be okay on your own for a while? I've got to play host with my partners for a bit, thank everyone in person."

Trooper that she was, she nodded. "Of course, go." She climbed carefully off my lap to find solid footing in her high heels. "I'm going to go down and see if Chloe and Daniel need help carving into the cake."

I stood, lacing my fingers into hers, intent on walking her over there. And beyond relieved that she'd be nowhere near Madison. Madison's claim that she wanted me still unsettled me. Especially with the too-coincidental timing and all the other shit going on. But with the way she continued inserting herself into my life at any opportunity, I worried about her true motive.

"Ready to make the rounds, partners?" I glanced at Dad, then Ben.

Ben nodded and joined us as we left the VIP section. Mom stood at Dad's side (after all, the night benefited her charity foundation), then we filed down the steps together onto the main floor. Ben and my parents split apart, heading in opposite directions and immediately engaging guests in conversation.

Hannah leaned against my side as we veered off toward the cake. "Why do you think Madison's here?"

Glancing down at Hannah, I arched my brows. "Honestly? To fuck with me. To fuck with you *and* me, more specifically."

Brows drawn together, she shook her head. "But why? She wants you now? She thinks this is the way to get you? I don't get it."

I hugged her closer. "Stop trying. I don't get it either, and it seems like a waste of mental horsepower. Sometimes there are no rational answers for things." I took another swallow from my beer as we approached the end of the bar.

Hannah tilted her head. "Or she's simply a Selfish Bitch." She maintained a stoic expression.

Hannah knew how badly Madison had hurt me. Because even though Madison wanted to be friends, said she'd changed, and donated a large sum of money to charity, it still didn't alter the fact that she'd hurt me. "Woman, you never cease to amaze me. Thank you for being you."

She gave me a flirty smile. "Only way I know how to be. Now go, mingle." She kissed my cheek, then shooed me away with waving hands. "I've got cake business to attend to."

Unsatisfied with her cheek graze, I wrapped my arms around her and gave her a hard kiss. She gasped into my mouth before melting into my arms with a tiny groan.

On a low growl, I released her. "There. Now I can go mingle."

I made my way through the crowd, periodically glancing back into the VIP section. Madison remained up there, this time seated on the end beside Kendall. They seemed to be discussing something funny, easy smiles lighting up their faces. I was fine with that. As long as Madison stayed far away from Hannah, I felt good leaving my well-behaving ex under the watchful eyes of my secret-agent sisters.

Someone bumped into me, and we both turned toward each other. "Dwight." I clapped the wild partier on the shoulder. "How goes it post-bunny bash? You get to keep any of those sweet things as play toys afterward?"

He chuckled. "You bet your ass I did—took four of them home that night. But after they saw my palatial digs, I nearly had to evict three of them."

My brows arched. "Only three?"

Grinning like the devil, he leaned in. "The fourth's a keeper. Maybe even a potential Mrs. Dwight." He turned and waved his fingers at a busty redhead dancing with three scantily clad girlfriends.

"You dog. Who knew I'd be the one to hook you up for the long haul."

On a head tilt, his eyes widened. "You should run a matchmaking service."

I barked out a laugh. "Ohhh, no. Kristen already thought your party bordered on escort service." I shook my head, grinning as I glanced over at Hannah. She and her team had begun to cut up the cake and spread plates along the bar. "I'm content playing businessman and advisor to Ben here at the bar and to my sisters, with Invitation Only."

"You given any thought to consulting others?" He took a sip of what looked to be scotch.

I shifted my full attention back to him. "Actually, I have. Why, got any connections?"

He nodded. "I'll email you next week. Two of my clients are considering startup ventures. But I know nothing about the risks involved and how they can minimize them. I'll pass along your contact information, if you're game."

Dwight had minted tens of millions of dollars in the short time he'd been doing portfolio management for the upper echelon of wealth worldwide. I blinked, surprised any of his clients would be interested in getting so hands-on in business. "The two clients are unrelated?"

He nodded. "Yep. Bored with watching dollars tick up as they play golf three times a week. They're wanting a challenge."

"Ah, gotcha. Yeah." I shrugged. "Why the fuck not? Give them my number. I'd love to hear what they're entertaining and how I might help." I glanced over his shoulder. "I think your bunny's getting lonely."

Dwight turned to catch the impending show. He waved his hands and charged over to her, shouting. "No, Vanessa. Keep your top on, baby. This isn't one of those parties."

I snorted, then made my way over to a few crew teammates from college. When I shot a quick glance back toward the bar, I froze.

Hannah was alone, Madison's face inches from hers with a sneer curling her lips.

I rushed forward through the crowd, and thank fuck, everyone scrambled out of my way. When I approached within hearing distance over the thumping dance music, I slowed.

Madison had no idea I stood in her blind spot. "...doesn't matter that you *think* he's yours. Nothing's permanent, honey. Certainly not with what you have to offer him. Look at you." Madison swept her gaze down and up. "How could any man be satisfied with that for long?"

"Enough," my primal growl vibrated in my ears.

Madison whirled around, eyes widening. With practiced control, she calmed. "Will it ever be enough, Cade? Will someone who doesn't understand who you truly are, what your social standing entails, satisfy you? You need someone better than that. Better than *her.*"

Someone like you? The harsh retort stuck hard in my throat. Instead, I spoke a greater truth. "You never understood who I truly am. You never will. You've overstayed your welcome tonight. Time to go—before security throws your ass into a skidding slide on the asphalt."

An indignant expression flickered over her face. "You wouldn't dare."

"*I* would." Hannah glared at Madison. "Try me. You have two seconds to vanish before you find out."

Madison huffed but wisely turned and strode toward the doors after glaring at me, then by the way the sea of people parted before her, it seemed at everyone and everything in her way.

She was gone, but that didn't mean damage hadn't already been done.

"Hey." I gathered Hannah into my arms, kissing her temple. "Don't let her get to you. She has *no* idea what she's talking about." Concerned, I pulled back, gazing down at her.

Her scowl intensified. "*Selfish Bitch.*"

"Exactly." I exhaled, relieved at Hannah's anger. Anger we could work with. But my gut told me the emotional obstacle course we'd face in the next couple of weeks had only just begun.

16. NIGHT AND DAY

The following Tuesday, like most mornings after 9:00 a.m., I sat in Ben's office, getting as much focused work done as possible for both Invitation Only and Loading Zone. Only at the moment, I struggled to ignore the loud clanking sounds from Ed and his maintenance crew as they performed their scheduled grease trap cleanout in the kitchen. By almost 11:30 a.m., I'd dealt with all my emails, put final notes in the business plan draft, and stood to stretch. A burger and fries were in my immediate future.

My phone lit up.

Madison.

Only she wasn't texting; a call was coming through. I debated ignoring it. Then I just answered the damned thing.

"Yeah?"

"Cade?"

"Yeah, Madison. What do you want?" I sighed. My gruffness came from the shit she pulled Saturday night. And the series of apologetic texts in the days since. Her behavior was bordering on stalkerish.

A sniff sounded on the other line. "Cade, I'm sorry. I...I

don't know what gets into me sometimes." Her voice caught. A whimper sounded.

Fuck. I sat back down. "Madison, are you crying?"

Silence. Another sniff. "Yes. I'm sorry. I'm trying not to. I've never felt like this before."

My mind spun. Memories flooded in of a time in our pasts, before we began dating in college, when she'd come to me after a bad breakup. But even so, Madison had rarely cried. Back then, her breakdowns began happening after the same upsetting situations with guys repeated themselves.

A twinge of guilt tripped through me, from treating her so harshly, over not giving the vulnerable girl I knew existed somewhere inside of her the benefit of the doubt. "Felt like what?"

"Out of control."

I huffed out a dry laugh. "We never have control. It's all an illusion. You know that." We'd talked about it many times on the lawn at Penn State, when she'd been trying to sort out her personal life with me as a sounding board.

She inhaled a shaky breath. "I just *want* so much. I want people to like me again. I want you to like me again. But all I keep doing is screwing things up."

I leaned back in Ben's chair, staring at the ceiling. "You're trying too hard, Maddie."

"Maddie?" Her voice wavered with a mixture of surprise and hope.

I cringed. I hadn't meant to use the nickname. But within the span of a couple of minutes, we'd fallen back into ingrained roles: Madison hurt and needing comfort, me providing it.

Not skipping a beat, I glossed over the slipup. "Stop trying so hard. You've done this before. You get so focused on the next thing you want, you forget how to treat other people. You forget yourself."

"I *have* done this before." Her amazed tone made it sound like a new revelation.

"Yeah. It's why you had such trouble keeping friends. Why you don't have any now. Relationships of all kinds, friends included, take acts of selflessness. Generosity. Your wants don't figure into that equation. If all you're focused on is what *you* want, and what you want involves people, you will never get it."

Ed popped his head into the office. "We're all set here."

I gave him a nod and held the phone away from my mouth. "The bill's covered?"

On a nod, he tore a report off a clipboard and handed it to me. "Yep. Part of the contract Ben set up. We're square."

"Thanks, man." He headed out as I put the report under a stapler on the center of Ben's desk.

"Sorry. Taking care of things at the bar."

"It's okay. I didn't mean to interrupt. So do you forgive me?"

I sighed. "Look, Madison. You say you want to be my friend, yet you verbally attacked someone I care about. Don't. Walk softer. Be kinder. No one will want to be around you unless you attract them. And that happens when you find the good in yourself and share it with others."

I heard her shaky inhale. Then she blew out a breath. "Okay."

"Okay?"

She sniffed again. "Yeah. I could do that. Slow down. Be nice."

Madison was so *not nice* to Hannah. Reforming would be difficult for Madison. But she had been nice for a time. I'd helped her get there once. "Nice would be a great start."

TUESDAY NIGHT. Another three-day stretch without seeing Hannah had gone by and it seemed like forever. Dinners had been suspended, and we communicated by text and phone call. She'd been slammed at the bakery, though, and I had inventory at Loading Zone and planning for the next two events. Shit had to get done. Yet even with our minimal contact after Loading Zone's party, it had become clear that although no lasting damage had been done with Madison's meddling, superficial wounds had been inflicted. Whenever we spoke about the double bar mitzvah, or my communications with Madison, Hannah's easygoing spirit hardened.

Sitting on Hannah's living room floor, my laptop and electronic notepad being furiously used with all the emailing and note-taking, was another one of those tense moments. On the cusp of an upcoming ten days of crazy, we had to buckle down and deal with collateral damage as best we could.

"...but Madison called you?"

"Yeah. Crying. She apologized for screwing things up. I feel sorry for her, actually. She doesn't know how to make friends like normal people do."

"Because she tries too hard." Hannah's tone deadened. "She could begin by apologizing to me."

"Agreed. But she may need shock therapy to make that kind of recovery."

Her gaze drifted down to the rug under us, eyes narrowing. "Did your sisters make any progress with Madison at the club the other night? Any discoveries?"

I shook my head. "Kristen said Madison was on her best behavior before she left the VIP area. Either she has nothing to do with the sabotage, or she's very good at deception.

Speaking from personal experience, I'm going with the latter."

"I wish you didn't have to deal directly with her." She lifted another piece of pizza out of the box from the pepperoni and mushroom side.

On a sigh, I stretched my legs out and crossed them. I perched my arm along the couch cushion above me, putting her within touching distance. Then I rubbed my thumb on the soft skin on her neck, bared from her ponytail. "I don't. Suzanne is my contact, but Madison replies when in a mood, which is a lot lately. Kristen offered to step in, but the extra burden isn't fair to her. She is point on my parents' party, and with Mom's demanding details, Kristen has her work cut out for her."

Hannah took a deep breath. "A week from Saturday. Then we're free of Selfish Bitch."

I clinked bottle necks with her. "Here's to a week from Saturday, when we have weeks and weeks with no plans."

She leaned her head onto my shoulder. "Eleven more days until freedom."

I nodded while I clicked out of the document I'd saved. "What *will* we do with all the time?"

She let out a soft laugh. "Sleep in bed for days."

Growling low, I lowered my mouth to her ear. "Only *sleep* in bed?"

"Mmm…" She turned her head, touching my lips with a soft kiss. "Passed out for days, after wild monkey sex for days."

"Wild monkey sex?" I snorted.

"You know." She leaned forward, got onto all fours, and slid her arms forward across the rug as she lowered her upper body. Then she folded them before resting her chin on her forearm to glance back at me. She wiggled her ass, and those little white shorts of hers slid higher. "Where I bare my engorged sexy-time goods, and you pound on your chest, howling."

I laughed and got onto my knees behind her. "First of all" —I ground against her, my jeans to her raised ass— "the only pounding that will happen is me into you." I gripped her hips, pumping against her twice in demonstration. "Second of all, I do not, and will never, howl."

She grinned, looking back as she rotated her hips, teasing me. "Grunt?"

I shook my head. "Growl. Roar. Snarl maybe, if I don't get what I want when I demand it."

Pulling away, she held my gaze. When she twisted fully around to face me, she crossed her legs. "Serious for a minute?"

"Anytime you want." I relaxed back into my sprawled position at the foot of the couch.

"Think you'll ever get bored with me?"

I held my sigh in check, wanting to do all those things I'd mentioned: snarl, growl, and roar. Not to mention crush one Madison Kensington for casting even a hint of doubt into Hannah's mind.

"I don't *think* anything. I *know* I won't get bored with you. Not in a few weeks, not in any amount of months, and not in the years I'll be lucky enough to spend with you."

Her expression softened, but then tightened again.

I leaned forward. "Look, Madison has no idea what love is. Don't accept what she *thinks* she knows. It's from her misguided perception."

Hannah's jaw tensed. "But you thought you loved her."

The physical distance stretching between us was brutal, even though it was only a few feet. Hannah had her legs crossed in front of her as a barrier, but we needed contact more. I pushed off from the bottom of the couch and crowded in close. She stared at my chest as I pushed her legs up and bracketed mine around hers.

With a gentle finger, I tipped her chin up, forcing her gaze to meet mine. "I loved a mirage of a girl back when I'd been young and foolish. Until that point, she was the best thing that had ever happened to me. But I didn't see that she only supported me when it suited her motives. The moment hers weren't aligned with mine, she no longer cared about me. No matter what I thought I felt for her at the time, that's not love. My time with her had been a joke. Her callous actions made me see her true self."

She gave a heavy blink. "How do you know I'm different? That you love me?"

Good question. Even better, how could I trust in what Hannah and I had? I'd been a great judge of people until Madison had pulled her con job on me. Back then, I thought she'd changed with me after she'd burned through all those guys. I thought she'd been capable of love.

But Madison and Hannah were night and day. Madison was hard-edged and manipulative. Hannah, easygoing and genuine. Where Madison found fault in others and turned a blind eye, Hannah saw the good in people, offering to help any way she could. And Hannah didn't have to try at all. It came naturally to her. There was no comparison.

And in hindsight, my proposal to Madison had been driven by logic. Feelings I'd had for her had been rooted from our childhood friendship. Beyond that, maybe they'd only been superficial. My grasp of life back then had been an initial version: Cade 1.0.

What I felt now was worlds-apart different. With Hannah, my heart both ached and soared. In every incredible way that made me never want it to end.

I inhaled deeply, smiling. "There aren't enough words to describe what you do to me, for me. Every day, I wake thinking about how I can make you smile, cause your laugh. I know I love you because of the things I want to learn about you, endless ways I want to touch your body, your heart. There are so many adventures I want to take you on, experiences I want to have with you—just to live in that moment with you."

Her mouth fell open slightly, but no words came out. I began to worry I'd overwhelmed her, when all I'd wanted to do was reassure her. Prove to her with words how I felt.

"You okay, Maestro? I think I stunned you speechless."

She nodded, throat working as she swallowed. Her voice rasped out. "I've never...that was the most beautiful thing anyone has ever said to me."

Lifting my hand, I watched her carefully as she closed her eyes in anticipation of the contact. My fingers brushed her cheek as she leaned in toward my touch. "I mean every word."

I sighed, wishing I could obliterate all the crap. Hannah didn't deserve to be dragged into the mud that Madison seemed hell-bent on flinging. A part of me thought *fuck it*, I'll kidnap Hannah to our tropical island, and the rest of the world would still spin, going on without us.

But I wasn't built to escape responsibility. Letting people down didn't exist as an option. Kristen may have offered to take over, but I knew she and the girls would struggle to handle it all. They needed me. Hannah needed me.

I just needed to figure out a way to keep the balance.

17. WEEKENDER

As I loaded the back of the Jeep Mase and I shared, the drama of last weekend and the pressure of getting two more events nailed out began to fade into anticipation for the party at my parents' place. I needed to relax more than I'd realized. The realization hit when my alarm sounded and I'd raced around, excited as I tossed last minute items together—without the jolt of coffee. Yeah, that happened before noon like...never.

I bent over and lifted the last box Kristen had dropped off yesterday, then slid it onto the only remaining open space on the floor. After scanning the tightly packed area, I wedged my leather overnighter into a safe place on a box between two bags of decorations. Almost set.

When I went back into the house to retrieve Ava's supplies (her leash, crate, bowls, and food enough to last the weekend), the pup trotted behind, jumping around, unable to contain her eagerness. That made two of us.

I laughed. "That's right, girl. We're goin' on a trip."

Mase followed us out front, barefoot with a half-full beer

bottle in hand. "If she stalls out, cut the engine, pump the gas, and count to ten before trying to start her again."

Confused, I turned around, brows drawn low. "What?"

The lazy shit busted up laughing. "Just messin' with ya', man. Tuned her up last week. She purrs like a kitten."

Amped about the trip, I shook my head with a snort. The Jeep was his daily driver, and I'd freaked thinking I'd have to scramble for transportation. "Do not fuck with me this early. I'm uncaffeinated. Uncool, man." I pegged him with a serious look. "Take good care of my bike. I'll take good care of your wheels."

"And my dog." Mase squatted, and Ava raced over to him and jumped against his chest. He fell back, pretending she'd had the force to tackle him. Then he tumbled over her, growling and roughhousing.

I chuckled. "And *your* dog? I figured our shared custody agreement allowed for a weekend at the parents'."

Ava and Mase really had taken to one another. Even though the dog was a gift to Hannah, Ava stayed at our place. But after all the months Mase had campaigned to get a dog, bringing her into the house had done wonders for the guy. Instead of being holed up in his room, morose when he couldn't ride waves because of the weather—or his woman, because of her law school studies—he spent time out in the yard, bonding with his new best friend.

I patted the passenger seat while calling, "Come on, girl!" Ava looked at it, decided it was too big a leap, and jumped onto the floorboard first instead, then the seat.

After closing the door, I saluted Mase. "Don't burn the house down."

He flipped me off.

I grinned, shaking my head. "See ya' Sunday."

Before picking up Hannah, I drove over to Loading

Zone, needing to drop off my draft of next year's business plan to Ben. I knew he'd be there this early; the man lived and breathed our bar.

I parked in the shaded spaces around back and shut off the engine. Ava tilted her head as she stared at me, one ear flopping to the side.

"I'll be right back girl." After I closed the door, I used the remote start on my keychain to lock the doors. Then I restarted the Jeep, letting it idle with the A/C on full blast to keep her cool.

I unlocked Loading Zone's back door and walked down the hallway to Ben's office. He wasn't in there, but I dropped the paperwork onto the center of his desk. Light shone down the hall from the bar area. I continued toward the front to investigate.

Ben stood behind the bar with a scowl on his face, arms propped on the edge of the counter. He glanced my way. "We have company." The warning look he gave me shouted that it wasn't the good kind.

"Who's here?" I racked my brain. The time of day threw me.

"Health inspector."

"Didn't we just have an inspection three weeks ago?"

"There was a complaint," Ben clarified.

I frowned. "About what?"

"Some bullshit about a bartender not handling the fruit with a gloved hand. She got sick a few hours later."

"She?" Couldn't be Madison. Or could it? No. The girl on the phone, crying, wanting to be different, asking for my forgiveness wouldn't be that stupid.

The inspector walked out from the kitchen area and approached Ben. "Here's a copy of my report. You guys run a clean shop, and I'm impressed with everything. Please remind your bartenders to wear gloves when directly handling food. Last time I was here, they were all good. It was during operating hours, and I didn't see any infractions."

"Hi, Spence." It was the same inspector we usually got. "Great to see you again." I shook his hand. "Did the complainant give their name, any other details?

"No. She remained anonymous. But by law, we have to respond to all complaints."

"Thanks. Just curious. We have a puzzle we're trying to solve and think it might be the same person who's doing everything possible to make life difficult for us."

Spence nodded. "We've seen it before. Competition. Angry employees. Just keep up the good work, and their efforts will be nothing but a waste of their time."

When Spence stepped out the front door, I shot a glance at Ben.

Ben shook his head. "Knew from the start something was up. I'm not even going there with the bartenders, other than to say the inspector came by and someone is gunning for us. Warn them all to stay on their toes."

I gave a short nod. "Good."

"You heading out?"

"Yeah. Just dropped the draft off on your desk. I emailed it too, but wanted to be sure you had my notes before the weekend. Is Lisa all set for tomorrow night at my parents' place? Everything covered here?"

Ben pushed away from the bar. "Yep. We're good. Get outta here and have a great time."

THE FIFTEEN MINUTE drive to Hannah's flew by. I vibrated more than the dog. Having Hannah all weekend at my parents', even though we had a party to run, seemed like a rare getaway—an unplugging we both desperately needed.

Before I pulled to the end of her driveway, she stepped out with a bag on her shoulder, waved, then turned to lock her front door. I jumped out, careful to close the door behind me, corralling Ava in and jogged over to Hannah. "Let me get that."

I took her bag with one hand and pressed the other into her lower back before bending down and kissing her. Then I dropped her bag onto the grass and deepened the contact. Wrapping both arms around her, I pressed small kisses in a line down her neck, inhaling her tropical scent. "Damn, I've missed you."

She leaned back in my arms, a pink blush coloring her cheeks. "Wow. What did I do to deserve such an amazing greeting?"

"You being here with a packed bag. Works for me."

Ready to head out, I picked up her bag again and held her hand as we walked toward the Jeep. Ava barked, front paws resting on the driver's door window frame.

I secured Hannah's bag in the backseat while she climbed into the passenger side. Wasting no time, I got in, started up the Jeep, and backed out of her driveway and onto the road.

Seconds later, laughter and commotion drew my attention to the right. I snorted, laughing.

Ava had overtaken her lap, and then some. "Look how big you've gotten. And such a good girl. Yes, you are." Hannah rubbed her ears, cooing and baby talking. Ava ate up the attention. Mase had been replaced.

Hannah hummed a relaxed tone. "How long of a drive is it?"

I glanced over at her again. Ava had settled down, resting her head into the cushion of Hannah's chest—a favorite place of mine too. Yanking my thoughts from the gutter, I blinked. "Ninety minutes, give or take traffic getting out of Philly. Maybe less today."

"And this is the house you grew up in?"

I nodded. "Mostly. Mom and Dad had both places by the time I was born. But although the apartment on Fifth had enough bedrooms, space was cramped for entertaining my parents' friends and clients while raising four kids."

"Sounds ritzy."

I smiled, remembering the humble upbringing Hannah had. Lack of normal family structure or wealth didn't mean she hadn't had a loving home. Both of us had been lucky compared to many less-fortunate children. "Only different scenery from yours. My parents were born into money, but they had generous hearts. So they made sure to leverage their money to help others along the way."

She sighed, nestling her head against the headrest. "I think Gran and Granpop would've liked your parents."

Hannah had said her grandparents raised her after her mom died. But she didn't talk often about her mom. Her tone seemed heavy when she did, and she usually changed the subject quickly. My curiosity wasn't a good enough excuse to bring up the topic though. When and if she wanted to share, I would be there for her.

I recalled what little I knew about her grandparents. "They loved chess and he loved old cars? They would've hit it off immediately. Too bad we couldn't have brought along Josephine. My dad would've loved to see her."

"Yeah?"

"A pristine black '67 Mustang Fastback? Oh yeah, no doubt. Wait until you see the surprise I've been dying to show you."

"Looking forward to it. By the way, I had an interesting morning. Got a phone call from Chloe at the bakery. There was a food and safety inspection prompted by a complaint. A lady said she got sick at the bakery. The inspector was there and wrapped up by the time Chloe called, or I would've gone in. The only ding on today's report was because Daniel wasn't wearing a hairnet or hat over his Mohawk while preparing food in the kitchen. Otherwise, we got a great score."

I blinked hard and glanced at her. "You're fucking kidding. Me too. A *woman* called in a complaint on us. Anonymously. Ours was some bullshit about no gloves with the fruit. All of our bartenders are religious about that."

"Really? Wait a minute...*Selfish Bitch*?"

I blew out a heavy breath. Hard to deny Hannah's theory with all signs pointing there.

She shook her head. "So she's stepping up the attacks." There was no question in Hannah's tone. Little room for doubt in my mind either, even though I'd tried to give Madison the benefit of it. Two hits in one day: Hannah's biz and mine? Even if it made no sense whatsoever, someone was out to hurt me and Hannah. A jealous ex was the most likely explanation. Could it be another ex of mine or Hannah's? Sure. But Madison was the only ex in play. "Apparently. Now she's going after our businesses."

"What's next?" She let out a dry laugh. "An IRS audit?"

"Bite your tongue, woman. That would be a nightmare."

She crossed her arms. "Maybe we should send the inspectors and auditors crawling up her ass. Two can play at her game."

I exhaled out a breath, grinning at the fight Hannah had in her. "I like the advice our inspector gave this morning. Keep doing our thing as well as we've been doing it, and let her waste her time."

She stared at me for a few beats. "You always take the high road. Is it only me that wants to punch her lights out?"

I coughed out a laugh. "Oh no. I'd love to give her a piece of my mind. But I won't battle it out on her level. Let her exhaust and frustrate herself. Our time will come."

On a heavy sigh, Hannah crossed her arms. "Days on end of being busy and then being randomly hit by her unnecessary drama is stressing me out. I can't wait for all of this to be over."

I fought a smile. "Look in the center console."

Hannah tilted her head. "Nice segue."

"Just open it. Trust me, it'll help."

She narrowed her eyes, but leaned over and opened the lid backward. Ava stuck her snout into the opening.

"No, no, girl." Hannah laughed and gently tugged on her collar. Then she reached in and pulled out the envelope I'd stashed in there.

"What is it?"

"Are you always this bad with surprises? This one's good for a change."

She stared at the envelope.

I snorted, amused with her suspicion. "*Open it.*"

Finally, she lifted the flap and pulled out the two airline tickets. She gave a couple of heavy blinks and stared at the tickets. "We going somewhere?"

I smiled, returning my gaze back to the road. "We *did* talk about private-island therapy. I booked us a week-long vacation in the Seychelles."

"Oh my God!" She squealed and Ava barked.

"So I guess that's a 'yes?'"

"Yes!"

The tension in the car dissipated almost immediately. Amazing what the promise of ocean and sand will do for a person. I wasn't the only one in the car who needed a complete break, away from the stress.

I frowned. "Wait. Do you have a passport?"

She nodded. "We traveled abroad to France during a cooking internship."

"Really? What was that like?"

"Incredible. We were there for two weeks. Lived in the homes of our host chefs."

The conversation went into the experience she had during her internship and all the things we planned to do on our upcoming vacation.

The last few miles of the trip drifted into a comfortable silence. I glanced over at her.

She stared out the front window with a faraway gaze.

My brows furrowed. "You okay?"

"Yeah. Just a little nervous, I guess."

"You've been around my sisters a lot. And my parents a few times now."

She shrugged. "I know. But this is bigger. I won't be around your parents and friends in *your* house for only few hours. This is *their* house and their friends for a whole weekend."

I shook my head. "Don't worry. This afternoon we'll be busy setting up for tomorrow. Tonight will be laid back, and I'll be with you the whole time. Tomorrow, we'll be up to our eyeballs with party details."

"Yeah, you're right. Guess it just helps to talk about it. I made it bigger in my head than it needed to be."

I gave her a pointed look. "Don't. My family shouldn't be

a cause of stress. They're all human, and they love me. By extension, my parents love you. And my sisters already do. Hell, I don't even know what I'm saying. You're already one of the family: Michaelson by adoption."

She smiled, happiness replacing the concerned expression she'd had only moments ago.

A few minutes later, we pulled up to the gate, then continued through, curving along the driveway. I didn't say a word, wanting her to experience the estate for herself. But when I glanced over, her eyes had widened. She rolled the window down and leaned forward to stick her head partially out, forcing Ava off her lap and scrambling into the back seat.

Hannah's mouth slowly dropped open as we pulled under the portico. Even though I'd grown up here, the grounds still took my breath away too. Well aware of what others lacked and we had in abundance, it always humbled and amazed me to take in the beauty of our home.

Built along the lines of a stately mansion, the front had four columns and wings that sprawled out on either side. Wider than it was deep, the house had an imposing presence to a visitor unused to the architectural style.

Eyes wide and blinking rapidly, Hannah opened her door, stepped out, and craned her neck, sweeping her gaze across the east wing.

"Hannah, watch" —Ava bounded out the door and bolted off, barreling around the side of the house— "out for Ava."

But little Ava wasn't brave enough to abandon us altogether. She swooped back into view in a wide arc, barking once at us before disappearing again.

I ran after Ava, shouting, "That pool isn't fenced!"

Hannah tore off beside me as we raced to restrain the

animal I hadn't warned anyone we were bringing. Hence the crate. And the long-forgotten leash.

Ava didn't appear again. By the time we made it past the side of the house and through the rose garden, I heard a loud splash.

The pool area near the barbeque was already filled with people: my sisters and Jason, my parents, even a few neighbors who'd been invited over for a casual gathering before we needed to set up for the afternoon. But all their attention centered on the pool.

Apparently Ava was a natural swimmer, or a survivalist who hadn't yet found the way out. I ran over to the end where the steps were and clapped my hands. "Come on, Ava. Over here."

Hannah appeared by my side and braced her hands on her knees while she sucked in oxygen. After a couple of gulps of air, she spoke between breaths, "Hoping you don't have to go for a swim?"

Ava swam our way, paddling from the center of the Olympic-length pool. I glanced up at Hannah, noting the others were outside of earshot. "Oh really, smartass? Who's the one who gawked at my parents' house instead of watching the dog? *You* should be the one swimming."

Her eyes narrowed. "You wouldn't dare. What happened to my knight, lifting me over puddles?"

I ran my fingers up her calf. "He's far more interested in seeing you make a big splash."

The smart girl sat down on the cool decking. Which meant in order for me to dump her, I had to stand up, scoop her up, and hoist her into the pool. All a lot of effort for a little bit of fun.

And so fucking worth it.

Hannah squealed, kicking when I snatched her up, but I

had a solid grip on her. The crowd gathered at the corner of the pool caught wind of my agenda and started cheering me on. Mom covered her eyes. Ava started barking.

I swung Hannah toward the pool. "One." Then swung back, over the decking.

She growled. "Put me down this instant."

"Two."

She locked her hands around my neck. "If you let go, you're coming with me."

I grinned. "Three." I hesitated on the last swing, catching her off guard enough for her to loosen her grip. Then I tossed her in.

She flew through the air, arms flailing, safely far enough away from Ava's position, and splashed into the water. I stood with my hands on my hips, grinning.

Hannah surfaced, sputtering, but with a big smile on her face, and I laughed.

Ava redirected her paddling, heading toward Hannah. She caught the puppy, cradling her with one arm. "That's right, girl. It's just a bunch of water, all kinds of fun."

While Hannah and Ava were preoccupied with their water-soaked reunion, I backed up a few steps, took a running head start, and leaped into the air, pulling my legs up to my chest. "Cannonball!" The last thing I saw before hitting water was the crowd scattering away from the splash zone with widened eyes.

Waterlogged jeans made for heavy going, but I swam underwater over to my girls. Hannah's toes barely touched the bottom, and Ava's four legs were free and paddling again. I broke through in front of Hannah, wrapping my arms around her.

A huge smile curved her lips. "You're crazy."

"And you love it."

She wrapped her arms around my shoulders and gave me a quick kiss. "Yeah, I do."

After a few minutes of reckless splashing and laughing, we climbed out of the pool. Beach towels were stacked in a pile on the nearest lounger. I scrambled over, unfolded one for Hannah, and bundled her up. Her hair was slicked back except for a few strands stuck to her cheek. I wiped them back behind her ears.

"You look great wet."

She side-eyed me, replying under her breath, "You've seen me wet before."

"Not fully clothed," I countered.

Her brows arched. "And a fully clothed wet is better?"

"Hell no. But that was fun. And besides, it only makes me want to get you out of them."

Squeals caught my attention. Ava had wandered into the admiring group and shook out her fur, spraying them.

"I've got her." I rushed over and scooped up the little swimmer. "We'll go shower and change. 'Bout an hour?"

Dad glanced at his watch. "A little longer, we'll start grilling at 1:00 p.m. No rush."

"Sounds great." I scanned everyone's amused faces. "Sorry for the messy entrance. For those of you who haven't been formerly introduced, the woman I nearly drowned is Hannah, my girlfriend. I'm sure she's thoroughly embarrassed and wants to make a quick exit, maybe set my hair on fire in retaliation. The little one is Ava." I held up a paw, waving.

Mom laughed. "Be sure to bring Ava back. We need to show her some love when she's a bit dryer."

I wrapped a free arm around Hannah's towel-covered shoulders. "Done. And feel free to gossip. We'll be gone long enough for you to talk about us and all the neighbors within a two-block radius."

We escaped to a fresh round of laughter as I tucked a drenched Hannah closer into my side and lowered my mouth to her ear. "That leaves us plenty of time to hose off Ava and blow her dry for a crate-time nap. Plus a whole extra hour for me to hose you off, get you wet all over again...maybe some blowing. Then we'll get to the drying."

She snorted and broke away, racing back around the side of the house toward the front. I put Ava down, and we chased after her. And as the wind hit my face, I thought that our weekend away was off to a perfect start.

18. FAMILY TIME

At 1:06 p.m., I ushered a blushing and thoroughly satisfied woman back down to the pool area. Hannah had begged me to take the sleeping Ava back out, since the dog would be crated at night, and of course, I caved to her and Mom's earlier request for puppy time.

And, after the lousy morning with dual surprise health inspections, I welcomed anything to distract us into enjoying ourselves.

We hadn't taken two steps onto the patio before I spotted Dad in front of the barbeque. Armed with tongs in one hand and a metal spatula in the other, he wore a black grilling apron and a white chef's hat.

"Mom make you wear that thing?" Grinning, I pointed at his head.

He glanced over at Mom, winking. "Maybe."

A breeze blew some of the smoke our way, and I coughed. Then I pulled Hannah away from the dissipating cloud, approaching the tables and chairs that were shaded with umbrellas. I took the leash from Hannah and tied it around the leg of the nearest lounge chair while Hannah poured a glass of water into an empty dog bowl she'd carried. The boundary gave the dog plenty of room to reach us where we sat at the far end of the tables, but kept her out of danger and the risk of getting underfoot.

Kendall handed me an open beer as she walked by. "Hannah, we're serving up mai tais. You game?"

Hannah nodded. "Yeah, I'll try one."

Kiki blinked, moving to a chair across from us, out of the sun. "You've never had a mai tai?"

"Nope." Hannah said the word with a popping "P" on the end.

"What about piña coladas? I know you've had strawberry daiquiris," Kiki replied.

Hannah took a sip of my beer. "I've experimented plenty with drinks."

Mom walked up with their guests. "Hannah, these are our friends and direct neighbors Lana and Kevin Thompson. And this is Walter and Amy Rivers; they live around the block."

"Nice to meet you." Hannah gave a little wave, since all the chairs and people between them made it impossible to shake hands.

Although Dad could've grilled something as pretentious as steaks, we didn't roll that way. Not at our house. Dad wined and dined any day, and many nights, for business. But he never brought any of that flash beyond the front gate at the curb. Our home was his sanctuary, a casual place filled with laughter and love.

And so Dad shouted out the menu choices, "All the burgers with cheese, say aye."

"Aye," I called.

"Aye," Kristen added.

"Any hot dog takers?"

Kendall, Lana, Jason, Kevin, and I all called out an affirmative. Kendall returned to the table with Hannah's tropical drink, complete with an hourglass-shaped glass, a blue drink umbrella, and a wedge of orange dangling on the rim.

Impressed with the presentation, I arched a brow. "You looking for a job at the bar?"

Kendall scrunched her face at me.

I laughed. "Could've fooled me. That's a five-star looking drink."

"Pffft." Kendall plopped into a seat across from us.

Kristen began to pass around two platters, one with burgers and the other with toasted buns. "When have you ever seen us blend a drink without dressing it up?"

I thought back, realizing Kristen was right. In fact, we'd all been making mixed drinks since we were tall enough to work at the counter without tipping over the glassware, long before we were old enough to drink them. It was a game we played when Mom and Dad were entertaining. And somehow their cute kids playing bartender had turned into amusement for the guests. "You're right. Totally forgot about that."

Kristen snorted. "No wonder why you wanted to open your own bar and tend behind it."

"Kendall, help me with the rest of the food," Mom called from the kitchen door.

I got up. "I'll help too."

Hannah scooted back, but I shook my head. "Stay here. Relax and keep an eye on Ava. She'll keep calm if you're here."

We returned with the side dishes, Mom and Kendall with bowls of chips and dips, me with a watermelon half filled with melon balls. Several conversations were underway already, my Dad and Kevin in a friendly debate over the proposed shopping mall a few blocks down. Ava had found a quiet spot in the shade under her lounger and had sprawled out for a nap.

At our three umbrella tables, our family caught up with one another and neighbors gossiped. Kevin mentioned admiring Clinton Iverson's new Bugatti Veyron. Mom whispered the news about David Stewart's new twenty-something wife.

When the food had been eaten, the gossip topics exhausted, and the energy dwindled down, we said goodbye to the neighbors. I purposefully hung back with Hannah and Ava for a few minutes before the rental trucks started to arrive for the party setup. I glanced at Hannah who sipped the last of her second mai tai.

"Well, what do you think?" I tilted my head, watching her peaceful expression.

Her gaze drifted down to her pale orange drink. "It's okay. Not my favorite."

Leaning in to brush a kiss on her cheek, I chuckled. "No, silly, my family. You were a little nervous when we drove up here. How about now?"

She blinked. "I totally forgot I'd even been concerned." A smile tugged at her lips as she looked up toward the house where everyone had disappeared. "I think I might love your family."

Stretching my arms up and locking my fingers together behind my head, I laughed. I let my ass slide down in the seat and crossed my feet on the chair seat opposite me. "All signs indicate they definitely love you."

Snorting a cute puff of air from her nose, she shook her head. "I still can't believe you tossed me in the pool."

I scoffed, unapologetic. "You needed that icebreaker. And with the entire cheering section goading us on, I knew you wouldn't be completely mortified. Think of it as a family initiation."

"Next time, warn a girl." She gave my shoulder a light shove. "So I guess I'm officially a Michaelson?"

The words came out of her mouth before she realized what they meant. I blamed it on her double dose of mai tais that I'm sure contained enough alcohol to impair her judgment and loosen her filters. 'Officially' a Michaelson meant taking our name—which involved proposals and weddings.

But her lighthearted demeanor told me she hadn't made the mental connection. And to make sure her thoughts didn't stray from her warm-and-fuzzy happy place, I chuckled. "Oh, yeah. You're a Michaelson alright, baptized by pool water, christened in the shower, and adopted while barbequing."

I lifted my beer. "Raise up that 'okay mai tai,' Maestro."

With a big smile beaming on her face, she grabbed her glass with the orange slice dangling from its rim.

"To new families and the security in knowing that with love, an entire army will always have your back." *No matter what obstacles we faced.*

Hannah's smile widened. And I swear her happiness brightened an already sunny day—burned right through all the nonsense that had clouded our morning.

AFTER STOWING Ava safely away in her crate for a nap, we went down to the kitchen to help with the last of the cleanup. I took over wash duty from Mom. Kendall tossed Hannah a clean dish towel, then joined my other two sisters, who sorted through Mom's serving pieces, deciding which items they wanted to use for the party. The rest would be purchased for pennies on the dollar from a restaurant supply store, who'd committed to Kristen to stay open this afternoon by private appointment.

Before we'd dried the last platter, 3:00 p.m. rolled around and the gate buzzed, signaling the rental trucks had arrived. Kristen ran off to the control panel to let them in. Then she rushed through the kitchen again and out the back door.

I took the platter from Hannah and set it on the granite countertop. "That's our cue. Showtime."

Two paneled trucks drove across the lawn and parked where Kristen directed them. Two-man teams began unloading dozens of chaise lounges and half as many market umbrellas. Huge concrete pots were brought out as well, then positioned in an alternating pattern, one in an empty space behind every few chairs.

Gardeners descended onto the pots, adding soil and planting assorted flowers into each one. After about forty minutes, all the chairs had been positioned and the gardeners had begun hosing down the tables and umbrellas, the cushions and chairs, and finally the decking around the pool.

Hannah nudged up beside me, smiling. "Those pots have snapdragons."

Even though my sunglasses were dark, I could see the brilliant colors. "It was one of two requests I made to the gardeners."

She tilted her head. "What was the other?"

"Purple pansies. Mom's favorite."

"Awww, how sweet."

I wrapped an arm around her. "I take care of my girls."

She leaned in, resting her head on my shoulder as we stood in the shade, watching the last of the activity. "None of your family is doing anything tonight, on the actual Fourth of July?"

I shook my head. "We've never been big on crowds. And we need a good night's rest to handle the nonstop craziness that will happen for the party tomorrow."

"So really, there's nothing for you and I to do today, other than make sure everything gets put in its proper place?"

Taking her hand, I led her down toward the pool area. The breeze picked up, and the fading sun made the temperature perfect. "Exactly. We oversee the client's vision to ensure that what we ordered arrives, and the way we imagined things actually occurs."

Hannah ran a finger across the top of the cushion on a chaise, the back of which rested at a perfect forty-five degree angle to match the rest in line, down the length of the pool. "Where did all the lounge chairs, tables, and umbrellas come from? They're a perfect match to the existing terra-cotta cushions and tan furniture."

I nodded as I scanned the pool area to take in the sixty-five chairs, thirty on each side and five in the middle at the end, spaced into wide groupings of two and four. "They're a perfect match because it's all their furniture. When Mom bought the collection a few years back, she bought enough for parties just like this, and she stores the extra pieces between events. She only throws one or two parties a year and wants things informal when it's family and a few neighbors."

Hannah blinked. "Right. Informal."

I chuckled as I roped my arm around her shoulder again and turned us back toward the house. We passed one of the planted pots that overflowed with flowers. "The pots are new this year. She may keep them, not sure."

Hannah paused in her step.

Trying not to laugh, I nudged her forward. "Go on. I know you want to."

I sighed, enjoying these quiet stolen moments we had together, away from the hectic pace of business, protected from the nastiness of exes. The weekend had only begun, but all the tension and stress that had been plaguing us had already washed away.

Leaning down to the pot filled with colorful blooms, she bit her lip in that tempting way that drove me wild, but glanced up with a joy-filled innocence—completely at odds with my guttered mind. And then the woman I loved embraced the little girl inside her and gripped a red flower by its jaws, making it sing while she gave it a voice.

"La, la, laa, la, la, laaa..." Her cheeks pinked by the time she released the flower. She nudged back into my side but kept her gaze down at the pool decking, trying to hide her widening smile behind the curtain of her hair.

But I'd caught a glimpse of it and an ache spread through my chest as I kissed her temple and led us back into the house. A selfish part of me knew why I'd insisted on snapdragons: not only because she loved them, but because I loved seeing the side of her she hid from the world—the uninhibited child she kept under lock and key, except for a rare occasion when she trusted and set it free. For me.

19. SURRENDER

After securing Ava into her crate for the night in the adjoining bathroom, we settled down into my double bed in the childhood room that had grown up with me. A Mets pennant hung on the wall from when Dad had made time on my tenth birthday to take me to a ballgame. A couple of trophies sat on the tall dresser in the corner, both from rowing crew. The wall also held photos: some from vacations with family, others from wild spring break trips I'd taken with friends. The only photographs of girls anywhere were of my sisters.

Hannah pulled the covers over her head.

I laughed, ducking under with her. "Whatcha doin' under here? Should I grab a flashlight? Are we playing fort?"

She made a frustrated noise. "I can't believe I'm sleeping in the same bed with you in your parents' house."

I dropped my voice low. "I think they *know* we're not sleeping."

Her jaw dropped, and she smacked my chest.

"What? I'm sure they had sex when they were our age.

Actually, they were younger than we are when Kristen was born."

"And did the two of them stay the night in the same bed in your dad's parents' house?"

"Don't know. Want me to go ask?" I ducked out of the fort and moved to get off the bed.

Her hand clamped down on my wrist, her whisper fierce. "Don't you dare."

Chuckling, I pulled down the covers, baring her pretty face. The T-shirt of mine she wore had slipped down one of her shoulders. I pulled the material up over her head, baring her breasts. Moonlight flooded in through the uncovered window, making her skin seem to glow. Her nipples hardened as I watched her.

"I'm not having sex with you in your childhood bed."

I snorted. "But the shower was okay?"

"That's different. You..."

"I..."

Her eyes narrowed. "You coerced me."

My brows shot up. "Coerced? That's a strong word."

She turned her head and glanced toward the bathroom, relaxing her expression. "Convinced."

I trailed my fingers along those tempting exposed breasts. When I brushed along the outer curve, her breath hitched and her eyes fluttered shut. I leaned over and teased my lips along the crook of her neck until she shivered. "More like seduced," I whispered.

She swallowed hard.

With a light touch, I swirled my fingertips over the swell of her breast until my palm grazed her nipple.

On a gasp, she arched up into my touch, seeking more. "You're doing it again," she mumbled.

"Doing what?" I murmured against her skin, teasing her earlobe with my teeth.

She smiled. "Coercing me."

"Oh, we're gonna play that game, are we?" I pulled my hand away and dragged the backs of my nails along her ribs. "We're arguing the subtleties of semantics. Your word sounds forceful. Perhaps you need a more thorough demonstration."

"Wh-what do you mean?"

"Easy, Maestro." I drew out the words as she relaxed her shoulders down. "No need to worry. I'll give you what you want. But by the time you get what you need, it'll be after I've teased you, slow and thorough. When I have you trembling and shaking, your words incoherent, then maybe we'll decide together that the word you've been looking for is 'seduced.'"

In a flash of movement, she shoved hard on my shoulder, and I found myself on my back. Before I could process the surprise, she straddled me. "Maybe I don't want to be seduced. What if I want to be the seducer?"

"I'm confused. You had an issue with our sleeping in the same bed only moments ago, but now you're ready to ride me with wild abandon?"

She looked breathtaking. Her hair fell around her face in dark waves, the ends curling above her chest. Plump lips glistened, begging to be kissed. I admired her body: the luscious curve of her breasts, the intriguing dip in at her waist, the sexy flare of her hips.

Her lips curved into a smirk. "Oh, no. There'll be no riding with wild abandon until you beg for mercy, until you groan and writhe, then plead for me to slide down onto you."

I'd surely died. This had become heaven. This dirty,

teasing side of her blew my mind. "Wait. Are you coercing me? Or seducing me?"

She gave a frustrated little growl. "You." She pointed to my chest, as if I would somehow misunderstand. "Will keep your mouth shut, or I will gag you. I'm not above tying you up either."

My cock kicked up against her. She groaned. Yeah, wasn't my fault, she turned me the fuck on with her talk of gagging and bondage. Shy little girl in the boy's parents' house had suddenly taken a wild turn into Naughty Land.

I thrust my hips up, angling perfectly to slide across her sensitized nerves. Her body shuddered, and her eyes drifted shut. I did it again, lowering my hands to her hips to hold her in place, then I flexed up against her, gliding over her clit.

Her hands fell onto my chest, bracing her weight. Her eyes remained shut. And without further debate, or any other word spoken, Hannah ground down on me, rocking along my length. Too much shock and sensation filled my system for me to utter even one witty retort.

I held back my movements, only flexing to give a great angle for her as I let her take charge and take what she needed. Her expressions flickered between pleasure and pain, as if she let the aching current guide her. With her panting breaths, I sensed that she took herself to the edge of release. Her skin was flushed and glistening.

On a gasp, she trembled, and her eyes flew open. "Cade, I...I need you inside me."

On a whisper, I arched my hips. "No place I'd rather be. So take it."

While I gave control over to her, she looked to me to provide her release. My heart ached a little that she trusted me so much—relied on me to guide her and only went there when I wanted her to.

With an imperceptible furrow of her brow, she did as I suggested. Only instead of grabbing my cock and guiding it in, she rocked her body forward, angling her hips to catch the tip at her entrance. Then she pressed down, but only an inch, no further. The tight pressure squeezed the tip, then her inner muscles clenched, gripping me so hard I almost popped out.

Fuck. My breath caught as pleasure ripped through me.

Inch by slow inch, she eased down on me. The intensity, the hot ache and need throbbing through my cock, nearly drove me out of my mind. A dozen panting breaths later, while I forced myself to hold back and let her have her way, she finally hit bottom, fully seating onto me. Then she pulled up, inch by slow inch, before doing the same agonizing descent all over again.

Damn. The woman would be the death of me, right here and now. I gritted my teeth through the torturous pleasure as she took me deep for a second time.

And that's when the real fun began. Seated on me, she rocked into this incredible rhythm, holding me deep as she ground her sweet pussy into my groin. Every dozen or so circles, she'd pull herself up my shaft, as if she needed the hard friction along the nerves inside of her, before coming down and grinding all over again.

Soon heat flooded inside her, rushing all around my cock. I groaned, pinching my eyes shut as she trembled and moaned. But then she stopped moving. I felt a twitch of her inner muscles, and she shuddered.

"Hannah...I might die right now if you don't move."

She did, sliding up my full length. But then she dropped down hard, taking me deep. Another pulse of her muscles.

Another shudder through her body. Her lips skimmed up my neck. "Are you ready to beg yet?"

My eyes widened. "Why, you naughty girl." And kudos to her for pulling something I would've tried.

But her hips moved again and dragged me under. Rational thoughts scattered. Until she stopped. She seemed determined to delay her own release just to deny me mine. And fuck, if her newfound tenacity didn't make things that much hotter.

I held out as long as I could, but this woman—her body and soul was like a drug to me. There was no denying the fact that what she wanted, she would get. And I would be the one happily giving everything to her.

A muted bang echoed outside. A long whistling noise trilled out before a second boom. The windowpane rattled. Hannah tilted her head and glanced back toward the window. The twist of her body rubbed us both with a sizzling friction of nerves, and we moaned.

"Fireworks." Her gaze returned to me, her awe-filled whisper hanging thick in the air.

Rubbing a thumb along her hipbone, I found my voice. "Out there, very near explosion in here."

The corner of her mouth kicked up a tiny bit as lust glittered in her eyes. Then in her measured, teasing pace, she inched back up before sliding down another endless time.

I groaned in agony.

She ground her hips against me again, a soft moan escaping her lips. "Do you surrender?"

"Yes. I'm begging you, Hannah. For the love of God, take your orgasm and give me mine."

A soft laugh. "What comes first?"

"Okay, I admit it. If this is coercion, then I coerced you."

A gentle smile on her lips, she lifted up, circling her hips as she rose, then slid back down. "But it is also kinda like seduction, isn't it?"

I gripped her hips, holding onto her for fear I'd lose control and start ramming us both into sweet oblivion. "Fuck yes, it's definitely seduction."

With a satisfied expression, she started slamming her hips hard onto me.

"Maestro." I ground out the word before she started to scream. My hand flew up, and I covered her mouth as hard spasms rocked through me. I bit down on my lip to keep my roar in check as I came.

To the sounds of fireworks, the pulses of our own explosions faded, and Hannah collapsed down onto me.

I tightened my arms around her, thankful for this weekend reprieve from our crazy lives, grateful for the love of the woman in my arms.

Resting my head against hers, I kissed her temple. "Thank you for seducing me, Hannah. Thank you for loving me."

Her hands gripped my shoulders for a split second before relaxing. On a long exhale, she hummed softly. "Thank you for loving me back."

We clung to each other, the chaotic rumble happening outside my room growing more distant with every breath as we drifted off together.

20. THE GREAT ESCAPE

An hour before the party, people raced around in Mom's kitchen, out on the patio, all through the pool area, and expanding onto the perfectly manicured lawn. Chaos surrounded me, but it was organized chaos, and I enjoyed getting lost in it.

Up on the patio, fifteen of New York's finest available sports models wore matching black-and-green board shorts that Kendall had ordered. They were busy rubbing something greasy onto their bare chests while Kiki bounced back and forth, directing them.

She stopped on the far left and actually assisted the poor guy, applying the shiny substance onto his chest.

More than a little concerned, I ventured out into the confusing scene. "Ummm, watcha doin', Kiki?"

She glanced over her shoulder, but made no move to remove her hands from the model's skin. He stared down at her, entranced by a pretty girl giving him a rubdown.

I sighed, trying to rein in my protective instincts and temper.

"It's coconut oil." She shrugged. "It'll make them glisten

in the sun. Plus they now smell like tropical drinks. All the more enticement to make the female guests' mouths water. It was Kristen's idea."

"Uh-huh." *Sure it was Kristen's idea.* But then, with every other left-field notion those girls had come up with over my lifetime, I didn't put it past any of them to be enthusiastic about rubbing tropical oil on man-candy.

I escaped back into the kitchen, fleeing the borderline-pornographic patio scene. Hannah leaned over the edge of the counter as she put the finishing touches on the cake Daniel had delivered earlier. In dire need of some normalcy, I moved closer to her.

While I stared out the patio windows, as the models wiped their hands in paper towels that Kiki was distributing, I bent down near Hannah's ear. "How long before we can run off together to that tropical island?"

"Parties first. Tropical island after." She pushed me away, focusing on her last-minute icing touches once again.

Like me, Hannah tuned out the rest of the world when she lost herself in her craft, tapping into her own kind of therapy.

Before my tasks for the event dragged me away for the next hour, I admired Hannah's latest creation while I had the chance. Because the party was a private affair for my parents, even though they'd officially "hired" us to coordinate and carry out the event, there would be no press here today. The only people who'd get to enjoy the cake would be us, which was perfect.

And so was her cake.

Depicting an explosion of fireworks over a dark body of water, the cake was incredible. The main field was a large sheet of dark blue. On the surface of the "water" was a reflection of overhead fireworks. Barely visible wires were threaded through dark chocolate posts that supported seven separate explosions in various sizes, colors, and three-dimensional patterns. Like snowflakes, each was different, spiraling off in sugared spheres of blue, green, white, red, and purple.

And on each end of the cake, mounds of green grass rose up from the water, where tiny spectators enjoyed the view. One couple stood by the water, hand in hand, gazing up; another sprawled out on a picnic blanket; and a third older couple sat, embraced on a park bench. "Which couple are we?"

Hannah paused, glancing over her shoulder. A shy smile curved her lips. "They all are."

My heart slammed into the backside of my ribs, and I exhaled slowly. Every time I let my guard down, Hannah surprised me in the best ways. I pressed in behind her and kissed her temple.

She dropped her hands to the edge of the counter and bumped her ass backward, crashing into my groin.

I groaned, but refused to let her hips go.

"Get out of here, Cade. You have things to do. So do I. Party first. Naughty later."

"Okay." I paused to hold her a moment longer and ground into her. "But you know you'll be thinking of me all afternoon."

She turned her head, glancing back at me. Her frustrated expression flickered into amusement as the corner of her mouth kicked up. "You know I will."

I stopped my grinding right as Kendall and Kristen rushed into the kitchen. Mom and Kiki followed. They all began arranging the flatware and lining up pitchers to one side. Two people from the catering company rounded the corner with trays of items and placed them on the counter. Then they disappeared again.

Before I left to take care of my responsibilities, I leaned forward, lowering my voice. "And don't forget the most important part: dark, sexy, claustrophobic closets..." I finally released her. "Enjoy your daydreaming, Maestro."

She narrowed her eyes at me, whispering, "There will *so* be payback."

"I'm counting on it. In a closet."

I winked, then left before my sisters' hard glares escalated to dagger-shooting levels for my loitering around their efficient flow. Yeah, whatever. If Kiki could rub down the waiters, then I could plant filthy fantasies into the mind of our baker—*my* baker.

I abandoned the kitchen, confident the girls had the catering under control and headed out back toward where the calypso band was setting up their equipment, diagonally off behind the barbeque area. We'd set up a plywood platform, ran extension cords out from the house, and had covered the area with seagrass rugs, but it was my job to make sure they had everything they needed.

As I passed through the pool area, the cabana-boy models were busy on either side of the pool, folding blue-and-green striped beach towels on the cushions of each chaise. Two gardeners watered the new large pots by hand, clipping and pruning any dead or wilting plant material as they went.

While I waited for the musicians to return from unloading more equipment, I watched the technicians as they set up smaller fireworks displays on the far side of the lawn. Only a few overhead explosions were planned. Earlier this week, I'd confirmed that the company had obtained a proper permit with local authorities, ensuring we were within the law and followed needed safety procedures.

The five musicians returned with the rest of their equipment, each carrying a different sized steel drum.

"You guys all set? Electric is good?"

One of them shook his head, bending down to a sound unit on the far corner. "No juice, *mon*." His accent sounded Jamaican.

I gave a curt nod. "No problem. I'll fix it." Following the cord up to the house, I found it had been disconnected, the plug lying on the concrete border. I inspected the prongs to make sure they were clean and dry, lifted the cover of the metal-capped outlet on the wall, and plugged it back in.

I turned around and raised my arms to get his attention. He bent down and flipped a switch on his unit. I got a thumbs-up signal a second later. I nodded, satisfied.

Then I scanned the area, searching for signs of panic or anyone in need of direction.

The cabana boys congregated on the patio again. I headed up there, unwilling to leave anything to chance or assumption. The group laughed about something the guy on the end said, but none looked guilty or uncomfortable by the time I approached within earshot.

"You guys have everything you need? Have my sisters briefed you on protocol?"

One nodded. "We're good. Half of us have experience. I used to wait tables all through college at a five-star Zagat rated restaurant. Your guests are in capable hands."

Impressed, I stepped closer. "What's your name?"

"Zach."

I nodded to Zach but addressed the group as a whole. "I'm Cade. Any of you have any questions, feel free to ask me, but follow Zach's lead and example. He's in charge if you need anything and can't find me. Oh, and Zach?" I clapped a hand on his shoulder, wincing at the coconut oil now on my palm. Yeah that shit would be wiped the fuck off in a minute.

I scanned their faces. "Gentlemen? By 'capable hands,' Zach meant metaphorically. No one touches any person here, guest or otherwise. No one propositions or accepts invitations. None of you are to drink a drop of alcohol; there are nonalcoholic beverages for you in the kitchen. Part of your personal responsibilities entails keeping the guests safe, even from themselves when the alcohol flows and filters disappear."

Zach laughed. "We got it covered. Don't we, gentlemen?"

The rest nodded in agreement.

"Good." Confident our guests would be taken care of, I turned toward the open door.

"Cade?" Zach arched his brows, and I paused. "Do we have to worry about any of the guests, regarding your concerns?"

I barked out a laugh, nodding. "All of the women, my two single sisters, and Bertrande." I pointed a finger at the group. "Watch out for Bertrande. He may distract you, then grope you, pretending like it was accidental. You've all been warned." Bertrande was a neighbor and an old friend of my Mom's.

Half the guys burst out laughing and the other half's eyes bugged wide open, wondering if they were in danger of stealth groping. I walked through the alarmed group. "Don't be so concerned about Bertrande. At least a quarter of those women haven't seen naked glistening chest muscles in years. Some touches won't be accidental at all. A few might take a lick." I smirked. "You simply step away and smile, flattered but polite. And are we clear that as long as you're being protective of our guests, none of what goes does down, unintentional or otherwise, is considered sexual harassment?"

They all nodded, many laughing.

"Good." No lawsuits with that cover-our-ass overview.

Chuckling to myself, I headed back up toward the house while I imagined one of our female guests chasing after one of our man-candy waiters with grabby hands. Those poor guys would have their work cut out for them today.

"Hey, Lisa." Loading Zone's best bartender had been sacrificed from the bar for the event. But Ben and I had both agreed that the other bartenders performed more than adequately when she had the night off. A full bar had been rented and set up outside the kitchen door, stocked with top-shelf liquors, a variety of barware and glasses, and a box of brightly colored drink umbrellas. "Have you taken inventory? Missing anything you need?"

Earlier that morning, I'd stocked the bar myself the way we did it at Loading Zone, with a few minor adjustments to allow for the variety of tropical drinks she'd be serving.

"Yep. And nope. All set."

I grinned, nodding over her shoulder as a small group strolled around the corner of the house. "Good. The first guests are arriving. Get ready to dance."

She raised her fist up for our kickoff ritual that we did at each bar opening. "Dance, monkey, dance."

I bumped knuckles with her. "Shout out at me or one of my sisters if you need anything."

Before the crazy began, I slipped back inside the house and found Hannah at the sink, washing her hands. "You all set?"

She nodded. "It's perfect. Time to go change?"

I planted my hands on her hips and spun her around toward the stairs. "I thought you'd never ask."

We raced up the stairs and down the hall, opening the door to my room. Ava let out a high-pitched whine from her crate in the bathroom, and Hannah rushed over to let her out. "Hey, Ava. It's okay, girl. Mommy and daddy are here."

I blinked, lungs stuttering on a breath as Ava's pink tongue coated Hannah's face. Finally, I sucked in a full breath of air. Kids and parenting were a distant someday thought with no bearing on present-day. I'd never imagined we *were* parents. But I guess, to a little German Shepherd puppy, when Mase wasn't mothering and spoiling her, we were, which was okay. Puppy parents I could handle without too much anxiety.

Hannah handed me the leash and clicked the other end into her collar. "Will you take her out while I change? She'll never make it through the party."

Now I whined. "But I planned on crowding you into my walk-in closet to make us late for the party."

She put her hands on her hips, giving me the classic impatient woman look.

Where did those annoyed looks originate, anyway? Women must've patented the damned thing and gifted the ability to each other when men weren't paying attention. I sighed, raising my hands in surrender. "Fine. I'm going. Shit patrol first. Naughty closet groping later."

Hannah snorted, closing the door after us with a firm click.

The mundane task of walking a dog turned into an adventure, but I enjoyed the low-energy break. Whenever Ava stood in one patch of grass, intent on grid patterning by the square inch to capture every distinct scent, I had intro-spection time, grateful again for our quasi-getaway weekend. In spite of the hectic pace of the party, I'd seen more of Hannah in the last twenty-four hours than I'd spent with her all week. And to be isolated from outside stressors, namely Madison's meddling, was worth the cost of Hannah and I having to share ourselves with others, even our dog.

By the time we returned from ten minutes of investigating every flower pot and bush for the perfect place to pee and take a doggy dump, and another ten minutes where sharp-as-a-tack Cade had to tie up an excited puppy while he went in search of a plastic bag he'd forgotten to bring, Hannah was fully dressed and ready to go.

And I couldn't even be mad. I stood in the doorway, staring in as she twirled with a beautiful smile on her face, happy.

"*Wow.* You look stunning, Maestro." A white dress with pink straps and a low neckline hugged her body until it reached her hips, where the material flared out.

My gaze traveled down to where those sexy toned thighs stretched out from the dress. "Are those petticoats?" I blinked. In Pavlovian response, my cock began to harden at the instant flood of memories. Hannah's petticoats and I had a naughty history. Our first closet encounter, actually.

"Sure are." Her eyes danced with amusement.

I pulled my T-shirt over my head and ripped open my button fly, gaping at her. "But I didn't even get to have any closet time."

She laughed, spinning me around toward the closet and shoving me forward. "*You* can take your closet time now, if you want. *We* can make closet time later."

I growled and shucked off my jeans in the cold, dark space, wishing her warm naked body was wrapped around me. "Fine. But I may be in a grouchy mood until later rolls around." With a yank that sent a hanger flying to the ground, I pulled a pair of black linen pants down and stabbed my feet into the fabric, before pulling them up, buttoning them, and zipping the fly.

Her light laugh sounded out closer behind me as I slid my arms into a linen shirt. I turned to find her standing mere inches away with a pretty little smirk. Shirt hanging unbuttoned, I bent down and crushed her lips in a heated kiss, wiping that smirk off her face.

She gasped, and I slowly grinned against her lips.

It wouldn't take much. Another couple seconds of kissing, a few strategically placed brushes in her most sensitive places, and I'd have her shivering, begging for more.

Before I got the chance to enact any of my covert plans, she broke away and pushed me back. With a stern look, she began buttoning my shirt from the top down, keeping her distance. "Later." Her single word was emphasized with an arched brow.

"Later. I'm beginning to like that word, actually. It's now weighted with all kinds of filthy thoughts."

She fought a smile. "I bet I could make you love 'later,' when we have all the time in the world to explore the dark closet you drag me into."

"Oh, *fuck* yes. Later keeps getting better and better." I growled low, chest heaving from thoughts drifting into my mind.

She laughed again and ran off.

My mood soared. My heart felt heavy in my chest, in the best way. Hannah's laughter did that. That megawatt smile. Her playful teasing. Everything about the woman running down my parents' hallway made any trouble out in the world seem insignificant.

I snorted, shaking my head, then chased an amazing girl

in petticoats out of my bedroom—for now—and back down to the unfolding party.

WITHIN THIRTY MINUTES, I'd become a one-man response team. The circuit breaker had tripped twice before we rerouted the band's power to a different outlet than one the kitchen shared. Mom had us move the umbrellas on the east side of the pool toward the foot of their corresponding lounge chairs for the angle of the sun, even though it obliterated a clear walking path along the edge of the pool. The Pearsons, my parents' new neighbors down the street, insisted I give them a guided house tour. Then Trina Hobbs and Stella walker, two of Mom's charity volunteers, wanted their own tour the moment I returned. Of course, my parents were busy mingling with guests, so I was happy to honor their requests.

When all flowed smoothly, I took a breather away from the party. Off to the side, I leaned up against a stone column on the patio. I glanced over my shoulder to see Hannah inside the kitchen. She had a smile on her face as she spoke animatedly with one of the caterers.

Everyone else was in party mode. Half of the sports-model waiters brought hors d'oeuvres back and forth from kitchen to guests. The rest balanced colorful drinks on their trays. Party goers laughed, mingled, danced. Some had jumped into the pool already.

I let out a slow breath, analyzing the scene from the big picture. We created an escape.

Hannah and I had looked forward to a distraction from the stress from the week, but so had all in attendance. Susie Carrington had just gotten over a messy divorce, yet she had an umbrella drink in hand and was laughing with Monica Kemp. The Olsons were at their first event since having to check their son into rehab for drug addiction. Gertrude Hoffman had just lost most of her fortune in an investing scheme, yet there she was, chatting and drinking. Forgetting. Escaping.

Out of the couple hundred guests on the lawn, I'd bet not one of them lived an actual rose-colored life. No one did. So with divorce, drugs, theft, and countless other life-altering events, dealing with the unnecessary drama of a stalkerish ex seemed more tolerable.

Mom moved into my line of vision.

I put an arm around her shoulder. "Party looks great, Mom."

"Thanks to you." She scanned the action down by the pool. "You looked deep in thought when I walked up. Is everything okay?"

"Yeah. Just thinking about how parties make us forget about real life for a while."

She took a step to the side and faced me. "What portion of real life are *you* trying to forget?" Her gaze was penetrating. The Mom look. That one where I could tell the truth or a lie and it wouldn't matter; she would see right through to the real story.

"Madison. She's inserting herself into my life. Unwelcomed. It's causing problems."

Staring back out to the party, she leaned in close, lowering her voice. "At the country club a couple of weeks ago, I ran into Madison's mother."

"Ah. I didn't know you and Shirley Kensington were still close. So that's why you weren't surprised to see Madison at the anniversary party."

"Yes. She shared with me the problems Madison is having."

"What kind of problems?" I couldn't imagine them discussing sexual addiction. Shirley would rather die than make that public knowledge.

"She's having a hard time adjusting to normal life again. One of her boyfriends in Europe put her in the hospital. From what Shirley had said, he'd beaten her pretty badly."

My heart sank. "Damn. I didn't know that." I paused and took a deep breath. "Madison shared a heavy secret with me. She is recovering from sexual addiction."

"Shirley didn't mention that. Apparently, the incident in Europe was instigated because he found out Madison was cheating on him. She said Madison isn't quite right from the whole ordeal. Madison always came to you when you were kids to help her solve her problems. Perhaps that's what she's doing now."

I blew out a fast breath. "Sometime later, you and I can have a talk about what happened between Madison and me." Now wasn't the time.

Inside of a few minutes, my empathy for the little girl I remembered from childhood multiplied. It wasn't only the people at the party who needed to escape.

Even those who caused problems had them.

21. CLOSETS AND CARS

The party had been going for hours. Women in bikini tops and gauzy pants paraded beside others who wore sundresses, like Hannah. Many who were clad in swimsuits stretched out on the chaise lounges under the shade of the umbrellas. A few lay in the full sun, taking advantage of the clear, warm day. A brave few women had joined a handful of men and splashed around in the pool, unconcerned with how their hair or makeup fared.

About half the men had dressed in casual linen, like Dad and me, but many were shirtless in swim trunks. I would've been among them had I not been a host tonight. Gone were the reckless days where I didn't care about responsibilities.

More vital to me, though, was that Mom and Dad were pleased with the event.

As predicted, many of the women got a little drunk and a lot bold with our man-candy waiters, but Zach and his team kept matters all under control, handling issues with professionalism. But Bertrande surprised me. He didn't chase after a single soul. Instead, he'd brought a date. And the two men only seemed to have eyes for each other. Good for Bertrande.

My other priority was making sure Hannah had a good time, distracted by the party or me—nothing else. And nervous excitement buzzed through me now that the party had gone autopilot enough for us to escape for a while.

After searching, I spotted her up on the patio. She sat slumped on a stool at the bar.

I slipped in behind her. "How you holding up?"

She straightened and turned into my arms, smiling wide. "I'm great. The cake was a hit. My feet? Not so much. These new shoes broke me in, not the other way around." She dangled the four-inch heels by their ankle straps.

I watched Lisa fill up a tray with drink orders, dropping a colorful umbrella into the top of each glass. "Everything going smoothly? Need anything?"

She shook her head. "Nope. I'm good."

A quick scan of the party confirmed all the guests had a drink or food. The tropical sound of steel drums played in the background. My parents and sisters were spread throughout the party, mingling with guests or relaxing.

Sunset was about an hour away, and I glanced down at Hannah. "Want to sneak away for a bit? I've got a surprise I want to show you." Plus I needed some one-on-one connection time. My gut told me she did too. Slipping away at the home stretch of our parties had become an addictive habit of ours.

Her eyes widened, and she smiled. "That's right. I forgot about that."

I helped her off the barstool, but furrowed my brow as I stared at her bare feet. "Maybe we should run you upstairs for a change of shoes."

"Nah, I can be barefoot for a while."

I ushered her back into the abandoned kitchen, and she deposited her shoes under a chair in the corner. Her gaze locked onto the Viking gas stove. She gravitated toward it, then ran her fingers along the edge of the gleaming stainless steel.

"Nice stove." Her voice held a breathy reverence.

"You act like you haven't been in this kitchen before. You were in here yesterday afternoon and most of today." The kitchen was almost quiet, the sounds of laughter and music muted. I smiled and leaned back on the far counter, bracing my hands on the edge as she swept her gaze around the kitchen.

She shrugged. "I know. But I didn't have a spare moment to stop and admire anything, which was fine. I'm glad I spent the time bonding with your sisters and Mom."

"And now?"

"Now that we've snuck away, I'm enjoying the scenery." She gave me a slow smile. "The kitchen's nice to look at too."

"*You're* the best thing to look at in here," I retorted. "Gorgeous." It took every ounce of willpower I had to remain rooted where I stood. Especially when my mind wandered, my gaze dropping down to the bottom of her dress, to the edge of those sexy-as-fuck petticoats.

Her head tilted as she stepped closer. "You look a bit mischievous."

I took a deep breath, tamping down the mischief. Then I shook my head and ushered her through the butler pantry. "Only looking forward to showing you my favorite parts of this house," I hedged, lowering my voice. "Besides my bedroom, of course. Which after last night's fireworks, has now rocketed to the top of the list."

She blushed as we reached two doors at the end. I wrapped one arm around her waist and reached the other around her, opening the door on the left. I released my hold as a warm gust of humid air flowed against us.

She took two steps into the bright room and stopped. "Oh, how cool!"

I smiled at her instant reaction. "Thought you'd like this space."

"What's not to like?" she voiced under her breath.

Safety glass spanned up the walls and formed the vaulted ceiling of a large greenhouse.

Hannah walked forward. After a few steps, she spun in a slow circle, eyes wide as she took in every detail. "Who's the gardener, your mom or dad?"

"Both."

"Really? What a great treasure to share with each other." Hannah glanced up at the glass ceiling, then down toward the tinted concrete floor. "What about winter and snow?"

"The glass is designed to withstand any type of weather. The room stays moderate all year with the constant flow of geothermal water through pipes imbedded into the concrete floor." While she scanned the room, I gently placed my hands on her waist and steered her toward the far wall of the greenhouse.

We passed Mom's colorful orchid collection as we approached a door at the end. Hannah glanced back and commented in the softest tone, "What a beautiful place."

"Care for a tour of Dad's toy collection?"

She nodded, her smile widening. "Absolutely." As I reached for the doorknob, she pressed closer to me and brushed a kiss onto my cheek, "Thank you for being my tour guide."

"Tour guide with benefits?"

Her cheeks flushed pink again, and I winked.

Clearing my throat, I opened the door and commented

in my mimicked tour guide tone, "For a rare treat, you will find the toy collection of Mr. Garrett Michaelson. Please watch your step and keep your hands inside the ride at all times—unless, of course, you want to touch your tour guide."

"If I do, we may never make it back to the party."

"Ahhh, I've been found out." I reached along the wall and flicked on the light switch.

As we entered the large garage, Hannah jolted to a stop a couple of steps in, and for a moment, I thought she took my comment of "watch your step" too seriously.

"Your dad has a *serious* toy collection."

I nodded. "Everybody needs a hobby; this is Dad's."

I grabbed her hand and led her down the center of the garage. Along both sides stretched a row of vehicles. In a perfect line, they were backed toward the walls, their chrome grills facing forward toward the center aisle. Each line held ten vehicles, reminding me of purebred horses in the stalls of their barn.

"It feels comfortable in here." She looked down, appreciating the polished concrete floor.

"The same heated water pipes run through this floor too," I explained.

"Amazing," she uttered under her breath.

"What part?" I asked.

"All of it, the planning, the way they thought of every little thing for their comfort and to protect the things they love. The plants in the greenhouse, these beautiful cars, and all the effort they went through to look after them gives me a stronger understanding of why you are the way you are."

"What? You mean my over-analysis, my OCD, my…"

Hannah interrupted my list with a gentle finger on my lips. "You mean your diligence in thinking through all possibilities, always protecting those you care about, forever looking after everything and everyone, even at the cost to yourself at times? Yes, the way you are. *That* is what I mean."

Uncomfortable with her comments, I changed the topic. "Which is your favorite?"

"My favorite what? Character trait about you?" Her brow furrowed.

I snorted. "Favorite car, Maestro." My matter-of-fact tone mocked her misunderstanding.

She shook her head on an eye-roll. Then she turned and walked down the centerline and was drawn straight toward a dark green convertible. I kept quiet, but followed until I stood beside her.

After admiring the front, walking along the driver's side, and looking into the passenger compartment upholstered in tan leather, she spoke, her voice low. "Breathtaking lines."

"And the car's beautiful too..." I struggled to tear my gaze away from Hannah's breathtaking lines, my thoughts racing toward curves hidden by petticoats.

Oblivious to my guttered thoughts, she glanced at me with an innocent smile, then rounded the rear and walked along the passenger side before standing next to me again. "Okay, I see it says Jaguar. What model is it?"

"She's a 1959 Jaguar XK150S."

"That's it, tour guide?" she asked with a smartass tone.

"What would you like to know?"

"Everything. I think I'm in love," she whispered.

Chuckling, I glanced at the car. "She started life in England of course, then came to the States and was sold to a gentleman bootlegger in the South. He was the sole owner until my parents stumbled across her."

"A bootlegger? You're kidding."

"Nope. She has quite the sordid history of running high-quality, homemade moonshine. Gives her a pretty cool and sultry provenance, I think.

"I like it. She's beautiful with a tough background." Hannah nodded.

"She had a complete frame-off restoration, made better with all stainless steel connectors and screws, and many other details only Dad could list from memory. Both my parents fell in love with her and thought she deserved to be brought back with an amazing restoration."

"Amazing is right. I can't take my eyes off her."

"Her name is Moon. My parents name their cars, like your Granpop with Josephine. A habit they started years ago. The name is in respect for her surviving through her moonshine-running life."

"Love the name." She tilted her head. "Hello Moon, very happy to meet you."

I wrapped an arm around her shoulder. "Ready to continue?"

"Lead on, tour guide."

I led her back to the center aisle, and we walked toward the rear wall of the garage.

She glanced up, her lips curving into a smile. "Does your dad work on all these himself?"

"He plays with them when he has a rare moment but has a trusted mechanic to keep them healthy and in shape. As you've probably noticed, Dad's a bit of a neat freak, but in a good way. He considers each one of these vehicles a work of art and created this protective space for them."

As we approached the lounge area at the back of the garage, Hannah stopped, tugging me to a halt. "Okay, this is seriously cool too."

I released her hand and dropped down into my favorite black leather chair.

She took in the inviting man-cave space, her gaze starting on the oversized leather chairs in the corner where I sat, drifting to the large plasma TV suspended on the wall, then sweeping across the three chrome barstools lined up along a small bar as she stepped onto the black rug. "Safe to assume no oil or grease is allowed in this area?"

I snorted. "Hell, no. Part of that neat-freak thing. This is where he relaxes with friends or clients that come to hang out in the garage to talk car stuff or solve the world's problems..."

She sat on a barstool, her bare feet dangling. "I could hang out here."

"Me too. One of my favorite places in the house." And seeing her sitting on the barstool, curves tempting me, luscious lips sending my thoughts under that pristine white sundress, it became favorite for one more reason. I had to take a deep breath to calm my reacting body. Almost...*later*. I vowed to remain patient just a little longer.

Hannah blinked, carrying on the conversation, again clueless about my sidetracked thoughts. "That's right, this vast space and the greenhouse beyond the door are still connected to the house. We seem like a world away."

"Yep. Mom and Dad wanted to pull into the garage and go into the house directly, protected from the weather outside and safer."

She tilted her head, staring at me intently. "Your parents are quite intelligent. Your dad with these cars..." A smirk twisted her lips, then she pointed at my chest. "Apple" —her hand opened, her arm sweeping wide to indicate the rest of the garage—"Tree."

I smiled, liking her comparison of me to my dad. He was a man with a few obsessive-compulsive quirks, but he was a dedicated businessman who loved his family with a fierce passion. With minor adjustments of career path choices and the whole family–business time allotment, I wanted to be just like him.

"What's over here?" She'd turned on the barstool, then hopped off and walked toward another corner of the garage.

I stood and caught up with her, wrapping my arms around her from behind. "Those are, well, kind of hard to explain. Many years back, my parents heard about a local young veteran who returned home with an injury that made it impossible for him to drive a car. They inquired and discovered the veteran could drive, but only if custom alterations were made to his vehicle. Through their attorney, they anonymously contributed funds designated to make the needed custom alterations to the vehicle he had driven prior to his war-time injury."

I stepped to the side and pointed to a picture up on the far left corner of the thirty-seven framed photographs. "After the first donation, they had their attorney contact the local VA Hospital and arrange for the administration staff to privately update him on any veteran who needed a customized vehicle due to sustained injuries. The pictures are of the veterans they've helped, men and women who kept their driving freedom with the help of my parents plan. Sometimes it was an alteration of the vet's existing vehicle, other times it was a contribution of enough funds for a wheelchair accessible van. They created a highly specialized anonymous giving-back thing."

Moisture sparkled in Hannah's eyes.

My brow furrowed, and I stepped back to her. "Hey, sorry, I didn't intend for any of that..."

She blinked and looked down, swiping a fallen tear from her cheek with her hand. "I know, just...wow. So...no words."

"My parents don't have a traditional 'I Love Me Wall'

displaying college degrees or life accomplishments," I further explained. "The first person they helped sent a picture and a letter through the attorney, thanking them. My parents started this photo collection to remind them of smiles they created. They helped give as much freedom as possible to those who put their lives on the line for all of us. My dad believes the classic man-and-machine connection allows us to enjoy life to the fullest, beyond having a car as transportation. If either of my parents get a bit down with life's challenges, they come here. Helps the soul."

Hannah grabbed my hand and gave it a squeeze. "Do their friends, or their mechanic, know about these and what your parents do?"

"Nope, whenever someone comes through here, if they're asked, they simply say they are pictures of happy people. The intended vagueness usually creates a curious expression on folks, but nobody presses the question."

"Wow. Your parents do so much for charity. The Unity Foundation for human trafficking and this. So, wait. You told me the secret about what they do."

"Yes, yes, I did. So if we ever break up, I'm obligated to kill you." I winked. "I need to be a thorough tour guide, don't I?" I gestured an arm toward the far wall of the garage, while crooking and offering my other. "Shall we continue the tour?"

"Lead on my good man." She held onto my arm.

"See any other favorites in the lineup? I know you're drawn to the Jaguar, for good reason. I'm curious what else you like."

"What's this one?"

"Oh, she's a beaut'. A 1929 Duesenberg. What attracts you to her?"

She crossed her arms over her chest. "Hard to say,

initially the collection of lights up front, the incredible amount of polished metals, how she sits with a presence of nobility. Is that silly?" She glanced at me. "What's her name?"

"Not silly at all. Now you understand why I appreciate the artistic lines of a vehicle, why I love your Josephine. Now you get a little more of what makes me tick." I nodded toward the car. "They named her 'Duesie.' More obvious than the others, but they love the nickname."

She smiled, leaning into me. "Thank you for sharing this special place with me."

It was the place I escaped to while growing up to feel closer to family, my dad especially, even all those years when he wasn't around. It meant a lot to me that Hannah felt the same, that she got it—got me.

"Wait, we're in a garage, and we entered through the doorway from the connecting greenhouse. But where do the vehicles come in from?"

"A secret."

Her brows arched. "A secret, huh?"

"Yep." I pointed along the same wall that had the doorway to the greenhouse. "See that floor-to-ceiling panel with the high windows in it?" We walked back down the centerline of the garage to take a closer look.

She nodded. "Yes."

"That's the vehicle entrance. Notice the metal track hidden along the wall, both in the edge of the floor and in the edge of the ceiling?"

Craning her neck back as we walked, she gave an imperceptible nod. "Sure, I see it now."

"That whole section of wall seals when closed but moves into the interior of the garage a couple of inches before sliding sideways when opened."

She blinked, examining the tracks as we approached closer. "Wow."

"What's on the other side of the door is even better."

"Really, what could be better than all this?" Her dark eyes held a curious glint.

I pointed to a red circle on the wall. "Push that button and see."

She pushed it, then walked over to the opening wall panel as it slid sideways. She cocked her head. "That's really quiet. I expected to hear a loud motor and gears grinding, like a garage door opener."

"One of Dad's inventions. Long story. He knows a guy..."

Her gaze returned to the open space, and she grinned. "You're kidding. I thought this opened to the outside."

"Nope. How else do you think the garage stays in neat-freak shape?"

She shook her head, then blinked. "They have their own indoor car wash area?"

"More like a big mud room for your car. Fully auto-mated. They pull in, close the exterior door before opening this interior panel, and push that green button if they need their car washed before entering the garage. That big blower system dries the car and the undercarriage. The whole thing is ingenious."

She chuckled as she stepped into the enclosed car wash room. "Then safe to assume that door on the other side of the car wash leads to the motor court where your Jeep is?"

"Motor court?" I asked, surprised.

She spun around and stared at me, dropping her hands on her hips, "Yes, Mr. Tour Guide, motor court. I know the name of a big-ass, paver-covered parking area when I see it."

"Okay, okay, impressive car knowledge."

When she stepped further into the space, I followed

close behind. My patience had run out. There was nothing else to see—tour over. Time for the *private* tour to begin. "You know, one could say this tunnel is kinda like a closet."

She spun around, eyes lighting up with challenge as those tempting petticoats beneath the skirt of her sundress rustled. "Oh? Could one?"

I stalked her as she sidestepped out of my reach and veered back toward the car wash entrance. "Oh, definitely. Plus there are several surfaces here sturdy enough to take even the most thorough pounding."

Her eyes narrowed, her head shaking slowly from one side to the other. "Oh, no. We are heading back to the party with my dress, hair, and makeup intact."

I cocked my head to the side. "I could work with that."

Her eyes widened, and she backed up another step, almost into the garage space.

"No."

I grinned, guttered thoughts flying through my mind of positions and surfaces to christen. All the innocent bonding had been something I needed for my soul after the couple of weeks of craziness. Now my body had other needs after an entire day of being a very good boy.

"Yes." I arched a brow, stalking another step forward for every one of hers back.

"Cade Joseph Michaelson, if you take one more step toward me, I will turn on the car wash." Her hand hovered over the green button.

It was no threat at all, because only two yards remained between us. I could easily clear that door and tackle her into the garage without a droplet of water hitting either of us. And *minimal* dress crumpling.

"Go ahead." I took another step. "As we've established, I do love you soaking wet."

22. ABOUT TIME

The following afternoon, with windows down and radio blaring eighties rock, we sped down the highway nearing home. Hannah held Ava in her lap with a thumb looped into her collar to prevent the pup from leaning too far out of the car.

And Hannah couldn't stop smiling. Which made me a grinning, happy-as-fuck idiot. I helped put that bright smile on her face. Yeah, being away from external stressors had taken a weight off of me too.

My hand rested on the gearshift, and she slipped her free hand under it, sliding her fingers loosely into mine. I rubbed my thumb over the soft skin on the back of her hand. Neither of us glanced at each other. We didn't need to.

We fit perfectly. Without needing to say a word, a calm had settled between us. We'd also worked out plenty of sexual tension over the weekend, giving us enough endorphins to buzz through our bodies for days.

When we passed the outskirts of town, Hannah let out a long sigh.

"You okay?" I squeezed her hand.

"Yes. No. Just...I'm not ready for the weekend to end."

When I glanced over at her, tears brimmed in her eyes. She took a deep breath.

"Hey." I lifted a hand up, brushing my knuckles on her cheek. "It's okay. The weekend isn't over yet."

"Sorry." She let out a short laugh. "I'm being silly. I just had such a great time—all the family, you and me, away from everything."

Away from Madison is what she meant. All the problems. And all the demands of both of our jobs that pulled us apart.

We turned into her driveway, and I parked in front of her garage before cutting the engine. Then I turned fully toward her. "*We* have a great time. We decide how happy we are even with real-life things happening around us that we can't control. There will always be that. But no matter where we go or what happens, we'll have us in the middle of it all."

She nodded. A tear escaped and tracked down her cheek. I brushed it away with my thumb before leaning over and kissing her softly.

When I eased away, she smiled and tightened her hold on my hand. "I love the 'us in the middle of it all' part. Makes us sound invincible. Thank you for understanding. All the good emotions from the weekend flooded in all at once."

I gave her another quick kiss. "I promise, Maestro. We'll make plenty of great weekend memories."

Below us, Ava interrupted with a yip. Then she stood on Hannah's lap, separating us.

I laughed as I leaned back and unfastened my seatbelt. "Remember to secure Ava." I arched a brow. "Unless you want to be tossed off your dock too."

Hannah grinned with mischief in her eyes, as if she

couldn't decide whether or not to heed my warning. After a moment, she twisted in her seat and corralled Ava back into her crate.

I grabbed Hannah's bag from the back, and she circled around the front of the Jeep, meeting me at the driver's door. As we walked up her front pathway, she leaned into me. Wordlessly, we slowed our pace, our steps dragging as we neared the inevitable good-bye for tonight.

She glanced up at me. "You know, you could get me a very different kind of wet..."

I watched that sexy lip get sucked in again. "Woman, you're insatiable." I dropped her bag onto the landing and pulled her close, staring into her eyes. "We could get all kinds of wet. But we both know, if I follow you through your front door, there will be no sleep. We've got a big week ahead of us."

And there it was, thrown out in the open—the crash back into reality. We faced our most challenging event to date, and one challenging wrench, who enjoyed throwing herself into our smooth-running gears.

Hannah nodded slowly and dropped her gaze down to a spot on my chest where her fingers dragged in a circle. "I know. The responsible part of me realizes we have a ton of work to do. But I'm still channeling my blissful, ignorant side. Can't we be bad and good? Sex and sleep?"

I groaned, closing my eyes, wondering if I had the willpower to indulge in her body for only a few hours, knowing we won't have the time to play for days. In the end, there really wasn't a choice. I opened my eyes and sighed. "Go grab Ava. I'll text Mase so he doesn't think we crashed while driving home."

Hannah squealed, wrapped her arms around my neck,

and kissed me hard. "Thank you! I promise we can get to sleep by a reasonable hour."

Laughing, I smacked her ass as she turned and ran off to retrieve Ava. I followed after her while texting a "home in the a.m." to Mase.

Hannah put Ava on a leash before pulling her out of the Jeep and plopping her down. I watched the two of them striding alongside one another up the walkway. Our picture-perfect family of three struck me as very innocent—totally opposite of all the naughty plans I had for the next few hours.

While she slid the key into the lock, I slipped my hands around her hips and lowered my mouth to her neck. She shivered under my touch.

I grinned. "I plan to do everything in my power to get you to break that early sleep promise."

THE FOLLOWING MORNING, I sat at my kitchen table in a fog. Too much sex and too little sleep made for a very satisfied, but groggy, Cade. I stared at the computer screen, but no valuable thoughts pinged between my ears.

I got up with a yawn, rubbed my eyes, and poured another cup of coffee—some Italian grind Mase's girlfriend, Laura, had given to him to make him more "civilized." I blew on the surface, then took a few sips on my way back to the table. Wasn't bad, although nothing beat a cup of reliable Starbucks in the company of Hannah.

But Hannah and I had collapsed sometime shortly before midnight and woken only a few hours later. When she left for her shop before 4:00 a.m., I drove home with

Ava, then sat down to start working through emails before tackling the to-do list.

Hannah's "wet" comment last night flashed into my mind. Maybe I hadn't tossed her off of her dock, but I had chased her into the shower. I smiled, remembering all the laughter. We'd had no problem extending our weekend fun. I looked at the time at the bottom of my laptop: 7:16 a.m., and I wondered what she was up to. She was probably running around in her apron, her arms covered in flecks of icing.

Damn. Now I want a cupcake for breakfast.

"Focus, Cade." I forced myself to go through the list for Saturday's event. There was still a shitload of stuff to do. Every item had been ordered, but inevitably things got screwed up without double checks. Sometimes wrong things got delivered even with them. Which left us to sort out the mess, flying by the seat of our pants with makeshift solutions.

And that was on a good day. We had Selfish Bitch to contend with on this one.

I sighed, a twinge of guilt running through me for reminding myself of the bad parts of Madison, like I did every time I thought about her. I got that it was my own self-protection, yet a part of me felt sorry for her. Her struggle after being beaten, wanting to be accepted, turning to me for help—tugged at me. She had a vulnerable goodness under that steel-spiked exterior. But the reasons why she hurt others—hurt me and hurt Hannah—didn't justify her reckless actions.

That's why I wanted to try to prevent as many glitches as possible. Not just because the double bar mitzvah was a big event, but also because I suspected I'd have my hands full with damage-controlling whatever next idiotic stunt Madison might pull.

As I opened the latest two emails from Suzanne and reread their contents, it struck me that no amount of preplanning would prevent every possible scenario. I couldn't even *be* at both of the events at once. There'd be no way to monitor Madison on top of all that.

Two. I need two of me.

We would all have to dig in and do our best for one hectic night. Then it would be over. And whatever stress we'd gone through to accomplish it would fade away.

Then Hannah and I would be on a flight to a tropical beach, all the chaos behind us.

I answered Suzanne's emailed concerns point by point. She was having difficulty securing the second photo booth. The vendor had two down for repair and the other two were previously scheduled at weddings that day. "Fucking weddings," I muttered. I surfed the Internet for other possible suppliers, but came up empty.

The photo booth issue reminded me of all the sabotage that had happened to date and how I had yet to bring Kristen up to speed with the two health inspections—they'd clearly screamed Madison. I fired off an email to Kristen with a copy to Kiki, Kendall, Hannah, and Ben, outlining the details of what happened on Friday. I also asked if anything new had happened to any of them. Within twenty minutes, I got replies from Kristen and Ben. Neither had anything new to report.

About an hour later, Mase stumbled into the kitchen while I reread Darren's email about the music. Darren detailed out the rental of the proper equipment for identical setups in each room, the sound buffer required to avoid having an all-out decibel war, and his suggested configuration for each room.

"Morning." I nodded without glancing away from the screen as I chased a thought hovering at the back of my mind. I pulled up the three different configurations: the one Kristen and I had initially suggested, the one Suzanne had countered with, likely as Madison's mouthpiece, and the one Darren needed for easy electrical access without guests tripping over wires.

A headache began to form at the base of my skull, and I groaned at the task of trying to get everyone to compromise into one workable configuration.

"You left Ava out all morning?" Mase snarled as he opened the back door.

"She's having a ball out there. Not one scratch or whine. From her, anyway," I muttered.

"Dick."

"Fuckhead." I smirked and flipped him off without taking my eyes off of Darren's diagram.

Mase snorted and sat down with a bottle of orange juice in one hand and a bowl of his custom granola blend in the other. As he poured the one into the other, my stomach lurched.

"That's messed up, man." I grimaced at the rank combination.

"Don't knock it till you try it." He held the bowl up to me.

I gripped my coffee mug like an anti-puke lifeline and raised it up in front of my face in self-defense. "No. Keep that shit to yourself." A deep inhale of my Italian brew prevented upheaval.

His chuckle was followed by dog claws clicking across the kitchen tiles while Ava chased her treat-filled toy around the room. All the noise scattered my concentration. I leaned back in my chair and gave up on work for a moment. I needed a mindless break anyway.

"How's it going?" Mase nodded toward my closing laptop, mumbling around a full mouth of orange-juiced granola.

I shrugged. "It's going. The usual obstacles, multiplied by two parties, along with trying to anticipate any shit my unpredictable ex might pull."

He leaned back in his chair, stretching his legs diagonally under the table, and dropped me a heavy look. "Thought Madison dumped you."

I huffed out a laugh. "Thanks for the reminder."

"So what's eatin' her?"

"Who knows. She cuts me loose, then what? Wants me? Crazy." Simple explanation. No details required. Mase didn't need to hear her deeper issues. And I wasn't in the mood to share my struggles about them.

He crossed his arms over his faded T-shirt. "Figures. Only wants you when she can't have you. Watch her. I saw the shit that went down at the bar. She gunned for Hannah the second you were distracted."

I sighed and pegged a hard stare at him. He mirrored my concerns. Mase cared about Hannah like a protective big brother. "Yeah, I know."

"You're gonna have your hands full on Saturday with even less time to watch out for your ex. Hannah gonna be up for that? Are you?"

I scrubbed a hand over my face, growling at the unknown clusterfuck ahead. "Yeah, I know. And fuck, I sure as hell hope so."

"You need to make room in your budget for security. I'd look good in one of those black 'security' T-shirts. And I would stick to Hannah's ass like a chair coated in Superglue."

I shot him a deadpan look. "Nice image. Who the fuck's gonna to protect you from me, with you being *one with her ass* all day?"

He slid his forearms across the kitchen table, staring hard at me. "To protect our girl from harm, I'd take a bullet. Even from you."

The corners of my lips twitched. "Thanks, man." Mase had our backs as a good friend. It meant the world. "Somehow I don't think Hannah would be thrilled about having a security detail. Try explaining to my woman that you're there to protect her from an irrationally vengeful ex."

He tilted his head, arching a brow. "I could pull it off."

For a crazy minute, I considered his half-serious offer. "Nah. Not needed. Hannah has expressed repeatedly she wants to knock Madison on her ass."

He nodded and leaned forward. "Sure thing. Offer stands. And whatever else you need, it's yours." He reached out a closed fist.

I nodded and knuckle-bumped him.

All the talk about Madison, and my earlier emails about Friday's health inspections, fired an urgent need under my ass to confront Madison. "Okay, man. I gotta get going." With a scrape of wooden chair legs, I stood, then grabbed my laptop and coffee mug.

An hour later, I showed up at the country club and phoned Suzanne from the lobby. "Hey, Suzanne, it's Cade. Got a minute?"

"Sure, Mr. Michaelson. I'll be right out."

A few minutes later, Suzanne appeared in the hallway that led back to her office. I met her halfway. "If you don't mind, I'd like to go back to your office to talk."

She gave me a short nod. "Absolutely."

When we got there, I followed her in and closed the door. Suzanne took a seat at her desk, looking at me expectantly while I sat in the chair positioned against the wall.

I took a deep breath. Normally, I was a good read of people. And I sensed deep in my gut that Suzanne wasn't loyal to Madison. Besides, Madison kept Suzanne on a really short leash with us, stepping all over her authority to handle our account. So I took a calculated risk.

"Suzanne, have you noticed anything unusual that Madison has done regarding our event—or us?"

Her brow furrowed. "I'm not sure I understand. Are you unhappy in some way with the event?"

"No. You're doing a great job. We're pleased in every way with how *you* have helped us. Let me explain." I offered the details of our sabotage over the last month, including the two complaint-provoked health inspections.

Suzanne blinked hard, then stared at me as if she'd seen a ghost. "The other day I heard Madison on a phone call. She said she'd become ill after eating at a local establishment."

Bingo.

She glanced down at her desk. "I have something to confess. When you were here for the sampling, Madison instructed me to bring you to my office and purposely delay you so she could speak with you privately. I overhead everything she said in the hallway afterward. I'm mortified that I had any part in that."

I leaned back. "Thank you, Suzanne. Your honesty and observations are appreciated more than you realize. We've been waiting for a break like this to figure out what the hell's been going on."

Suzanne continued, "That's not all. When I couldn't

secure the second photo booth, I looked into the two that were reserved for the weddings. I thought maybe we could double book one to be able to both use it that same day, if the times didn't conflict. I found out one of the weddings was fake. It didn't make any sense before. Now it seems to have an explanation."

"Sure as fuck does." Damn. I wanted to kiss Suzanne.

I blew out a hard breath, my mind racing. "How much do you have on Madison to be able to report her actions to the club's board members?"

Her brows drew together. "With what you've said, and the things I've witnessed, it's enough. Our board takes our members concerns very seriously. Madison is harassing you, professionally and personally. That hallway conversation she had with you could be considered sexual harassment: our general manager made a sexual advance to a subcontractor hired by one of our members. I'm pretty sure the board will want to talk with you though."

"I'm good with that. Give them my cell and email." I leaned forward, resting my forearms on my knees. "Other than the board, please keep this between us."

"I will. By the way, I was finally able to secure the photo booth once the rental company confirmed there was no wedding at the reserved location. So we're on with two for Saturday."

"Perfect." I let out a sigh of relief. "I'm going to talk to Madison, confront her. I want her scrambling on defense; she's been on offense for too long. I won't mention a word about our conversation though. You do your thing with the board members."

"Do you think it's wise to meet with Madison if part of our complaint is about sexual harassment?"

I stood and gave her a nod. "Give me a few minutes.

Then tell her I asked to meet with her in the front lobby. There will be plenty of witnesses there to see and hear our conversation."

"Okay. I will."

"Oh, and Suzanne?"

She glanced up at me.

"Thanks again. We owe you one. In fact, if you ever need a job at a country club, I will give you a glowing recommendation for ours or any of your choice."

She smiled. "Thank you, Cade. I appreciate your support."

As I walked back to the lobby, a flood of details combined themselves, puzzle pieces clicking into place. The most upsetting one being Madison's confrontation with Hannah at Loading Zone. Although I had some empathy toward Madison with what she'd been through, her damaging actions were all I could focus on at this point. In full protection mode, a hard edge toward Madison was all I could manage.

When I got to the lobby, I stared out the back windows, watching as waiters spread white tablecloths onto patio tables to prepare for lunch guests. Then I turned and scanned the half dozen people who were in the lobby area. A young female concierge was behind a desk, thumbing through the latest issue of Vogue. Two businessmen sat with papers held high. The coffee drinker held a *Wall Street Journal*. The one with a *USA Today* appeared to be sipping a whiskey sour. A pair of teenage girls dressed in tennis uniforms stood a few feet down from me along the glass wall of windows, gossiping about a new instructor and his endless muscles.

A good mix of people in the room served as perfect witnesses—close enough to prevent Madison from feeling comfortable. And as if on cue, heels clicked along the marble floor in a tight-ass rhythm until Madison stepped onto the expansive woven rug beneath my feet.

"Cade." An irritated expression accompanied her head tip. "What is it you need to discuss that couldn't be done in my office?"

My eyes narrowed in warning.

On an inhale, she softened her features. "Could we at least have a seat?" She gestured to two empty chairs.

"No. This won't take long enough to warrant getting comfortable."

Her lips firmed into a line.

Good. I had her attention.

I crossed my arms over my chest. "You're busted, Madison."

She gave me a hard look. "At what?"

I almost laughed. Her crimes probably numbered so high that she wasn't sure which one I was talking about.

"We know it was you."

When she opened her mouth, I shook my head.

She shut it without uttering a word.

"We know you pretended to be Kristen. We know you canceled and rescheduled shit. We know you called the health inspector on my bar and Hannah's bakery. Give it up. My company and your club are about to host an event in a few days. If you value your job at all, focus on cooperating for the duration. Do it for your club members' sake, if nothing else."

Although I hoped they'd fire her ass before Saturday, I couldn't be sure they would move that fast, or that they would believe the evidence we had and act on it at all. So covering our asses by attempting to diffuse the situation before anything else happened seemed the wisest course.

Madison stared at me for a few seconds. Which was plenty long enough for confirmation of her guilt in my mind.

She glanced around the lobby, then shot me a fierce glare. "Will there be anything else, Mr. Michaelson?"

"No. I think we're good here. Have a nice day."

On my way out to my bike, I dialed Kristen. She picked up on the first ring. "Sis, you're not gonna believe this. I just spoke with Suzanne. She confirmed it's Madison."

"Holy shit. That's awesome."

"Right?" I filled her in on the details, including the confrontation with Madison. My phone vibrated. I glanced at the screen, which showed that Mase was calling in. I let it go to voicemail.

"So that's it? You think she'll back down?"

"Hell no. But maybe we bought us time to get past Saturday's event without drama. Keep your guard up just in case."

A text came in from Mase.

Emergency. Get to the house now.

"Gotta go, sis. Something's up with Mase."

23. DEALING WITH DISASTERS

I raced home on my bike, trying to wrap my brain around what the emergency could be. In the couple of years we'd been roommates, Mase had never sent a dire message like that. Clearly he hadn't lost a hand in some freak accident; he'd texted me. The only other thing I could think of was something had happened to Ava. Or the house was on fire.

As I stepped through the open front door, the cause of the alarm became clear. It wasn't a fire at all. The exact opposite had happened. Water had flooded everywhere.

Fuck.

My boots slogged through water on the wood floor in the entryway. Down the hall, Ava sat upright on dry tiles, tethered to Mase's bedroom door by her shortened leash. Her fur glistened—wet.

I took in the scope of the damage in the living room and cringed, my heart sinking. The leather sofa and entertainment center stood in several inches water. Smaller items which usually sat on the floor were stacked haphazardly onto them.

"Mase?"

"In here."

I walked into the kitchen, every step splashing water. Mase stood near the kitchen sink, arms braced on the counter edge, head hanging down. The wood dining table and chairs were stacked in disarray, some upside down, some upright, on every spare counter surface.

"Dude. What happened?" I struggled to process the mess around me.

He shrugged, then stared at me under heavy brows. "Came home to water pouring out from behind the dishwasher. Tried turning off the valve under the counter, but it wouldn't budge. I had to run out and shut the water off at the main."

"So the bedrooms are okay? Why didn't the water go into the hall?"

"Oh, you haven't seen the worst of it. The reason Ava is on the dry island in the hallway is that most of the water poured into the basement, either through the floor or down the steps. Almost the whole ceiling of the basement is trashed. Brace yourself before you go down there."

"*Shit.*"

"Yeah. The pool table and foosball table are toast—both are lakes. It's raining down there."

I took a deep breath in the humid air and gave Mase a hard stare. "Thanks, man. Sorry you had to deal with this on your own."

"I did my best. Shocked the shit out of me."

I clapped a hand on his shoulder as I walked by. "You did great. I'm gonna survey the damage down below."

When I stepped through the doorway and onto the landing, it was dark, and I instinctively reached for the wall switch. I paused. "Hey, Mase? You cut the electrical too?"

"Yep. Right after the water main."

No amount of warning prepared me for the devastation. Sunlight streamed into the basement from the narrow windows. Ceiling to floor, wall to wall, the room was soaked through. The bar was ruined. Every surface within my line of sight was wet or covered in water. I stopped a few steps shy of the bottom of the stairwell to avoid the rainfall still dripping down.

I blew out a hard breath and went back up the stairs. I'd seen enough. I pulled my phone out from my back pocket.

"What are you gonna do?"

Scrolling through my contacts on the phone, I shook my head. "No clue. My first thought is the contractor who did the remodel. He should know a good water damage company."

I hit CALL on the screen the moment his info pulled up. He answered his cell on the third ring, and I exhaled in relief, glad it didn't roll over to voicemail. "Joe. This is Cade Michaelson. I have an emergency I hope you can help with."

I explained the key points to Joe, and he immediately offered to call the emergency response company he knew and send them over. Thank fuck I had a great contractor. And besides, he'd be getting a ton of dollars flowing his way once the insurance company started cutting checks.

That was my next call. While I was on perma-hold through several people at the insurance company, I watched Mase dry off Ava with a beach towel then get her situated in his room with fresh food and water bowls.

A couple of hours later, our furniture was all either in the garage or on the back patio. A crew had begun removing the water using Shop-Vacs on the upper floor and a pump in the basement. The insurance adjuster had just left after initiating the claim.

Joe swung by to assess if it would be safe for Mase, Ava, and me to stay in the house. "As long as you leave the electrical breakers off for the basement, kitchen, dining room, and living room, you should be safe staying in the bedrooms. I'll have my plumber swing by this afternoon to replace the frozen valve under the kitchen sink and the burst dishwasher hose. Then he'll turn your water main back on and double-check everything."

"Thanks, Joe. We really appreciate your help."

When he left, Mase and I went back to our rooms. I had no idea what Mase planned to do, but I collapsed on my bed, exhausted from the stress of the entire day. I laid there, staring at the ceiling, thinking about all the tasks I'd wanted to accomplish today that got bumped to tomorrow, along with new time-suck obligations for my house—now a construction zone.

All I wanted to do was find comfort and fall asleep in Hannah's arms. But Mase and Ava didn't have anywhere to go, and this was my house. The mess and cleanup was my responsibility to deal with, not Mase's.

My phone vibrated from the nightstand. I reached over and grabbed it.

Hannah had texted.

Busy day. What're you doing?

I laughed out loud. In the day's mayhem, I hadn't had a chance to breathe, let alone contact her. *Nothing* was what I was currently doing. It would take an hour to explain what I'd *been* doing. But I didn't care. I needed to hear her voice.

I gave her a call. "Hey."

"Hey." Her voice was soft, and I swear she smiled on the other end.

Just hearing her voice made me relax, dropping my shoulders an inch lower from my ears. "Well, looks like I'm building you another walk-in closet in the basement." Mentioning our closet joke helped lighten my mood.

"Another? What's wrong with the first one?"

"It's under water."

She gasped.

Yeah, that about covered it. And still, I went over all the details with her: seeing Mase's stricken face when I'd walked in, the ruined leather couch, the destroyed *everything* in my now-rainforest basement—I could almost hear the mold starting to grow.

"Cade, that's awful. Anything I can do? Bring Chinese food? Pizza?"

"No. Thanks, but Joe, my contractor from the remodel, brought sub sandwiches and drinks to feed us and the emergency crew about an hour ago. It's almost six, and you have early busy days ahead. Besides, I'm so tired, the second I get off the phone, I'm gonna pass out." I sighed heavily. "I just want to forget this day."

She gave a low sympathetic tone. "I wish I could make it go away."

I closed my eyes. "Me too. I wish I was in your arms right now."

"Me too."

"Just keep thinking about those tickets to our tropical island. Six more days. First, five insanely busy days ahead of us. On the sixth? Beach."

"Or, we could just add sand to your living room. Insta-beach. "

I barked out a laugh. "Thanks, Maestro. Only you could make me see humor through this."

"Anytime. Wish I could help more."

"Tell me about your day. Help me focus on something else."

I listened to her tell me about new customers, then Daniel and Chloe's latest antics. Lila had invited Hannah to lunch on Wednesday. A new resort client had contracted with her shop to supply gourmet desserts for their dinner and room service menu, which all came about from a walk-in customer who happened to be the resort's food and beverage manager.

As Hannah talked animatedly about everything that had happened to her since I'd left her this morning after an incredible night of sex, topping off a wonderful getaway weekend we'd had at my parents', I began to nod off.

I interrupted her when she took a breath. "Maestro, I'm so sorry, but I'm about to pass out."

"It's okay, babe. Sleep. Sweet dreams, Cade."

"Thank you for talking with me. You've just guaranteed I will."

ALL DAY TUESDAY, I worked nonstop from before sunrise to well past dinner. I caught up on to-do items for Saturday's event and met with both Joe and the owner of the remediation company to create a plan for the house repairs and restoration. The list was overwhelming, but I took each thing one at a time on a priority basis.

Wednesday morning brought more of the same. Hannah texted to remind me that she was meeting Lila for lunch today. I'd been stuck at the house since Monday afternoon in the humidity with fans blowing 24/7, so I escaped out of the house for some peace and fresh air.

Before an afternoon meeting at Loading Zone, I dropped

by my favorite coffee spot. It was second only to Hannah's front lounge in Sweet Dreams and only a few blocks away from her bakery.

The coffee aroma was a welcomed break from the staleness of my house. As I took a sip from my cup, waiting for my sandwich to be delivered, I stared at my laptop. Several items on my combined to-do list had been taken care of already. But I still had over a dozen more that needed attention by the end of the day.

I glanced up when someone stepped into my peripheral vision, thinking it was my sandwich order. Instead, Madison moved into the empty seat in front of me.

Fuck me.

I sighed. "Don't sit, Madison. It's not a good time." My words came out guttural as I glared at her.

"Wait, I come in peace." She set two plates down on the table, cautiously pushing a cheesecake brownie my way. "I remember this was your favorite." And ironically, a devil's food doughnut sat in front of her.

"Things change. Not my favorite anymore. I'm into cupcakes now."

My comments didn't faze her. She kept a smile on her face as she put a napkin onto her lap. "I'm sorry. I didn't mean to cause you and Hannah so much trouble."

I narrowed my eyes at her. "Bullshit."

She broke off a piece of her doughnut and put it into her mouth. My sandwich arrived, and I pushed her peace offering back toward her side of the table.

"Cade, I get that we have to get along to make everything go smoothly Saturday. I'm willing to do that."

Damn straight you are. Had she been contacted by her board yet? I hadn't heard anything more from Suzanne, and in the chaos that had become my life, I hadn't had a spare moment to follow up on it.

When I just stared at her, she leaned forward. "I was foolish. I know that now. You were the best thing ever to happen to me. I miss us. I'm willing to be what you need."

I laughed at the ridiculousness of her words. "You could never be what I need."

She gave me an honest-to-fuck sincere look. "Give me a chance. I could try."

With a wide grin, I leaned back in my chair and laced my hands together behind my head. "Madison, you have to know that I don't believe a word you're saying. I can't. And I already have a girlfriend. I'm not interested in changing that. I'm tired. I've had a fucked-up couple of days, and I came here for a break. And that doesn't include you at the table with me. So either you get up and leave, or I will."

With a nod, she stood and picked up her plate. When I glared at her cheesecake-brownie peace offering, she picked that up too. "I'm going. I don't want to upset you. Just think about what I said."

No chance in hell. With Madison showing up unexpectedly yet again, I was unable to do anything but think defensively.

She walked up to the trash, slide the food off both plates into it, then set the dishes on the counter. She turned and gave me a quick smile with a wave before walking out the door.

I stared in the direction where she'd disappeared to make sure that she was out of my space and not coming back. It took a few more minutes after that for my shoulders to relax down.

After a deep breath, I picked up my sandwich, ready to begin the relaxing lunch break I'd come for.

LATER AT THE BAR, as I sat in Ben's office looking over our second-quarter financials, my phone rang. An unfamiliar number flashed on the screen.

"Hello?"

"Is this Cade Michaelson?" a deep male voice asked.

"Yes. And this is?"

"Doug Phillips. I'm legal counsel for Lakemont Country Club. Do you have time for a few questions regarding the complaint against Madison Kensington?"

"Sure." I'd clear my afternoon, if that's what it took.

"I've read Suzanne's complaint and have interviewed her for more details. Can you describe the events starting from the beginning? I understand you and Madison were once involved personally?"

Nice. So had Madison also been interviewed before she'd surprised me at the coffeehouse?

I spent the next thirty minutes giving him the highlights of the important events and answering any questions as we went. He asked me if I had anything further to add or if I had any questions.

Then he posed a question I hadn't expected. "How would you like to see this matter resolved?"

I blinked. Could it be that easy? "I want it to end. I want her to leave me alone. I want her to leave our companies alone. If you really want to know, I want her fired and to never see her again." Harsh? Yeah. Could Madison use a break? Probably. But not from me. Not in this situation. She had multiple chances to redeem herself, but failed. Maybe she needed a fresh wakeup call to realize she had *much* farther to go in her recovery.

"I do want to know. We are protecting the country club

and its members. That means doing whatever it takes. Will you be seeking any other remedies in this matter?"

"No. I'm not looking to sue the country club, if that's what you're asking. But if she keeps surprising me like she did today, I will seek an order of protection against her."

"What did she do today?"

"Sorry, I was so focused on the upcoming event and our companies, I forgot about earlier today. She had to have followed me. She showed up at the coffeehouse I frequent to basically reiterate the hallway conversation that Suzanne overheard."

"Which part of it?"

"That Madison wants to get back together with me."

He sighed. "Okay. Got it. I spoke with her first thing this morning. She should not have contacted you, and she knew that. Thank you for your patience and providing me with all the details." He paused. "By the way, are you related to Garrett Michaelson?"

"Yes, I'm his son. You know my dad?"

"I've known him for years. He's helped me individually, and also our firm, with our financial portfolios. He's a great guy. Say 'hello' to him for me."

"Will do."

When I got off the phone, a text showed on the screen that had come in during the call. It was from Hannah.

> Want me to bring dinner over tonight?

I replied without hesitation.

> Fuck yes.

AT THE END of another long afternoon stuck in my email box and on my cell phone, we sat on the back patio around the fire pit in the middle of our relocated-furniture zone. Hannah had brought over two pizzas and cream cheese frosted chocolate bacon cupcakes. I slid a couple of slices onto my paper plate after giving Hannah what she wanted.

Ben ignored the pizza and went straight for the dessert. He took a bite, then rolled his eyes into his head, moaned, and collapsed backward onto the decking where he'd been sitting. "I've died and gone to food heaven. That is officially the best thing I've ever tasted."

His happiness ended when Ava bounded over him and snarfed down the rest of his cupcake, paper wrapper and all. Mase's shoulders shook in laughter while he chewed a mouthful of pizza.

Hannah quickly gave Ben a replacement cupcake when he stared at Ava in disbelief. Then she glanced over at me. "Okay. Thanks for sparing me trauma by having me come in through your side gate, but I'm going to have to see the kitchen sometime. How bad is it?"

I stood and tugged her up by the hand. "Words will never do it justice. Prepare yourself."

Mase, Ben, and Ava hung back in the yard as Hannah and I walked through the back door and entered the disaster area that had become the kitchen. Large fans were still blowing to dry the place out, but I shut them off for a minute so we didn't have to shout over them.

Needing body contact with her after two challenging days away from each other, I wrapped my arms around her from behind and held her close. "All the flooring and some of the subflooring is being pulled. The lower maple cabinets are totaled, along with all the drywall and baseboards."

Hannah moaned softly. "It was such a dream kitchen."

"It will be again. Don't even bother looking in the basement. It's a total redo, game tables and all."

She turned in my arms and stared up at me. "You and Mase can sleep here while all this is going on?"

I nodded toward the hallway. "Take a look. The living room, kitchen, and basement took a hit for the rest of the house."

Hannah kept shaking her head, like she couldn't believe what had happened. That made two of us.

After I turned the fans back on, I led her into my dry bedroom. The moment I closed the door, I felt the stress on the other side of it begin to fade. All because Hannah was here again.

I pulled her into my arms and just held her, breathing. "Damn, Maestro. I've missed you bad."

"Missed you too. I'm so sorry you had to handle this alone."

I pulled back and kissed her softly. "Not alone. You were here, if only by text and phone. Mase has been awesome with this. With him here, I had the time to escape for a couple of hours today."

When I released her, she stepped over to my bed and sat on the edge, looking up at me. "That's right, you went out to lunch."

"Yeah. And I went to Loading Zone afterward to help Ben out a bit."

"Who'd you have lunch with?"

"No one. How was your lunch with Lila?"

Hannah didn't reply. Instead her eyes narrowed imperceptibly. For a few seconds we stared at each other. And I had no idea what was happening as her expression hardened further.

"Cade, you were with Madison at Starbucks. I saw the

two of you together when I drove by from Lila's back to the shop. She was sitting across from you at a table. You were leaning back and laughing."

I shook my head. "She stopped by, uninvited. I didn't have lunch with her."

Her brows drew together. "Why didn't you just tell me she was there?"

"Because you asked me who I had lunch with."

"So I have to ask when you see Madison? I know you've talked to Madison before without telling me. Why are you still keeping things between you and Madison from me?"

I blew out a hard breath. "I'm not keeping anything from you, Hannah. This is the first time I've seen you alone since lunch, and Madison surprising me for a few annoying minutes didn't pop into my mind—I'd blanked it out."

She frowned. "What about the other time?"

"You mean on Monday?"

"Yes. Monday. When Kristen and I were going over cake details last night, she mentioned that you spoke with Madison on Monday. I just went with it, acting like I already knew about it. But I felt blindsided. I should've known about it. *You* should have told me."

I thought back to the nightmare of Monday afternoon. "Yeah, I confronted Madison in the lobby of the country club."

Her brows raised. "Yeah. I got that part."

Whoa. I took a deep breath, trying to remain calm. She was pissed. I got it. "As I was leaving the parking lot, Mase called and texted. My house was going under water. I shoved all things Madison into the back of my mind to deal with everything else."

She still held a deep scowl on her face. I tried to read her but failed. In a sudden movement, she burst up from the bed and nearly knocked me over. I took a step back as she paced back and forth. When she stopped, she stared hard at me. "Cade, I need to be able to trust you."

I blinked. "Hannah, you should trust me. I haven't done anything wrong."

"What about the hallway conversation after the tasting that I overhead? I had to pull that out of you too. When your ex tells you she wants you, and you don't tell me that happened, what am I supposed to think? That's three instances where you and Madison have been face to face that you haven't told me about. How many others are there?"

Fuck. Do all women have an ingrained ability to remember old resolved screw-ups to recycle at a later date?

Not wanting to miss another detail, I scanned through my memory. "None. And I didn't mean to keep any of them from you. In my mind, none were an issue worth mentioning."

She scoffed. "Bullshit. If my ex told me he wanted me back, you don't think you would have a right to know that? Don't you think I would want to share it with you?"

My shoulders slumped. "You're right. I would've been pissed as hell. And it was wrong of me not to tell you. I'm really sorry."

She huffed out a breath through her lips. "I've been trying to blow off Kristen's surprise comment, but it's been bothering me—why you hadn't told me, if there was a reason you were hiding it from me. With my past scar tissue, I pushed it into the back of my mind, trying to trust you as I waited for you to tell me. After today's lunch with Madison, it all came rushing back."

I took a step closer to her, softening my voice. "I had no idea. And I had truly forgotten with the craziness of the week. Guys can be dense sometimes. I'm a world-class idiot for not realizing how important the information was to you."

Moisture welled up in her eyes. Her face tilted down to the floor before lifting back up to meet my gaze. She lowered her voice to a near whisper, repeating, "I need to be able to trust you."

She didn't need to say anything more. I pulled her into my arms, and instead of fighting me, she clung tightly. "I know you do, Hannah. Please, believe me. There is *nothing* going on. Madison is a nonissue for me—for us. But I promise to do a better job of keeping you in the loop. Speaking of which…"

I went on to update her with all the details of the conversation with Suzanne, the complaint she helped initiate with the board, and my subsequent phone call with the club's legal counsel.

On a shaky breath, she nodded. "What do you think's gonna happen? Do you think we've just pissed her off that much more?"

"I don't know. I voiced my wishes to the attorney: that she be fired and that I never see her again."

Hannah pulled back and gave me a tentative smile. "I *totally* second those wishes."

24. FINDING ORDER

There's a certain rhythm in orchestrated chaos.

Technicians rushed back and forth, carrying wires and electrical tape. Rows of chairs were directed on wheeled carts. Two dozen helium-filled black-and-green balloons bumped together as they floated by on strings connected to their handler before veering off left. Another two dozen silver-and-blue went off right.

The second photo booth that had been so much trouble to hunt down finally arrived. Two men struggled with an industrial dolly as they negotiated it down the hallway. The man facing my direction lifted his brows, and I pointed to the room on the right, checking another item off the list on my tablet.

Ankles crossed, ass planted against the wall in the hallway across from the entrances of the two event rooms, I'd claimed the perfect vantage point to direct traffic while remaining out of the way. In the room on the left, Kristen and Suzanne directed the room arrangement according to our agreement. Kendall and Kiki manned the room on the right.

And thank fuck, Madison was nowhere to be seen. Maybe she'd heeded my warning after all—or the attorney's. Regardless of the reason, things going smoothly today were in both of our best interests.

Darren had been busy all morning setting up sound boards and equipment in each room. We'd created soundtracks, but the boys insisted on live DJs, their mom waved a big fat check, and we smiled, nodded, and complied like smart little business owners.

Thanks to meticulous planning, unending emails, and double-checking confirmations, each component involved in running, servicing, or supplying the event had a role, knew their timing and task, and completed it with little additional direction. I served as the failsafe, monitoring the progress of both rooms to make sure nothing fell through the cracks.

I turned my head as movement rounded the corner, and a very important component began rolling my way. Forgetting all about lists and party coordination, I pushed off the wall to greet Hannah and her crew.

She directed Daniel and Chloe in steering a large cart that held one of the cakes. A smile lit up her face the instant we made eye contact, and my heart lurched into the backside of my ribs.

Every time she walked into a room, she struck me. Dark hair, bright eyes, killer smile the moment her gaze met mine. I'd cause that smile. And she had the same effect on me.

"Well, what do you think?" She gestured to the cake they were wheeling in.

Daniel glanced over his shoulder as he steered the front end of the cart, walking backward. "Hey, Cade."

"Hi, Bossman." Chloe grinned.

"Hey, guys. This one goes in the room on the left." I pointed, holding the tablet toward the correct doorway with an extended arm.

I wrapped an arm around Hannah as she stepped into my side, and we followed the two into the room. Pressing my mouth and nose into her hair, I inhaled deeply, grounding myself in her tropical scent.

Then I looked over the brightly colored cake to answer her question. "I think it's brilliant. Soccer, huh?" She'd grilled me nonstop about the likes and dislikes of both boys: hobbies, taste preferences, colors. I'd compiled the list of questions, then had the mother complete two profiles to give Hannah inspiration.

"Yeah. I went with a sports theme for both. That way each gets a unique cake, but neither can say they got something better than the other."

I chuckled. "Wise woman."

The cake was simple in theme, yet intricate in design. On one side, an empty orange-and-white goalie net bracketed a grassy soccer field. Players ran midfield across the turf. The other side had a life-sized black-and-green soccer ball flying up off the field. A sugared air wave with whitish swirls supported the ball.

"Looks great, Maestro." I kissed her temple. "We're about thirty-five minutes out from party time. You all set with the other one?" Daniel and Chloe finished positioning the cake on the far table and wheeled the empty cart by us and out the door.

She nodded. "Minutes away. I'm excited to see your reaction to Jared's cake."

I arched a brow. "Oh? I'm intrigued." Winking, I smacked her ass. "Go. I'll meet you in the other room."

Before leaving, I double-checked room set up for John's

bar mitzvah celebration. Per our instructions, ten tables with ten chairs lined the perimeter of the dance floor. Between the tables near the side wall that adjoined to the other party sat the photo booth. Along the back wall were long banquet tables covered in black tablecloths with a line of chafing dishes that would hold the food. At the end, on its own separate table, the soccer ball cake was displayed.

Suzanne and Kristen each carried a handful of streamers attached to balloons, and they deposited small groupings of them around the room. The tables held a variety of masculine centerpieces, from black baseball caps with green-and-blue "J & J" scripted on them to commemorate the boys' day to green foiled party crackers. Not a single flower was anywhere in the room, by the boys' request.

Darren finished setting up along the other side wall. A friend he'd brought bent over the equipment, making adjustments. I walked over to check on their progress. "How's it going?"

Both men looked up. Darren kicked his chin up toward me in greeting.

I extended a hand to the newcomer. "Cade."

"Rick. Nice to meet you." He gave my hand a quick shake, then shifted his focus back to the equipment, sliding a dial down the sound board.

"I'll be next door for the duration if you need anything," Darren commented to Rick as he stepped out from the booth they'd created. He turned toward me. "All set in both rooms."

We headed out the door. "What, didn't want to 'pop-out' in the Bieber room?"

The hard-edged rocker shot me a deadpan look, his shaggy head of hair and tribal tattoos making the question comically rhetorical. "Wearing earplugs at the party is rude, right?"

I barked out a laugh as we stepped into the other room. Darren headed straight for his sound booth as Kiki and Kendall descended on me at once.

"The photo booth's not working," they complained in unison.

Before I had a chance to ask if they'd plugged it in, they ran off shouting orders at people in different parts of the room.

I pulled out my phone, texting Suzanne.

Need electrician in Jared's room. STAT.

Seconds later, a reply popped up.

On her way.

The parents of the guests of honor appeared in the doorway, John and Jared coming in right behind them, along with an entourage of what looked to be family and a group of boys and girls their age.

"Mr. and Mrs. Stewart, Jared, John." I spread my arms wide, welcoming them. They were twenty minutes early, but we were on schedule enough to accommodate the incoming flow.

Taking a needed few seconds, I sent rapid-fire texts to my sisters and Suzanne.

They're here.

And Madison still wasn't.

Straightening my shoulders, I took a deep breath. Then I

smiled at our clients. *Showtime.*

25. EBB AND FLOW

Hannah and her crew wheeled in the second cake right before I escorted Jared and his father into their room. Both boys already had their official bar mitzvah at their temple, and, as if by divine proclamation, each boy held an air of importance, like the experience had elevated them.

My only comparison was when I'd gotten laid: *my* official induction into manhood.

But I understood their custom. My family had never been overtly religious, but my Roman Catholic grandmother, Irene, God rest her soul, had insisted that her grandchildren have exposure with the Church, even if we chose not to belong. To which my mother promptly exposed us to a variety of other religions, ensuring we were well aware of our choices.

In the end, neither Mom nor Dad went to church regularly or often, and none of us had ever been exposed to the Jewish religion, aside from a couple of friends at the club growing up. My learning curve for this double bar mitzvah had been a trial-by-fire, Google-aided endeavor. But the Stewarts had been eager to help whenever I stumbled or found a roadblock. Having helpful and understanding clients, who were invested in their kids' happiness, made all the difference in a successful event.

As Hannah's crew positioned the cake into the back next to the buffet, I gravitated toward this mysterious cake Hannah had teased me with. Catching flashes of sugar crystals in between Daniel and Chloe as they inched it safely onto its designated table, it wasn't until I approached closer that I made out the theme of the cake.

Magnified into quadruple ordinary size, a regal black-and-silver chess set stood in cake form. As Daniel and Chloe wheeled the cart away, and Hannah inspected the cake for any needed last-minute repairs, I stepped behind her.

Needing closeness, but unable to sneak away with both parties revving up, I put my tablet down on the table beside the cake and slid my hands onto her hips, pulling her back into me—nothing lewd with kids and parents arriving, but enough to establish connection, possession.

She hummed a low note and leaned back against my chest, covering my hands with hers.

I bent my head down and brushed her hair back with my chin, sliding my lips across her jaw until I found her ear. My rumbled growl made her shiver. "I love the cake, Maestro. Reminds me of games we've played."

My tone was illicit. While my mind meant the chess games I'd taught her to play, my body touching hers, behind hers, made me wish we could play all kinds of less-innocent games.

She turned her head and gazed up at me, smiling. "Thought you'd like it. With every stroke of icing, I thought of us. "

My mind guttered yet again. I swallowed hard. "Stroke. Icing."

"Mmm-hmm..." Her low tone was loaded with sensuality.

The new frosting condiment she'd recently added to our naughty pantry had a world of possibilities. In my struggle to be good, I tried to focus on the cake.

"Break it up, lovebirds. We've got a party to conduct." Kiki grabbed our shoulders, separating us and shoving me backward.

I laughed and pulled both girls into a big hug. "Go be wonderful, girls. Here, Kiki, hold on to this." I gave her my tablet for safekeeping.

An hour later, both parties were buzzing with energy. Music blared—*thank fuck* in my room that meant rock music. We all stood by the cake again, the one spot in the room that seemed to be home base when we needed to catch our breath and oversee the party as a whole.

My gaze locked on to a potential hazard. "A chair is being dragged onto the dance floor. I need to make sure no one gets hurt during the hora."

A crowd gathered on the floor, ushering the man of honor into the center and onto the chair. I glanced up at Darren who'd just faded out a song from Metallica. The popular song of "Hava Nagila" streamed out as the room cheered and gathered to form a circle, holding hands.

Three sturdy men hoisted Jared, who was seated in the chair, high into the air and began the traditional chair dance. We all clapped along, shouting as they paraded their newest man around the floor. Jared had a perma-grin slapped onto his face, arms bouncing toward the ceiling, as he surfed above the crowd.

A couple of hours passed with various activities and

dancing. I thought about checking on Kristen and Suzanne, but we'd decided to remain in our corresponding rooms to be available for anything the client needed. In the event of an emergency, we'd agreed to text, but my back pocket hadn't vibrated once.

Kids lined up for the photo booth, ours done up with an edgy background for the theme. Thankfully, the sound-dampening panels of the walls and our room configurations offered enough sound buffer to keep Bieber away from the rock, as it should be.

Not one incident to report on either side. And still no sign of Madison.

After searching the crowd, I spotted Hannah behind the chess cake as she and Daniel carved out slices onto dessert plates. Not needed anywhere else, I strolled over. "Where's Chloe?"

Daniel glanced up, the tips of his Mohawk vibrating. "She volunteered to serve the soccer cake."

"She a closet Bieber fan?"

Hannah and Daniel exchanged a quick glance, then busted up laughing. "That's exactly what we said."

Narrowing my eyes, I glanced toward the other room. "I knew it. I sensed that about her."

Hannah wiped her hands in a cloth napkin. "You got this, Daniel? I need to go to the little girls' room."

"Yeah. I'm good."

Hannah grinned as I fell into step beside her. She arched a brow. "Gonna help me lift my skirt?"

I exhaled slowly, dragging my gaze over her body. She wore jeans and a dressy tank top that begged to be pulled down, but her lack of skirt was beside the point. "Thought you'd never ask."

"Cade!" Kiki called out from behind me, sounding panicked. "The photo booth froze up again."

I groaned, pulling Hannah in for a tight hug. "Damn electrics are cock-blocking me."

She laughed and shoved me away. "Go. I can lift my 'skirt' by myself."

A cascade of other images flooded into my mind, naughty innuendo-induced things she could do by herself, and my jaw dropped.

She shook her head as she walked backward out the door and mouthed, "Bad boy."

Yeah, I was. And she loved it.

I headed over to the photo booth, then popped open the electrical door in the back like the electrician had done earlier. Last time all she did was press the reboot button, so I tried that fix before calling her back in. All the lights in the outer portion of the unit flickered off. I waited a few seconds, then pressed the button again, and the unit hummed back to life.

Satisfied, I walked around to the front and peeked in to find a young boy and girl inside. "Give it a few seconds, then you can try again. She nodded and my gaze drifted down to where she sat on his lap, his hand resting comfortably on her hip. They couldn't have been more than twelve or thirteen. "Your parents know you're here, sitting on each other?"

The girl blushed.

The boy shook his head. "You won't tell, will you?"

I snorted. *Fuck no.* But I acted gruff anyway. "Keep your hands outside the ride at all times."

His face turned white as he nodded. "Yes, sir."

I turned away from them and grumbled, "Sir." Something way too old for me to be called. Well, maybe by anyone other than Hannah...

I scanned the room, searching for her. At least five minutes had gone by, maybe ten, and she hadn't returned. There could've been a line in the ladies' room, but I doubted it. The men's bathroom had half a dozen stalls in addition to a trio of urinals on the wall.

Madison's glaring absence, along with Hannah's extended one, choked a sudden cramp into the base of my throat as I watched the closed door leading into the hall. Kiki was hanging out by Darren at the DJ booth. "Kiki, you're in charge until I get back."

When I stepped into the corridor, it was empty. I headed toward the lobby area, where the main bathrooms were located. Rounding the corner into an adjoining empty hall, movement flickered in the corner.

"Cade."

Madison.

As I turned, she stepped out from behind a potted palm. I arched a brow. "Getting your hands dirty gardening?"

"Ha, ha." A seductive smile crept onto her face.

A scrap of a dress barely covered her body. Her shoes had to be five inches high. Interesting choice for a kids' party. "You running a party or going clubbing." My statement fell flat, omitting my loudly thought *or going whoring.* Definitely not hitting a Sex Addicts Anonymous meeting.

"I'm being a good girl." She stalked forward, her steps weaving a little.

I scoffed. "Impossible." Not with that outfit or her predatory sexual demeanor.

Instantly, the trauma from my past hit me hard. The vile version of Madison that I'd never known while dating her had come to horrific life before my eyes.

Repulsed as she eased closer, I edged backward, keeping

distance between us. My elbow hit a wall when I ran out of hallway real estate.

A corner of her red lips lifted. "As you ordered, I'm staying out of your way. And you're right. You *know* I do bad best."

Furious, I exhaled slowly, refusing to let her affect me, even though she'd cornered me against a wall between her body and another damned potted plant. The scent of alcohol lingered on her breath.

As she pressed closer, I held fast—instead of shoving her with the body check I wanted to give to her. But no woman deserved physical abuse, regardless of the form, including Madison. So I kept my reaction chilled and my voice low. "Get off me, Madison."

A slow smile curved her lips as she raised a hand, brushing her fingers over my forehead. She ran them through my hair.

An angry shudder ripped through me. With measured words, I growled in warning, "Back the fuck up."

She purred. "Awww, no need to be nasty, Cade. Give in to it. I know you want me."

I snorted. "You're delusional."

"Am I?"

Her hand went straight for my crotch and fuck if my traitorous dick didn't twitch in recognition as she gripped me there. (Stupid-ass men's dicks with minds of their own.)

"I'm warning you, Madison. If you don't step back, you're gonna get shoved on your ass."

Her smile widened, and she pressed into me.

Reining in my temper, because I refused to lay a hand on her, I pinched my eyes shut, jaw clenching.

My eyes popped open the second her lips touched mine.

I stared into hers; they were wide open, gazing back as if she knew me. She knew nothing at all.

My hands flew to her shoulders, gripping her hard, right as her tongue flicked across my opening mouth. "Stop this game."

A whimper sounded down the hall.

My head snapped left.

Hannah stood with a stricken expression on her face, her hand flying up to her mouth.

"*Fuck.*"

"Ooopsie." Madison finally stepped back. She looked anything but sorry.

"Kiss your job good-bye," I growled. Maybe the attorney had dragged his feet. I wouldn't. I wiped the back of my hand over my mouth, which left a red lipstick smear across my hand.

Madison had the nerve to laugh. Either she didn't believe I'd carry out the threat or was too drunk to care.

In a blur, Hannah charged between us and shoved Madison hard, knocking her drunk ass to the ground. "*Selfish Bitch!*"

Madison stared at Hannah wide-eyed. So did I as Hannah leaned over Madison with her hands clenched into tight fists, looking fully prepared to finish what she'd just started.

Tears welled in Madison's eyes, then she glanced at me. Her vulnerability surfaced. She'd fucked things up royally, but still, beneath it all, was the girl I once knew. The girl who existed beneath all the impenetrable shields only wanted to be loved. She was just clueless on how to make it happen. In fact, her games had pushed *me* right to the edge of violence. Although nothing justified a man hitting a woman, it could've happened with a man less in control.

Instead of attacking Madison, Hannah whirled around. She shoved a finger at my sternum, tears brimming in her eyes. "You. Just..." She growled and turned, storming back the way she came.

"Hannah, wait!"

She spun around. "No. Leave me alone."

Approaching slowly, I shook my head. "I won't do that. This wasn't what you think. And neither is Madison. She—"

My mind flashed to Mom's explanation, news I hadn't yet shared with Hannah. *Fuck.* Well, it was do-or-die time now. All or nothing. I lowered my voice, "She has more issues than sex addiction, Hannah. I'd forgotten to tell you what my mom shared with me at the Fourth of July party. Madison had an ex-boyfriend in Europe who'd beaten her to the point she had to be hospitalized."

Hannah's expression turned pained. Her voice dropped to a fierce whisper as she took a step closer. "You're defending her? And the list of things you keep 'forgetting' to tell me about her keeps growing."

"No. I'm not defending her. I'm only explaining that Madison isn't well. And I didn't realize how messed up she is until just now."

"She's crazy."

"Maybe. Damaged, at the very least."

Hannah shook her head and pinched her eyes shut. Her tears finally fell.

I moved closer, needed to hold her.

She took quick steps back. "No," she snarled.

Not wanting to upset her further, I froze in place.

"Don't. Your instincts ran to keeping me on the outside with everything. All I asked was for you to let me in, make me a part of what you struggle with. But all the little things you 'forget' to tell me add up. How can I trust you when you don't automatically feel that I'm important enough to help you with what you face, what affects you—what threatens us?"

"Hannah, please."

My heart pounded. A cramp formed in my throat. I'd fucked up. But not as a major event. I'd failed with all the little things along the way while I hadn't been paying enough attention. And because of it, Hannah wasn't slipping away—she threw herself with everything she had in the opposite direction.

"No," she ground out. Her gaze hardened. "I don't want to be around you now. Plus, you've got *her* all over your face. When I see you, I see that." She pointed back toward Madison. Then she spun and strode down the hall.

When I turned around, Madison wore a shit-eating grin on her face. I glared at her. "All this because you wanted something you could never have?"

"I always believed I could. We were so right for each other back then." She sniffed as she pushed herself into a seated position, curling her legs to the side.

I let out a heavy sigh, dropping my hands into my pockets as I gave her a hard stare. "The image you have of us back then was a mirage. The real you was hidden from me."

She stared at her lap on a shrug. "I didn't have the courage then. Really, I had no idea that I had a problem. That there was a clinical definition for it."

"Madison, look at me." When she lifted her face, her gaze locking with mine, I continued, "You have more than a sex addiction. You have a compulsive personality. Obsessive. You never explained why you fucked with our businesses. I'm not even sure you understood. But it all makes perfect sense now."

Her brows drew together. "It does?"

Yeah. She had no idea. Which made her all the more dangerous. "Sure. You wanted to get close to me. When you had no control over that, you scrambled for anything you could affect. Maybe some twisted part of you wanted to hurt me, like you felt it connected us in some way. I don't know. Don't really care now. You need help. And thanks to you, someone I truly care about is in pain."

"I'm sorry, Cade."

I didn't ask what for. In her narcissistic world, she would only be able to have remorse about things not working out in her favor. I pegged her with a warning look. "Just keep away, Madison. From everything."

She gave me a short nod. "No problem there. You got me fired."

I stared at her a beat longer. "No, Madison. That was all on you."

Without another thought, I left her on the rug in the hallway. If guests saw, so be it. After the stunt she pulled, and her blood alcohol level, security needed to escort her ass off the property.

I fired off a quick text to Suzanne.

> Send security to the hallway past the lobby.
> Madison. Drunk.

I needed to find Hannah. She thought we needed space, but we needed to sort it out together. The few minutes of time I'd given her was all the alone time I could afford. I hoped she would realize that Madison had been ambushing us and me all along—not only the business sabotage, but also the other day at lunch and tonight in the hallway. I'd fucked up. I got that. But I hoped Hannah had faith in me, the man beneath all my screw-ups that she'd fallen in love with. That she'd trust in her instincts—trust in me.

In the seconds it took to reach the lobby area, my heart raced. I stopped to scan everyone mingling in the wide-open space and those who sat in the chairs. I passed by a mirror and paused when I caught the damage. Red still stained my lips and smeared off of one corner. No amount of wiping with my hand removed it entirely. "*Goddammit!*"

Searching for Hannah, but not finding her anywhere, I rushed into the men's room and grabbed one of the rolled wash cloths, wet it, squirted a shit-ton of soap onto it, and washed my mouth, face, and hand off.

Then I crossed the hallway to the women's bathroom and barged in. "Hannah!" I ignored the indignant looks of two younger guests and one older woman, who seemed shocked but not alarmed.

No one answered. I bent over and peered at the shoes under the only two closed stalls like a pervert, in plain view of the women now washing their hands who eyed me with guarded interest. None of those feet belonged to Hannah.

I stormed back out and leaned a shoulder against the wall, pulling my phone out, texting Hannah.

Where are you?

No text bubble popped up in reply on her end. Nothing. A few seconds later I sent her another.

Please, Hannah. It wasn't what it looked like.

Which is what everyone says when they get caught, guilty or not.

You know Madison. This was her plan all along.

Impatient, and worried with her nonresponse, I backtracked through the lobby and down the corridors. I approached the two ongoing parties, muted sounds of their competing music filtering out their closed doors. Then I realized I'd gone the wrong way. She'd never want to be around other people when upset.

But she wasn't in the bathroom. Not in the lobby. We'd driven separately, and she'd parked her car near my Jeep in the front parking lot. I raced out, bursting through the front doors of the air-conditioned lobby into the muggy night air. Five running steps down the pavement, I stopped. Her car was still parked next to mine. Hannah: nowhere to be seen.

Firing off duplicate texts to my sisters, I sent them an emergency all-call.

If you see Hannah, text ASAP.

Madison pulled a twisted stunt.

Hannah upset.

"*Fuck.* Think, Cade. Think." My chest grew heavier with every second that ticked by.

Not knowing where else to look, I yanked the main entrance doors back open. The same people milled about in the front lobby. A concierge sat at his desk, and I walked up to him.

"Who's the person directly above your general manager?"

The young man blinked. "I'm not sure, sir. The board members I think."

Blowing out a breath in frustration, I texted Suzanne again. She hadn't responded yet.

Call me. Urgent.

My phone rang seconds later. I shoved out through the back patio doors for privacy as I picked up the call. "Madison is drunk, in a skanky dress, and she just cornered me against my will, kissing me in front of Hannah. Now Hannah is MIA. Madison told me she was fired, so you may want to have security kick her out if they haven't already."

"O-oh, Cade. I'm so sorry. I hadn't heard. I did call security after your text. Hold on a second." The party sounds in the background faded, and I heard a door close before she came back on. "Here it is: an email from the board confirming Madison's termination. It was sent just before the parties started. I'm sorry I didn't stay on top of her issue. I could've warned you."

I shook my head. "No, don't worry about it. Knowing that in advance wouldn't have stopped Madison."

"Okay. I'll follow up with security to make sure they've handled it. And again, I'm so sorry."

I ended the call and went outside, prepared to search every square inch of the grounds. As I walked down a lit path, I thought about the spa. But when I got there, I found the doors had been locked at the late hour. Then I searched around the building, sticking to the sidewalks and paved surfaces.

After thirty minutes of searching the grounds, I came full circle, ending up at the front parking lot again. Hannah's car remained beside mine. I crumpled down onto the curb, finding it hard to breathe.

I was a Grade A asshole. There were so many other ways I could've have handled Madison. I'd been offered an out by my sisters for the entire night. But no, I had to be king. Being cool, calm, and collected in the face of adversity had always been my strong suit.

To admit I needed help wasn't written into my DNA. My

instincts ran with taking on everything at once, juggling to make sure every ball got caught and tossed back up, seamlessly.

Only this time I'd dropped something fragile, irreplaceable.

26. WRECKAGE

M inutes blended into hours as I sat on the curb in the humid night. Waiting. For what, I hadn't a clue. My death sentence, I supposed.

Texts had come through from each of my crew, chiming in with updates. No one had seen Hannah. Right when I was about to retrace my steps and start the search all over again, Kristen texted. Chloe had called Daniel to let him know she'd run into an upset Hannah right after the incident and taken her home.

Whose home? Chloe's or Hannah's?

Not that it really mattered. Hannah obviously didn't want to talk to me, or she'd be here now. Would have texted me at least, to let me know she was okay.

But I knew my sins, and they'd been grave.

Possibly fatal.

None of the problem had to do with Madison, although she'd certainly been an instigating component. Part of it had to do with the difficulty Hannah had in opening herself wide and trusting again. Not only that I wouldn't cheat on her, but that I would protect her—confide in her with everything, for fuck's sake. I'd been irresponsible with that. Hadn't given it the attention it rightfully deserved.

And maybe a million things could've happened, impossible to predict, but I knew in my gut something bad had been coming, that Hannah and possibly our relationship were in danger. Even with all the warning bells going off the last few weeks, I could've put Hannah first above everything else—all this worthless shit—but I'd chosen not to.

Maybe that said something dark and tragic about me. My therapist would probably call it a "hero complex." Because guys like me thought we could save the world, handle it all perfectly. But the world had crashed down around me when I failed to keep safe the one person who counted on me the most.

At some point, with how great Hannah and I had been doing, and with how busy things had gotten in our lives, I'd forgotten the challenging path she had walked to get to this point—and how fragile she still remained in many respects beneath that tough front of hers.

"Cade." Kristen sat down next to me on the curb.

"Hey." My lungs burned, like every drag of oxygen scorched them.

"I'm so sorry, bro." She hugged me with one arm. "What're you still doing here?"

I closed my eyes and shook my head before dropping it onto my folded arms. "Nowhere to go."

"What?" Her hand squeezed my shoulder when I sighed.

"Home has Ava, *our* dog. Hannah doesn't want to see me. And I can't make my legs move to leave this spot. Her car is sitting next to my Jeep. It's like the moment I leave, that's it."

"So talk to her."

I shook my head. "I can't. She's made it clear she doesn't want me to. And maybe I don't have the right to. She deserves better than me. I knew her issues. Had I stopped to really think about her needs and fears for just a moment, and she'd given me plenty of opportunities to do so—she'd even asked me to relinquish the reins with this in her own way for Christ's sake—then she wouldn't have gotten hurt. But I was pushing forward too hard too fast, without making sure Hannah was there with me. Now it's too late."

She rubbed my back. "Cade, that's ridiculous. It's a misunderstanding. Give it time, she'll come around."

I sighed heavily. "Don't think so. I knew the stakes, but ignored them. I blew off the signs. My ego got in the way. I should've handed the event over to you and protected her. It was a huge thing for her to trust herself in the first place, let alone trust me. She went through weeks of therapy over the issues she'd had. I was reckless." I should've been more careful, kept Hannah in the forefront of my mind with all things, especially where Madison was concerned. "All her scar tissue, all the trauma she'd finally healed over and moved on from, got ripped wide open today."

"So that's it? You're not going to fight for her, fight for what the two of you have?"

"Not tonight. She needs time. And I need to get my head screwed on straight. I thought I could be what she needed. I'm the one who asked her to try. But I pushed her concerns aside. I'm the one who failed her."

"Oh, Cade." Kristen pulled me in tighter.

I clung to her. My entire world had imploded, and the small comfort of family support in the midst of ruin helped me to breathe for a moment.

"If I disappear for a while, you good to handle everything?" Hannah didn't want to be around me now. And I didn't trust myself to stick around and not force the issue to see her.

Her long pause made the air even heavier. "Yeah."

I lifted my head finally, looking into eyes I hadn't been ready to see yet. A world of sympathy gazed back at me. I gave her a hard unblinking stare until she reined it in and nodded, understanding.

Working past the choking cramp at the base of my throat, I swallowed hard. "Take care of Hannah too. She needs you. Needs all of you."

"We will, Cade. She's family." A tear tracked down her cheek, but she quickly wiped it away. "You're family too, baby brother. Don't you disappear for long. We need you too."

I gave her an absent nod. Because I was adrift and had no idea what I would do. Even if Hannah came around tomorrow, next week, next month, I didn't know what it would take for me to be what she needed. But I sure as fuck didn't want to be something she didn't need.

I nudged a gentle fist into her chin. "If for nothing else, to kick your asses at Monopoly." I forced the corners of my mouth up, but the attempted smile fell.

"Will you tell the others I'm heading out for a while? Kendall and Kiki? Mom and Dad? Ben...Mase?"

"I will, Cade. I'll give them all your love."

Good. Because the thought of composing a text to each of them was overwhelming.

I felt empty.

27. RESIGNATION

In the darkened hours of early morning, I stood in my hallway after an insomnia-filled night. The dim lighting distorted what I saw at first. Something white lay on the darker wood flooring in the entryway by the front door. The rectangular paper had been folded neatly, and I bent down to pick up the note in the dark space. The edges were sharp, almost scored at the crisp bends.

I stared at it, as if through sheer will the contents would transform into something good. Only a foreboding that weighed heavy around me caused a sickening pit to churn in my stomach. To prevent myself from throwing up in the hall, I walked toward the kitchen as I unfolded it.

I scanned the note.

In utter disbelief, I read it again, more slowly.

Hannah had written a letter of resignation. Not only from me. Not just from Invitation Only. In a clear overreaction, she hadn't quit me and the business; she'd cut all ties. With Mase and Ben, with Ava, my sisters.

"Oh, the fuck you are." I bit the words out as I crushed the damned note in my fist. Seething, my breaths came quick

and shallow. I paced twice, before heading straight back to my bedroom.

After stabbing my legs into a pair of jeans, I yanked my desk chair out, sat, and tossed the crumpled ball into the center of my desk. Then I forced deeper breaths into my lungs as I stared at her note.

She didn't mean what she'd written—couldn't possibly want this. In the midst of the love from my family and friends, Hannah had come alive. No way would I let her give that up.

Taking my time to spread the paper back out flat, I stared at the amount of wrinkles in it. Let them be. Let her see the evidence of my immediate anger with her ridiculous notion. Having a powerful message to send, I flipped it over to bare the blank side: a tattered canvas, perfect.

I grabbed a pen off of my stack of unpaid bills then began my reply.

Hannah,

I'm sorry. I didn't protect you. I should've made you first. You're the most important thing, and I failed you.

I reject your resignation.

When we started down this adventure, we both committed to giving it a go.

One of your greatest fears was risking our friendship and losing not only me, but Mase and Ben. My sisters. My parents.

They are all there for you. Yours as much as they are mine. The girls need you with Invitation Only. Mase and Ben need you. Ava needs you.

Fuck, I need you.

But I know I lost the right to have that mean anything. I know I fucked up.

But this note isn't about that.

You want your space. I get it. But do it surrounded by your new family. Take care of them. They'll need you while I'm gone.

Because you need your space, I'm heading out of town. I don't trust myself to stay away from you. But I will be back for you.

No matter what you believe, I love you more than I love anything in this world.

I will love you forever,

Cade

With a burning lump in my throat, I folded the note, her words ending up on the outside.

One side of the folded rectangle had an entire blank surface, so I wrote a word that summed up my feelings about the whole damned thing.

Grabbing my leather duffel, I shoved a couple of pairs of jeans and a handful of T-shirts into it. I looked around the room, but there wasn't a fucking thing I felt I needed. I grabbed only the bare necessities.

Passport. Tossed it in, along with my driver's license and a single credit card.

I grabbed my checkbook and ripped out two checks, then signed the remaining blank ones. I zipped the bag shut and slung it over a shoulder, scooped up the unpaid bills, and dumped them onto the kitchen table with the checkbook on top. As an afterthought, I grabbed a yellow sticky note and scrawled Mase a message.

> *Had to bolt. There's money to cover expenses for a while.*

I peeled off another square and stuck it below the first. Damn tiny things.

> *Contractors have deposits. Should be on autopilot with remodel schedule. Joe will take care of it all.*

On a third note I wrote:

> *Bike in airport lot by elevators. Extra key in bottom desk drawer.*

I cut the kitchen light, casting the room into darkness again. How I felt on the inside.

A mind-numbing twenty minutes later, I stepped onto Hannah's front porch. I didn't ring her bell or knock. She only ever came and went through her front door, so I shoved a corner of the recycled note into the rubber molding surrounding her door.

That one word faced outward, reminding me of how I felt about this shit going down. She deserved her time, and I needed to finally listen. To push at this point risked me fucking things up further. If that was even possible.

She had made a decision. And I was honoring the consequences. For now.

On her driveway, I sat on my bike. Stared at her door. The pull to stay and fight was tremendous. Didn't matter though. Walking away for the time being was the right thing to do.

But the part of me screaming inside, the man who'd finally found the woman meant for him, and then lost her, stared at the folded note that showed the only word echoing through my head.

"*No.*"

28. A WORLD AWAY

I stared at what had now become my escape hatch—a first-class airline ticket stub. The original two airline tickets meant for both Hannah and I to seek calm after all the chaos had been sadly exchanged. And the seating choice wasn't because I wanted comfort. I sought separation. Isolation.

Sitting in my airline seat, I grabbed the headphones the flight attendant gave me and asked for a double scotch. The passenger who sat beside me put on headphones too. Good. I didn't want to have to growl at him to enforce my do-not-disturb mood. I downed the scotch and closed my eyes.

After a connecting flight and hours of being passed out from lack of sleep, I arrived at a destination most people would go to for an amazing vacation. I looked at it as a soul-searching mission.

The staff at check-in must've sensed my detachment, because they efficiently did their jobs without much small talk. Inside of an hour later, my ass was planted on the beach. I stared at the horizon. Then I looked around. White sand stretched in either direction. Several palms curved their trunks over the beach before swooping up, green fronds pointing toward the sky.

This place would be as good as any to figure my shit out. I sat there, trying to open my mind. Nothing happened. But at least I was a safe distance away from Hannah. Half the world between us meant I couldn't be a stalker and sit on her front doorstep, asking her to talk with me. Begging forgiveness.

Slow torturous days went by. Each the same. Me sitting on the beach. Walking the beach. I paced back and forth, creating a rut in the sand, as I searched my mind and heart for answers.

There were no revelations, though. Only memories of failure that constricted my chest, making it difficult to breathe. I had tried to handle it all, control the universe around me. But doing all that got me into this mess. After trying to do everything, I had nothing. Because I didn't have Hannah. In thinking I had it together, yet being totally wrong, I barely knew what to trust in myself anymore.

Figuring out what I truly wanted would take sorting through what was really important in life. Yet I kept coming full circle. Hannah mattered most. But nothing else seemed to solidify on how it could all work together. What path to take.

I'd blown it on the whole balancing-work-and-life thing, very similar to what my dad had almost done with our family years ago. And I'd sworn to do it better. A fine job I did of that. It snuck up on me. My own ego had taken me down.

I blinked as a realization hit me. Done with trying to sort my shit out on my own, I jumped up off the beach and headed to the Four Seasons concierge.

A polite brunette wearing glasses glanced up at me as I

approached. I looked at her name tag. "Adrienne, I need to use my cell phone. Can you help me make a call to the States?"

"Oui, monsieur. Our hotel offers technology to make your personal phone work here. Or I can assist you in connecting the call through our phone systems."

"My cell phone would be great."

"Would you like me to do it for you?"

I nodded. "Yes. Please." My mind was already blown with too much thinking. I didn't need to struggle with learning something new.

After a few minutes, she handed it back to me. "Let me know if you need anything further."

"Thank you, Adrienne." I walked outside onto the patio and dialed the number.

After a few rings, a calming voice answered. "Hello?"

"Dad."

"Cade? Good to hear from you. Kristen told us what happened. You okay?"

I let out a heavy sigh. "Been better. Being stuck on an island is giving me plenty of thinking time but no answers. Hoping you could help me out with that."

"Anything I can do, I will."

"You were a workaholic when we were kids. I know it put a strain on your and Mom's relationship. How did you figure it all out?"

His deep chuckle sounded over the line. "You're right. I was focused too much on work, and all of you suffered for it. But 'figuring it all out' didn't happen overnight. Hell, I still have to work hard at pacing myself. Your mom helped me realize a few things along the way."

"Like what?"

"Intimacy doesn't take a lot of time, but you do have to

make the time. You can't work long hours, days at a time, only keeping the prize at the end. A healthy relationship needs constant attention, daily, even if just a few moments to connect. Like a pot on the stove—you want to keep it on simmer so it doesn't boil over."

I nodded, even though he couldn't see me. "That makes sense." So many days in the last weeks, I hadn't seen Hannah because I knew I would in another day or two. Texts were great, but maybe it should've been more connection.

"I see so much of myself in you, son. Hard charging, driven, wanting to succeed by being the best. But everything comes at a cost. Be sure the sacrifice you make is on the business end instead of your personal life. I saw the reverse too often with business associates; many grew distant with their spouse and children in order to advance in their professional lives. I knew I didn't want to lose my family."

"What about communication? I've fucked up there. When so many things were being juggled at once, I pushed out of my mind things I felt were nonessential shit to try and focus on tasks that had to be done. But turns out, some of what I thought was unimportant was critical for Hannah to know, but I didn't see it. I missed huge things and hurt her in the process."

"Every relationship goes through that. It's not easy balancing out what used to be two separate lives into one relationship. For years, I pushed so hard at work to make sure I was providing for and protecting your mom, even before you kids were born. But it took me a long time to realize that the women in our lives want to do the same things for us. Protect. Provide."

I started to see the connection. "Ahhh, guys think *they* have to do it all."

"Exactly, Cade. That's the difference, *that's the key*. You have to do it together."

The sun was suddenly too warm, and I sat down on a chair in the shade, letting his words sink in. "Great perspective. I think that'll help. But what I'm still rolling around in my mind is the success thing. At school, they did a great job in teaching us how to create something out of nothing, how to really work hard to achieve results. How did you balance love and work?"

"You've heard the phrase, work smarter not harder?"

"Sure. Ben and I say it often at Loading Zone."

"Just because you're working smarter, doesn't mean you should pile on more work to fill in the extra time. That's *why* you're working smarter. To be able to have time with her."

Shit. The simplicity of it nearly overwhelmed me.

Frustrated at my idiocy, I blew out a hard breath. "And all I did was take on one more thing, then another one more thing, until it was my time with Hannah that suffered. That's how I let things slip through the cracks. If I'd set aside more time for her, we would have communicated everything."

"Maybe. Sometimes we have to learn the lesson to know what to focus on. I know I did. We incrementally lose control with each new responsibility we stack on our shoulders. But in the end, we're the ones who added the stressors into our lives. And we're the only ones who can take them out."

"Yeah." I let it all soak in, grateful as fuck I'd called him. When the silence stretched on, I leaned forward, resting my forearms on my thighs. "Thanks, Dad. This has helped more than you know."

"Anytime, Cade. And trust me...I know. I wasn't smart enough to learn that I needed to ask these questions when I was your age. So does that mean you're coming home?"

I laughed. "Soon. I still have a few more days before the return flight. And I think the extra time will help me figure everything out. Now that I've talked with you, I have a roadmap to get there."

"Call me if you need anything else. Good luck."

"Thanks, Dad." I hung up. And after the call, I experienced the first calm I'd felt in days. And...a little bit of hope.

The following day, I sat on the beach again under the shade of a palm tree after having the best night of sleep I'd had since I'd arrived. In small bursts of clarity at different moments, I remembered what Dad had said and thought about how it applied to my situation. Around lunchtime, I realized I needed to stop trying to figure out how to correct the past mistakes. Instead, I began to focus on the future.

I tipped back my beer bottle and took a long pull while watching kids splashing around in the waves. A line of pelicans glided low over the water, searching for fish in the shallows. The beauty of the place started sinking in as I got out of my head for a moment.

And in the peace of it all, with my mind relaxed, my confidence grew. I didn't have it all together. I probably wouldn't do everything right the first time, but since my dad was still learning, I figured I didn't need to. I just needed to want to, be aware that it would take effort and attention. A relationship wasn't an autopilot, take-for-granted thing. And the rest would have to work itself out.

Someone shouted, sounding alarmed. I sat up, planting my bottle into the sand. A woman stood at the shoreline, shouting something in French while she pointed to an abandoned paddleboard floating on the surface about a hundred feet straight out.

I ran up to her as did others. Tears were streaming down her face. No further translation needed. I raced into the surf after another man, who'd already taken off toward the paddleboard.

By the time we made it out there, no one was around, and we began diving on separate sides of the floating board. The water was clear enough for me to see a form beneath the surface moving with the ebb of the tide. I grabbed an arm and pulled him up.

Thank fuck I'd rowed crew and our coach insisted on Advanced CPR Certifications for the entire team. I swam quickly back to the beach, pulled him safely away from the waves, and laid him onto the sand as I yelled toward the small crowd gathered on the beach. "Tell the hotel to call for help!"

With no time to waste, and no pulse or breathing detected, I started with the breaths. The other man fell to the sand beside me and began chest compressions. He and I spoke no words, instinctually working as a team to save the man's life.

After what felt like forever, but was likely only about ten minutes, an emergency crew arrived and took over for us. They opened up their automated external defibrillator, hooked the leads up to his chest, and asked us to step back. Seconds later, they pushed a button and his body jerked. When no response came from him, they checked his breathing and pulse. They repeated the process once more.

The crowd had pressed in around us as the man finally began to move. He coughed out water, and the emergency crew rolled him onto his side to help him clear his lungs.

I took a couple of steps back, hands shaking, as I tried to get my own breathing and racing heart under control. The French woman came up to me, one hand covering her mouth as the tears continued to stream down her face. She placed her other hand on my chest as she swallowed hard.

She looked too choked up to find words. That made two of us.

I pulled her into my arms, and she held me tightly while the emergency crew strapped the man onto a backboard to carry him to an ambulance that was parked on the edge of the beach.

As they lifted the man and began to walk off, she pulled away from me, speaking rapid French as she glanced between me and the other man who'd assisted me. I shook my head, not understanding, then nodded anyway and motioned toward the man we'd saved. She gave me a weak smile and ran off after him.

The other man who'd assisted in the rescue stepped closer toward me. "She thanked you. Thanked us. For saving his life. She said her husband is her world."

My lungs froze. Then I forced in a deep breath. Moisture welled up in my eyes as I stared toward the emergency vehicle. Everyone around me faded away, dispersing into different directions as I stood alone.

Hannah *was* my world. It wasn't about trying to fit her in to what already existed. It all needed to *begin* with Hannah.

29. MESSAGE IN A BOTTLE

The Seychelles Four Seasons concierge had taken great care of me, making arrangements so I could take a flight back home two days early. At my request, I'd been supplied with a gel pen and parchment stationery. And during plenty of contemplative time on the plane, optimism ruling my thoughts, I'd drafted Hannah a letter—the most important of my life.

Although definitely no poet, I spoke from my humble heart, the boy inside me desperately needing the love of the girl inside her.

After traveling the long journey back to the States, I finally pulled the rental car into an empty angled space in front of Sweet Dreams during what I knew would be a slow time for them. Her fastback was parked out front in its usual space. My heart ached at the sight of her car, at a cherished piece of her.

Knowing how to open her front door without triggering the squeak that she'd been meaning to oil, I slipped into her shop without giving away my presence. I approached the front counter, deposited my message on the center of it, and gave the letter one last glance.

A rolled parchment page with a slender red bow stood inside of an empty wine bottle that the flight crew had been gracious enough to give to me. A cork they'd politely provided had sealed my message inside.

For a split second, I contemplated ringing the service bell on the counter, but decided against it. My needs were spelled out inside, and I wouldn't ask for anything more, not even to disrupt her day. Hannah, or one of her employees, would find the bottle sometime this afternoon when a customer needed help.

I could wait. I'd been suffering for almost a week. I was willing to wait a whole lot longer.

So I left.

I should've gone to Kristen's place to let my sisters and family know I was back and geared up to piss them off on a regular basis. Tired and hungry, however, I went back to my place.

I couldn't find my keys and had to knock on the door. The Jeep was parked in the driveway, and it was a weekday, so I hoped Mase was home. The inside entryway light flicked on. The door opened.

I laughed at his shaggy hair and wild-eyed expression. "Damn, I've missed you, Mase."

"Holy fuck, dude." A hundred and ninety pounds of lean surfer tackled me to the concrete on my front landing. "You disappeared with only a note. That's bullshit."

I grunted. "Get off me, cretin. And didn't Kristen tell you?"

He climbed off and stood. "A note from you and a cryptic voicemail from her that you'd be gone awhile. Lame. Next time I expect a call from you." He glared at me, then offered me a hand up. Ava barreled through the open front door and jumped onto my chest before I fully grasped his hand. Her weight knocked me back onto the ground, as if seconding Mase's complaint.

Mase laughed, pulling his hand back. "We both missed you, you stupid fuck. You don't get to just up and leave your life. You worried the shit out of us."

Ava kept licking my face. "Hey, girl." I laughed. "I missed you too, ya' little menace." I looked up at Mase. "Yeah, sorry. Just needed to physically and mentally check out for a while."

I scooped Ava off my lap, shooed her into the entryway, and rolled up off the ground. Then I followed them into the house.

"Do me a favor and order us a pizza? I need to text everyone and let them know I'm back."

"Of course, man. Whatever you need."

I nodded and disappeared into my room, shut the door, and collapsed onto my bed. I wanted the first text to be Hannah, my fingers hovered over her name, but I held back. She had my letter. That would be better than anything else I could do. I created a group text and added everyone in.

> Hi, guys. Back home now. Exhausted.
> Eating then passing out. Will get together
> with everyone soon.

I closed my eyes while I waited for the pizza to arrive. When I woke, it felt like a few hours later. Turned out, it was almost sixteen hours later. Bright sunlight streamed through the windows as I stumbled into the kitchen.

I scrubbed my hands down my face, getting my bearings before I opened the fridge. I grabbed a bottle of water and a takeout pizza box that had edible-looking contents.

As I sat down at the table, half a pepperoni slice shoved into my mouth, my eyes drifted over to the corked empty wine bottle sitting on the center of the table. Inside the bottle was a crumbled wad of paper. Not rolled like mine had been, or folded like the one from Hannah, just a crushed note sitting in a sad heap on the bottom.

My heart sank.

Chest heavy, it was everything I could do to pull another full breath into my lungs. I chewed my mouthful carefully before doing anything further, thinking it would be ironic for me to choke to death on cold pizza before I read my death sentence.

Then, as if the tragic comedy thus far hadn't been ridiculous enough, it took a full five minutes to manipulate that damned wad of paper through the narrow bottle neck and tiny opening without destroying it. I mentally sent out every positive vibe and thought possible while trying to breathe, praying that good things came to humble men who'd wronged, suffered, and were determined to be better.

I finally pulled the crumpled mass free.

Nothing on its surface indicated a fatal prognosis. With care and hope, I pulled the corners free, flattening out the paper with my hands (only after I'd wiped my sweating palms on my jeans.) The side facing up was the letter I'd written to her on the connecting flight to Boston from Dubai. I took three deep breaths to steady myself before flipping it over.

To a blank page.

I blinked.

I flipped it over again, back to the side of my letter, scanning it thoroughly to be certain I hadn't missed a note in the margin or an underlined word. But nothing new had been written.

So that was it then. My heartfelt letter crushed *was* the reply.

I flipped it back over, closing my eyes, fighting back tears.

A door opened. I heard shuffling and the rapid clicks of puppy claws running across the wood flooring.

"Hey, man. Welcome to the land of the living." The fridge door opened. Shut.

Hardly. The land of the living dead was more like it.

Mase sat across from me.

I sighed and opened my eyes, shoving the rest of the pizza slice into my mouth, even though I'd likely puke it up in a few minutes with how my stomach churned.

"What's that?" Mase pulled the note out of my reach.

"Nothing," I grumbled. He didn't turn it over, just stared at the crumpled blank page, so I didn't get too territorial over what might as well serve as my obituary.

Mase pointed to the center of the paper. "Doesn't look like nothing."

I narrowed my eyes at him, then the paper. *Asshole better not be fucking with me.* I swiped the page back from under his pointed finger. When I leaned over to have a closer look, all the air wheezed out of my lungs.

On the reply to her note that I'd left in her door almost a week ago, I'd written a huge "no" on one folded side.

But on the wide expanse of my wine-bottle parchment letter in which she could have written her reply—an entire blank side of paper for her to let me know how she felt about my request—she'd only sent back one tiny word.

A very small "yes."

I exhaled a relieved lungful of breath, grateful for the tiny sliver of hope.

(And realized I needed fucking reading glasses.)

—————

THE NEXT MORNING, sitting at a table at the coffeehouse felt like déjà vu. Only this time, Madison walking toward me had been my idea. Closure.

Coffee in hand, she sat down across from me, a somber expression on her face. She knew what this was about, even though I hadn't spelled it out in so many words. My heavy tone had been enough.

"Hi, Cade."

"Thanks for meeting me, Madison. We have a few things to discuss."

She nodded. Said nothing.

"Please understand why we're meeting like this. I'm giving you this time because we grew up together. But it has to be the last time that we see, or even communicate, with each other. I'm not your therapist, even though you came to me all the time to fix your problems when we were kids. I think that's why you're so attached to me now. But it needs to end. You need professional therapy."

She took a deep breath. "I know. I need help."

"I hope you truly understand what you need help with. It's not just sexual addiction. You seem to have replaced sexual addiction with obsession. And I was your target, for whatever reason."

"I discovered too late that you were the only one who ever really loved me."

I gave her a nod. "I did. I loved the woman I thought I knew. But you're broken right now. You need to get fixed. Not for someone else. Not to 'get' something out of it. For you."

Tears welled in her eyes. It seemed my words were getting through to her.

"I mean it about the no communication. This is it. You

can't contact me again. Or interject yourself into any part of my life. Ever. You need to move on. Learn to be better for you. Alone. Once you're healthy, someone who sees and loves you for *you* will come along."

"I'm so sorry. I regret what I've done, how I've hurt you. And Hannah."

For a fleeting moment, I saw the little girl I once knew in the eyes of the woman sitting across from me. "Thank you. Please know I always want you to find happiness in your life."

I stood. The meeting was done. But she looked up at me with the eyes of a lost little girl. I pulled her up from the chair and gave her a fierce hug. She had a hard road to travel. And she wouldn't have me to run to anymore. The least I could do was give her a solid memory of the boy who'd once cared for her as she worked toward finding another.

I pulled away and gave her a hard stare. "You can do this. The Madison I knew growing up was fearless. Find her again."

30. A WALK IN THE PARK

The following afternoon, I walked along the curving sidewalk in our tucked-away section of Fairmount Park ten minutes early and spotted the empty park bench. My pulse kicked up a notch from excited to frenzied, and I broke out in a cold sweat. Anxiety and I had never gotten along very well.

"Calm the fuck down, Cade," I muttered. "You're no good to her dead from a coronary."

Ava trotted alongside me, happy to be in the middle of so much activity buzzing around, but amazingly mindful due to Mase's new leash training. And I couldn't decide which I wanted more: Ava running in every direction chasing grasshoppers and butterflies or the pup on her best behavior. The latter seemed easier on me, however, and I was grateful. Besides, best behavior seemed to be the theme for the day.

I sat down on the park bench, watching the sidewalk in the most likely direction Hannah would come from, and Ava sat beside my left leg. Not even thirty seconds ticked by before I stood and began pacing. Misunderstanding my actions, Ava scampered up and followed for two circuits of pacing, before giving up, sitting down, and watching me wear a groove in the sidewalk.

A gravelly deep voice sounded out behind me. "Have a seat. She's going to say yes."

Blinking, I turned around. An elderly man leaned on the top back slat of the park bench. "How do you know—"

He snorted. "A man this nervous? Only a woman could make a man so crazy. Relax. Breathe. And speak from your heart. Women understand that language."

Distracted by the man, my erratic pulse began to calm. I arched a brow. "You seem wise."

A hard laugh was followed by a rattling cough. As I took the seat he suggested, he clapped me lightly on the shoulder with his frail hand. Ava settled next to my leg again.

"Only fools play the game of love. The lucky few get caught by it and never let go." His bony finger pointed along the sidewalk. "There she is, my boy. Go get her."

And there she was.

I sucked in a breath, my heart jumping at the sight of her walking toward me in a bright yellow sundress. Her hair was pulled up into a high ponytail, a few dark wisps catching in the breeze, teasing across her pinked cheeks.

In the first brief second, I could see she fared well, if perhaps a little on the thin side, but my focus lingered on her tentative smile. Ava broke all her good behavior and bolted toward her, yanking the leash out of my hand. I laughed and stood, glancing behind me to thank the older man.

He'd vanished. I scanned the park behind me and off to the side where I'd come from, but he was nowhere. Furrowing my brow for an instant, I wondered if he'd been real.

Soft laughter chimed out from the sidewalk reunion, and I spun my attention forward again. Hannah's megawatt smile struck me.

She knelt down, then laughed as Ava licked her face. "I've missed you too, girl. Yes, I have. Oh yes, I have."

A pang of jealousy speared through my heart. But I banished the nuisance feeling as quickly as it had come.

The innocent deserved unconditional love.

The rest of us had to earn it.

Ava's new red leash trailed along the cement as Hannah lifted the gangly puppy into her arms. "She's almost too big to pick up now."

Unsure if I'd be able to keep my hands to myself if I let them hang free, I shoved them into the pockets of my jeans. "Yeah. Mase's been feeding her some kind of premium organic puppy chow."

She nodded. Her smile softened as her gaze lifted to meet mine. Hesitant hope reflected back to me in those bright green eyes. She threaded her hand through the loop of the leash before plopping Ava down onto the sidewalk. They walked the rest of the way to the bench. "Don't forget how he loads his plate with extra food, just to be able to drop her table scraps."

I snorted. "Delinquents."

Hannah sat on the bench, and I pulled my hands out of my pockets, lowering to sit beside her.

Her eyes narrowed as she examined my face. "You look too skinny. And very tan."

"Yeah. No appetite."

Her eyes softened. "Cade, I—"

"Hannah—"

We both laughed quietly out of nervousness.

I took a deep breath. "You first."

She nodded and dropped her gaze down, staring at her folded hands in her lap for a moment. After a slow inhale and exhale, as if steeling herself, she raised her gaze to meet mine. "Cade, I was so wrong to do what I did. Cut you off like that. Running from the best things in my life had been an idiotic thing to do. I panicked and closed in on myself. But most of all, I hurt you in the process."

I blinked. So not how I imagined our reunion going. "Hannah, I'm the one who was wrong, on multiple levels. I was an idiot to begin with, not putting you first above the business. Above everything. I should have removed you from harm's way with the threat of an ex who we *knew* could cause problems. On that night, after your note—when I left —I didn't feel worthy of you. You trusted me to keep you safe, and I failed you."

Her clasped hands moved from her lap, the fingers of one hand reaching out to touch my knee. "But you came back."

I glanced up. Her expression was unreadable. Open, but nothing more.

"I did. On the beach, a fight rose up from my gut and into my heart that hadn't been there before. I left for you, because I didn't think I could be what you needed me to be."

"And now?"

"Sitting on that sand for days on end gave me clarity. The man who fell in love with you wants to fight for us, not for selfish reasons, but for you. If you'll give me another chance, if you understand sometimes I'm an idiot and slap me upside the head, I will fight to be worthy of you."

Tears welled in her eyes, threatening to spill over.

A cramp choked my throat at the sight of her barely held emotions. My vision began to blur from building tears.

"I'll give you a second chance Kincade Joseph Michaelson. I'll give you a second, and a third, and on and on. But only under one condition."

A tiny flame of hope flared to life, and I exhaled in relief. "Name it. It's yours."

"The next time I run. And there *will* be a next time; I *am* going to run—this we've established."

She paused, and the corners of my lips twitched as I fought a smile.

Her hand squeezed my knee. "You have to chase me. I'm so fucked up when I'm lost in the middle of a panic attack, I don't think. I *can't* think. You have to think for me. Chase after me. Always fight for us, even when I can't." Her voice fell to a pleading whisper, her tears spilling over onto her cheeks. "Promise me."

My tears fell too, not manly, but I didn't give a fuck. Hannah was here, pouring her heart out, asking me to love her.

I lifted a hand to cup her cheek, wiping away her falling tears with my thumb.

"I promise, Hannah. I promise to think for you when you can't, I promise to chase after you when you run, and I promise to fight for us no matter what obstacles come our way."

She inhaled a shaky breath. "We need to remove an obstacle now. Before I feel comfortable moving forward, we need to be on the same page about something."

Warring emotions gripped my heart. Panic. Hope. I wanted to soothe her fears, and there was so much left to say, but I needed to listen first. I held her gaze and gave her a firm nod with my full attention.

"We have to talk more. I need you to *know* what we *need* to talk about. In fact, don't decide what is and isn't important to share with me, it all is—from the mundane to the shocking. If something upsets you? Tell me. Make me a part of your life in such a deep way that I don't feel separate from it. I don't ever want to feel like you're keeping things from me again, even if it's unintentional."

A choking cramp locked up my throat again at the pain I'd caused her even as I exhaled a relieved breath at what she needed from me. "I agree. One hundred percent. On the island, I realized we could've avoided all the heartache if I'd made more time for us, not just hang-time or sex, but *real* time where we connect and share. Things got so busy, I let *us* fall through the cracks. The time we make for each other is where we solidify us, where we communicate. I'm going to fucking communicate like you wouldn't believe." I took a deep breath. "Can I ask you one favor?"

She nodded.

"Please be patient with me. Sharing every little thing is new for me. I want to be everything you need me to be, but they don't make an instruction manual. I'm learning as I go. Just trust in me, no matter what."

"I will. I do." She gave me a hesitant smile, and it was all the invitation I needed. I leaned forward, capturing her lips with mine. Warm, salty, trembling, both a reunion and the seal of a promise, the kiss was the best of my life.

When I pulled away, she smiled brighter than I'd ever remembered. I grinned, the happiest man on the planet. "That's why I came back."

Laughing, she tilted her head. "My soaking wet kiss?"

I tapped her nose. "Nope." I arched a brow. "Although I do like you wet..."

She shoved at my chest with little force. "Neanderthal."

"You know it." I grinned again. "I came back because I want to be the cause of your smile, every lucky day of my life." Remembering I had a gift for her, I grabbed her hand

and tugged her up off the bench. "C'mere. I've something to show you."

Nervous and excited at the same time, I led her down the walkway to the opposite side of this section of the park. As we rounded the bend, her surprise edged into view.

She gasped the moment she caught sight of the spectacle. Her smile widened and she squealed. "Oh my God... Cade!"

A meadow of rainbow-colored snapdragons in small clay pots stood in rows, stretching across the grass. The hill rose up on the far side, and the flowered pattern on the grass canvas formed the irregular shape of a heart.

Children ran along the edges, playing among the flowers. Butterflies flew above the blooms. Even a few iridescent dragonflies glided by, finding perches on the peaks of the flowered stems.

Instead of running into the middle of the flowers like I'd expected her to do, she pressed against my side, lacing her fingers together with mine. I sighed, comforted by the gentle gesture, happy she wanted to be here with me.

"It's amazing, Cade." Her soft words held the tiniest tremble. She sniffed, and I looked down to find her crying.

"Hey, hey. No more tears. Only happiness, okay? I hoped this would make you smile and laugh."

A choked laugh came out. "It does. I am happy. I'm just overwhelmed. What an incredible bouquet of flowers. It's just...I'm the luckiest..." She buried her face against my chest when her words started to croak out.

I held her tight. "No, Maestro. I'm the lucky one."

We stood there for an eternity, both of us holding each other tight. Even Ava respected our need for privacy by stretching out in the long shadows of the flowers for a late afternoon nap.

Finally, I rubbed a hand up Hannah's back. "Might be hard to stick 'em in a vase."

She huffed out a soft laugh, turning toward her snapdragon meadow. "We can collect a few favorite pots. Maybe Chloe and Daniel can deliver the rest to friends and family."

"I like that idea: share our celebration with others."

I smoothed my thumb up her arm and tilted my head. "I could've done a meadow of cupcakes and run naked through them. But I bake for shit, and arrested for streaking seemed like the wrong message."

She busted up laughing—music to my ears.

She gazed up at me, her sparkling eyes bright green in the sunlight. "Some fantasies are better left to our imagination."

My face fell into a pout. "But I like the idea of the cupcake meadow. I'm looking forward to licking frosting off your body."

Mischief danced in her eyes, and she bit the corner of her lower lip. "I'm looking forward to that too."

Unable to believe Hannah was really here with me, I pulled her into my arms again, burying my face against her neck, inhaling the tropical scent I hadn't realized I'd become dependent on until just now.

With soft tender kisses, her lips trailed a line up my neck. Teeth tugged at my earlobe. "What do you say we go back to my place?"

Exhaling, relieved to the point my knees nearly gave out, I squeezed her tighter.

"I say *yes*."

31. SWEETEST TASTE

My heart raced as we entered her dimly lit entry, and I closed the front door behind us. Without saying a word, she slipped her hand into mine and glanced over her shoulder. A gentle smile curved onto her face and lit up my world.

She squeezed my hand, and I couldn't tell if she did it to make sure I was actually there with her, or because she felt me shake with nervous excitement. Fuck, probably both. The adrenaline of the last couple of hours still had me shaking.

We stood in the dark space for a few seconds, just breathing.

"I have a surprise for you too, Cade." Her low voice held a sultry note.

She could've been talking about something mundane, like last month's profit and loss statement from Sweet Dreams, and I still would've been mesmerized.

My mind guttered. "Does it have anything to do with us naked in a cupcake field?"

She pressed against my side. Her voice softened. "In a way."

"You're killing me, Maestro. If you keep me in suspense much longer, I *will* pass out."

She leaned up and pressed a kiss to my cheek. "No passing out. I've got plans for you, Mr. Michaelson." She reached behind me and flicked the light switch on.

I blinked at the sudden brightness and tried to focus.

Her small but well-appointed kitchen was immaculate, as always. On her marble-topped kitchen island, four condiment items stood, lined up in a row toward the back edge.

Exhaling hard, I moved forward and examined them: a glass pot of honey, gourmet jars of chocolate, and caramel sauce. I lifted a finger to touch a chilled a red-and-white can of whipped cream that peeked above the rim of a filled ice bucket. A lump formed in my throat, but I swallowed hard past it.

"How long have these been on your kitchen island?"

"When I realized I'd made a terrible mistake. When I gave up on us and let you leave."

The corner of my mouth kicked up. "You've missed me."

"Yeah, I did."

Not willing to spend another second without touching her, needing her connected with me, I brushed a stray lock from her forehead and leaned down. Her darkened hazel-green eyes softened, then fluttered shut. My lips brushed over hers, and a soft sigh escaped her lips.

Savoring her taste and the feel of her warmth, I wrapped my arms around her, pulling her closer. With a slow suck, I tugged her lower lip into my mouth, then kissed her more deeply as I held the one woman in this world who made me whole.

"I'm blown away that you made a condiment shrine."

Her lips twitched as she fought a smile.

I shook my head. "No, really, Maestro. All the fun and kidding aside, you have no idea what it means to know you missed me as much as I missed you. And the condiments aren't about the physical. Nothing between us has ever been that simple."

She gave a nod as her eyes glistened with tears, her smile finally showing. "I know."

My gaze drifted over her shoulder, and I blinked. "Ummm, what is all that?"

She turned around and released her hold on me. "Well, that's part of my surprise."

Uncertain what that meant, I stepped closer to her table. Six glass bowls, some large and some medium, lined up across the tabletop with clear plastic wrap over their wide tops. The bowls held what looked like different colored frostings: pink, yellow, green, blue, dark brown, and white. A collection of small glass bottles stood beside the bowls, toppings: shiny metal balls, rainbow sprinkles, and some kind of snowflake dots.

"Frosting?" I still couldn't believe it, and the word croaked out past a throat gone dry as I pictured Hannah whipping this together with her hair pulled up into a messy ponytail, a cute ruffled apron over a baby T-shirt and short cotton shorts.

I swallowed hard. When I turned back toward her, she looked up at me with an adoring expression, not the naughty I'd initially imagined. Caught in a mix of lust and love, torn between wanting to tear open those bowls and gathering her back into my arms to simply hold her, I blinked hard, attempting to reset my brain.

Lust won.

"Clothes off."

She huffed out a breath, her eyes widening. "What?"

"Like that hadn't been your plan all along." I arched a brow, daring her to argue.

Game on. And I was beyond ready to play.

When she made no move to shed the bright yellow sundress she wore, I took a step toward her, staring hard at her, silently threatening to remove it myself.

She simply stared back at me, holding her ground.

My nostrils flared. "Off. I'm not going to say it again. Naked. Except for your little vintage apron." I pointed to her feet. "And those strappy shoes."

Her body shuddered, but she gave a slow nod, mischief flickering in her eyes.

When she moved to untie the thin straps holding up her sundress, I nodded. I relaxed in relief a split second before lust tightened through me as she completely bared herself. Perfect curves tempted, breasts swaying, hips shifting. She stared at me, a beautiful pink flushing her skin while the cotton fabric pooled at her feet.

"The apron is in there." She pointed to the drawer next to me, trying not to smile.

My gaze locked with hers, I jerked it open and grabbed whatever was on top. Luckily it was the apron in question. I handed it to her and watched wide-eyed as she pulled the blue polka-dot ties over her head. Then she fastened it behind her at the waist, doing incredible things to her breasts.

Shaking my head in disbelief at a fantasy finally turned reality, I had no idea what to do next. But when I focused on the fun about to begin, left-field thoughts fired into my brain. Frosting was about to become a contact sport.

I'd been in her kitchen often enough to find what I wanted. I yanked open the drawer beside me, sending metal and wood utensils crashing into one another. One flew out, clattering onto the floor.

The corner of her mouth twitched, her luscious lips twisting in amusement.

"What are you smirking at?" I glanced down and grabbed a metal whisk with my right hand and a long spatula with my left. "Choose your weapons, Maestro."

She blinked, eyeing the slotted metal spatula. "That's for flipping hamburgers."

Tilting my head, I arched a brow at her. "Says you."

Dropping her hands onto her hips, she tipped her chin up at me. "What about you?" She continued to stare at the spatula and took a step backward.

I stalked toward her.

She took another step back.

"What about me?" I held my weapons of choice in front of me as my menu item took another step toward the buffet of frostings. "This is my fantasy, remember? Instead of saying 'thank you' for making my dream come true, why don't I show you a great use for this spatula?" I smacked it onto my thigh, making a loud whack against my jeans.

Her eyes widened. "Neanderthal."

Moving suddenly, she ripped the plastic wrap from the tops of the bowls. Then, as if I wasn't frayed enough, or maybe because she wanted to push me further, she swiped a finger through the pink frosting before sticking it into her mouth. She made slow work of sucking that lucky frosting off, hollowing out her cheeks as she pulled the finger between her lips.

I growled low. "You got that right. Nothing civilized about to happen here."

32. MOMENT TO SAVOR

Hannah...

Wild mischief glinted in Cade's eyes, and I watched closely as he stalked forward. Caught off guard with his sudden playful mood, my muscles tensed. Then I feinted left and lunged right, darting past him and snatching the first two things from the utensil drawer that I wrapped my fingers around. I thrust them up between us in defense—my dual weapons against his.

He snorted. "A ladle? What are your plans with that? Glop hunks of frosting onto my head?" He shifted his gaze to my other hand. "And what the hell is *that*?"

Narrowing my eyes, I glanced at my hand. The pea-green tool had flat rubbery "bristles" on its end. "Usually, a silicone basting brush. But tonight, it's a first-class frosting flicker." I snapped my wrist toward him, making the rubber ends quiver.

His blue eyes flashed in the bright lights of the kitchen. Which made me glance at the darkness outside the windows and realize anyone peering in could see my near-nakedness. And watch everything else about to follow.

"Ummm, maybe we should close the shutters."

He glanced over his shoulder, following my gaze. "Why?"

"Anyone can see in." I chewed on my lower lip, flushing with sudden shyness.

He dropped his classic deadpan look at me. "Anyone, meaning 'peeping-tom neighbors' who trudge through your backyard at night?"

I scowled, lowering the ladle and basting brush down to each of my hips. "Or kayakers rowing by."

"In the pitch dark?"

"What about my neighbors across the water?" I hedged, beginning to feel stupid with my weak stalling ploy.

His stare hardened as one corner of his mouth curved up in a smirk. "If your neighbors across the water have high-powered binoculars mounted on a tripod to catch us the first time we fuck in your kitchen, good for them."

My lips twitched as I fought a smile. I'd missed him. This lighthearted exchange, his quick wit laced with naughty intentions, was but one of the many facets to Cade that I needed. But underneath all the sexual bluster was a man who loved me.

His absence—the needless separation I'd also played a part in—had been rough on us. And beautiful moments of crazy fun were a part of the courting again, our ritual to celebrate being together, full of life.

In a flash of movement, he whirled around and stabbed the end of each of his utensils into a different bowl. "Get over here, woman." His eyes narrowed. "Or stay there." He shrugged, pulling his loaded weapons from the bowls. "I'll nail you with frosting no matter where you stand."

I arched a brow, smirking. "Only with frosting?"

He gave me no warning. Soft wetness splattered my cheek, my chest above the low neckline of the apron, and the inside of my left knee. I glanced down to see streaks of pink and green on my skin.

Gaping at him, shocked at the unexpected start of the all-out frosting war, I maneuvered around the kitchen island, taking cover while he reloaded. Hovering at the corner of the barrier between us, I waited.

Amusement glittered in his eyes, and in that split second, time slowed, my heart warming with a heavy ache in my chest. Cade unleashing his true self—the no-holds-barred, vulnerable boy behind the man—made me fall in love with him even harder.

Yeah, these moments were what I missed most when I'd nearly blown it by running again.

Never again. I hoped. I repeated the mantra in my head a few times, willing it to be true. I'd admitted to Cade that I ran when spooked, but he was worth the attempt at rewriting my knee-jerk panic reaction. For once, it would be nice to trust in someone to be my strength when I faltered—trust in Cade.

"Hellooo, Maestro." He arced the whisk in a slow wave in front of my face. He'd taken another step closer while I'd been zoning. "Where'd you go?"

I smiled. "Just got lost in this wonderful moment. I really missed you."

"I missed you too. Bad." He snapped his wrists, flicking me with the yellow and blue this time.

Pulled back into the present in that split-second frosting flick, I laughed, darting to the other side of the table, shoving the ends of my weapons into the nearest bowls, chocolate and mint green. "You're going down, Michaelson."

He froze, blinking. His gaze locked onto something behind me, so I glanced over my shoulder. My entire naked backside was reflected in the windowpane. The blue polka-dot ties dangled down from my waist across one of my ass cheeks.

I turned and unloaded my weapons, firing frosting streaks onto his face, shirt, one bicep, and jeans.

"Hey." He scowled, glancing down. "I was distracted."

"You wanted me naked in an apron. Serves you right. I'll use any advantage I have." I reloaded.

He shoved his tools into the bowls too.

We proceeded to launch all the colors in an extreme frosting close-quarters combat, spattering each other, along with every surface around us. The bowls and utensils clanged as we knocked them into each other. When we'd exhausted ourselves with laughter, and the frosting supply dwindled, we stopped for a temporary truce, trying to catch our breath.

I gasped for air, pointing to the untouched bowl. "You didn't use any of the white frosting." For some reason, I hadn't either, preferring to show my superior skills by painting bold colors all over him, but we'd actually sustained about equal damage.

"Nope. I've got plans for that white frosting." He crooked his finger at me. "C'mere."

I hesitated, but he cocked his head—a subtle warning to either obey, or he'd see to the task for me. I smirked and surrendered my weapons, laying them on the table, while sauntering around the other side.

When I came within reach, he wrapped his hands around my waist and pulled me close, bending down and kissing me breathless. In a sudden move, he broke away and lifted me up, seating me on the marble top of my kitchen island.

I gasped at the cold stone under my bare ass.

Yeah, I'd be cleaning and disinfecting all day tomorrow.

With determined focus, he relocated the condiments from the small surface beside me to the counter next to the stove, then brought over the last frosting bowl and the bottles of toppings. The bowl hadn't remained entirely untouched during our skirmish; a pink streak and a blue glop marred the frosting's smooth white surface. He glanced back and reached an arm toward the utensil drawer, pulling out a yellow silicone spatula. Then he dipped it into the frosting.

Time stood still. My breaths grew shallow while he stared at me.

He held me locked in a gaze so all consuming, I felt devoured, cherished, and freed at once. Never again would there be doubt of where I'd run when panic set in. My safe place, existed with Cade, in his arms.

A devilish smirk twisted his lips as his free hand slid warm and firm over my thigh, inching the hem of my apron higher. The spatula in his other hand tilted sideways and fell against the skin high on my inner thigh.

"Ooops." He pulled the spatula off my leg and tossed it back into the frosting bowl. "I've made a mess."

"You better clean it up." My bossy tone surprised me. Cade always took a dominant role with our play, and I loved that.

A dark brow arched. His chin inched to the left, his eyes narrowing on me in disbelief. "Did you just give me an order?" He gripped my hips, lifting them clear off the counter and yanking me to the edge. I fell back on a soft laugh. He wanted it clear who wielded control here.

I propped an arm under my head, gazing down at him. "Yeah, I did."

His blue eyes darkened with desire. He tore his frosting-covered black T-shirt off, revealing his tanned chest. Sleek abdominal muscles tightened, drawing my gaze to the dark dusting of hair that led down beneath the unbuttoned fly of his jeans. I stared at the length bulging against the underside of that denim.

Rich and low, his tone nearly came out as a growl. "Okay, smartass. Now I plan to make a much bigger mess before I ever think about cleaning it up."

My eyes widened, feigning shock. "Oh? Promise?"

He sucked in a lungful of air, chest expanding. "Wow. Maybe I should disappear more often. I can't decide whether to spank you or pound into you."

I grinned, so incredibly happy to have him here with me, the fact we weren't mindlessly having sex up against the wall already didn't bother me. I'd missed him too much to care. Teasing and taunting had been the foundation of our friendship and courtship before we'd ever gotten naked. And the fact that we lingered here in this wonderful place of intimacy, of reconnecting, meant a great deal to me. To both of us, I imagined.

Neither of us rushed the moment.

But my smartass couldn't help itself. "I'm so afraid. That floppy spatula looks dangerous."

He snorted. "First of all, do not say the word 'floppy' when we're naked. Second, that is not the spatula I would spank your feisty ass with."

His tone was edgy, serious. My playful expression fell away. I gasped in surprise as an ache throbbed between my legs. "No?"

He gave a slow shake of his head. "No."

Then he shoved his hand back into the drawer, metal utensils crashing together. He rummaged a second before pulling out another metal spatula, only it was wider and solid. The hard surface glinted as he turned it in his hand beneath the overhead pendant lights. "This is the spatula I'm gonna use."

"Going to?" I stared at it, visualizing the cold unforgiving metal smacking my skin. Another flash of pleasure speared between my thighs at the thought, forbidden, unknown.

"Definitely." He placed the not-so-harmless kitchen utensil beside my hip. "But first, I plan to heat up your front side. Then I'll flip you over to sear your backside."

I groaned at the thought as he dropped his head. His teeth met the skin inside of my bent knee in a gentle bite, hot breath fanning up my thigh as he exhaled.

Tender kisses followed the fogging air, teasing a trail up my inner thigh.

My body flushed hot as I fought to catch my breath. Desire, laced with something greater, pulsed through my veins. Vulnerable and exposed, spread for Cade on his condiment alter in the middle of my kitchen, I offered myself to him. Body, heart, soul, were his.

As if sensing the gravity of my thoughts, he paused in his hot trail of kisses and gazed across my body, into my eyes.

"I meant what I said earlier, Hannah. It's not about the sex for me. No matter how wild we get, or how much I tease, what we do sexually will always be about the deeper connection between us."

Warmth spread in my chest and I smiled. "I feel the same, Cade. You are to me what no one else on Earth ever has been, or ever will be."

For a few beats, we held each other's gazes.

But the moment for action had come, and I couldn't stand to wait any longer.

"You plan on only using the frosting?"

He blinked. "What?"

I smiled, enjoying his sudden confusion. "You teased me for months about honey, chocolate sauce, and caramel." I pointed to the red-and-white can. "Whipped cream. There is a brand new can of whipped cream, and you grab *only* the bowl of frosting?"

"This is my show." He pointed at the lineup of condiments he'd moved earlier to the counter beside the stove. "That is my arsenal of pleasure to use how and when I see fit. And I will not be mixing them."

I arched a brow, trying not to laugh at his adorable OCD-ness. "Yes, sir."

He chuckled under his breath. "There's a good girl."

To my surprise, instead of returning his attention to my inner thigh he grabbed my right hip and turned me to the side. Seconds later, a sharp sting fired through my ass cheek.

I gasped in shock, twisting toward him.

He smirked. "I will however, mix up whatever tools I choose to use."

Soothing fingers brushed across my throbbing skin as he rolled me back over onto the counter. But as the slow burn eased from my skin, it traveled between my thighs, settling into a delicious ache.

His eyes searched mine, and an unruly part of me couldn't decide whether to be disobedient again, or let him take the reins.

"Do you trust me?" He put the spatula back down onto the counter.

I held his intense gaze, my heart melting all over again. "With all that I am."

"Then lie back, Maestro. Let me love you...*with all that I am.*"

———

Happily Ever After
for now . . .

———

Cade & Hannah's romantic adventures continue to unfold in the **No Weddings** series...

No Weddings
One Funeral
Two Bar Mitzvahs
Three Christmases
For Valentine's

Thank You!

Thank you for experiencing Cade and Hannah's romantic adventure with us in *Two Bar Mitzvahs*.

If you enjoyed the story, please express your love for *Two Bar Mitzvahs* by recommending it to friends in person, by email, on Goodreads, and through book clubs and reader groups.

And if you value reviews to help guide you into your next book, as we do, please help other readers by sharing your review of *Two Bar Mitzvahs* on your favorite retailer and book community sites.

Incredible thanks to everyone for extending your love of *Two Bar Mitzvahs*.

Reviews are cherished love notes to authors
and tantalizing invitations to readers.
Appreciated by all. ♥

Want to Read More?

Dive into the steamy romantic comedy of the
No Weddings Series...
No Weddings
One Funeral
Two Bar Mitzvahs
Three Christmases
For Valentine's

———

Read more of your favorite characters from the No
Weddings series in the steamy spinoff
Unbreakable Series...

Kiki & Darren's romance ignites in...
Heartbreaker

Mase & Leilani's passion flares in...
Rule Breaker

Ben & Shay flirt with danger in...
Lawbreaker

———

Escape into award-winning time travel romance
in the steamy novels of the
Highland Legends Series...
Forged in Dreams and Magick
Bound by Wish and Mistletoe
Born of Mist and Legend
Found in Flame and Moonlight

Adventure in paranormal short stories
in a spinoff of Highland Legends
THE TRAVELER: Initiate Years ...
Veil of Realms
Secrets of Alexandria
Panther Rising
Stones of Power
Highland Magick

Want to Read EVEN More?

Icebreaker and *Ball Breaker*
AND
an epic romantasy series are all coming soon!

Be the first to receive preorder alerts, exclusive bonus gifts,
and occasional free stories...
Join our Bastion Family Adventurers!
katbastion.com/email-subscription

ALSO BY KAT & STONE BASTION

No Weddings Series

No Weddings · One Funeral

Two Bar Mitzvahs · Three Christmases

For Valentine's

Unbreakable Series

Heartbreaker · Rule Breaker · Lawbreaker

Forthcoming: *Ball Breaker · Icebreaker*

Highland Legends Series

Forged in Dreams and Magick

Bound by Wish and Mistletoe

Born of Mist and Legend

Found in Flame and Moonlight

THE TRAVELER: Initiate Years

Veil of Realms · Secrets of Alexandria · Panther Rising

Stones of Power · Highland Magick

Half-Baked Holidays

Half-baked Holidays:

A Romantic Comedy Holiday Collection

Comic Book Date Series

The Accidental May the 4th Comic Book Date

The Unbelievable Made on a Dare Comic Book Date

The Irresistible 4th of July Comic Book Date

Standalone Novels & Novelettes

Brand New Year · The Espionage Effect

Romantic Poetry for Charity

Utterly Loved

Kiki...

For a blessed few hours, I forgot.

Loading Zone did that to me. The nightclub's Industrial Grunge feel, which I'd helped design with its exposed brick and rusted steel, wrapped itself around me like a comfortable blanket. Heavy bass thumped, vibrating into my bones. My thighs burned from dancing back-to-back songs. Three lemon drop martinis in the last two hours hummed warmth through my veins.

"C'mon," my sister Kendall shouted above the loud music as she grasped my hand, then tugged me forward. "My toes are numb."

Out of breath, I nodded and we headed toward the corner booth the eight of us had crammed into earlier. I dance-walked in the narrow path through the crowd behind her, each step a hip shake and head toss to the pulsing rhythm.

The moment we reached the table, our oldest sister, Kristen, pulled her husband from the booth. "Time for us to go. Jason has an early flight tomorrow."

Cade, our brother and silent partner of Loading Zone, guided his new wife, Hannah, out right after them. "Last dance, Mrs. Michaelson?"

Which left Cade's two best friends: the scruffy prodigy surfer Mase, his former roommate; and clean-cut businessman Ben, the other owner of Loading Zone. I slid over the black distressed leather before landing in the center of the wide, shallow booth to face the dance floor while Mase abandoned his spot on the opposite side to anchor the end next to me.

I grasped the stem of my martini glass, sipped the last bit of the tart lemon drop, then let out a happy-buzz sigh. Being around these three—including rising-star architect Kendall —all of them with their shit together, lent some grounding *yin* to my artistic *yang*.

"Sex on a stick, twelve o'clock," Kendall announced.

My heart suddenly slammed into my ribs. But I exhaled slowly, trying to hide my reaction.

I'd been excited about tonight for several reasons: banish my secret problems from my head, surround myself with my favorite peeps, and *Darren Cole*.

Ben snorted out laughter while Mase dropped me a deadpan look. "'Sex on a *stick*'?"

I shot Mase a sidelong glare and elbowed him in the ribs.

He grunted and nudged my arm away.

By the time I glanced up, corded forearms shot over the outer edge of the table. Large hands planted with a hard smack on the brushed metal tabletop. A familiar folded strip of paper skittered out from his fingers, sliding in a wide arc toward Ben.

My breath caught as I stared into Darren's dark green eyes. A lock of his shaggy black hair fell over his forehead as he tilted his face downward. He set his jaw, expression hardening, as a scuffle between four guys unfolded right behind him, the apparent cause of his sudden hand-plant. He gave me a piercing look. "Twenty minutes."

Then he turned and grasped the nearest offender by the scruff of his shirt. Security arrived an instant later and manhandled the others into submission.

As Darren flexed his left arm while leading his guy toward the exit of the club, the tapered point of a tribal tattoo peeked out from the back collar of Darren's black T-shirt. My imagination began to paint what lay hidden from view: thick black ink arcing across sculpted back muscles, a woven design that twisted downward toward his tight...

"What's that?" Kendall leaned over the table.

I tore my gaze away from Darren and reached for the note, but Kendall snatched up the slip of paper first. She unfolded it and read its message aloud, "'*Gimme a* ride? *K.*'"

"Oh, sure." Mase took a long pull from his beer, then swallowed. "Kendall gets to innuendo the fuck out of this, but I don't?"

Ben arched a brow. "Twenty minutes. That's one helluva ride."

"Shut up. Both of you. Guys objectify women. We can do the same. And it's a ride home, smartass." I tried to shoot Ben an annoyed glare, but the corners of my mouth twitched into a smile and ruined the whole thing.

"*Suuure*...a ride home." Mase winked at me, then glanced over to where Darren strode along the edge of the room as he headed back toward his DJ booth. "I suppose he qualifies."

"Worthy of objectifying? Darren more than qualifies." I pinched the message *meant for Darren's eyes only* and ripped it from Kendall's grasp. "He doesn't say much," I continued. "Leaves the club with different women. Built like the perfect male specimen..."

Ben choked on his beer. "And what are we? Male rejects?"

"Ewww." Kendall scowled. "That's incestuous."

"You're like our brothers. Can't even..." I scrunched my nose and blanked out my mind, willing myself not to visualize it.

"Not looking for love?" Ben asked, tone softening.

At that, all of our gazes drifted toward the dance floor. One of the last songs of the night streamed a fast tempo from the speakers, but in the center of a thinning crowd, Cade and Hannah stood oblivious. Wrapped together, they swayed to a slow rhythm only they seemed to hear. The look of adoration on their faces as they stared deep into each other's eyes spoke volumes.

"No," I said with absolute conviction. "Heartache lies down that road."

Mase laid a gentle hand on mine. "As your pseudo-brother, I'm warning you: Be careful."

I had no idea whether he meant Darren specifically or men in general. It didn't really matter. I'd learned my love lesson early. And I'd never trusted a guy enough to let one hurt me since.

Darren? The only kind of guy I was willing to play with. A beautiful man I refused to form any attachment to—easy to leave.

The quintessential heartbreaker.

In Darren's truck. Again. A vast awkward distance between us. *Again.*

The drive took only about ten minutes. But the ride home from Loading Zone in Philly's Old City Arts District to the outskirts of sleepy Glenhaven—the third since last summer—stretched eternal.

Why? A hookup shouldn't be this difficult.

My gaze shifted toward him. Powerful hands gripped the steering wheel, thumbs knocking some unheard drumbeat into the silence of the cab. Sculpted forearms stretched up toward cut biceps that vanished under the thin black fabric of the T-shirt that hugged them. His expression was serious, but relaxed. As if he didn't feel the weight of the moment like I did.

Now or never, Kiki.

I took a deep breath and ran a flattened hand over the gauzy material of my skirt, trying to calm myself. Then I inched closer to him, needing some sort of validation that whatever tenuous thing we had between us was moving toward something...fun...instead of away from it.

Tonight didn't have to be a big deal. He either wanted me or didn't. Two other platonic drop-offs didn't mean anything significant. Maybe he was shy. Or a gentleman.

As we drove, yellow pools of light from wrought iron lampposts marked the passing time in a visual cadence. *Light...dark. Light...dark.* The streetlights soon began to feel like a countdown, as if they mocked me for just sitting passively in their spotlights.

Yet how to breach the uncomfortable silence? My mind tumbled over the possibilities: *How did your sound board glide tonight? Wow, how 'bout the heavy bass on that last song?*

He cleared his throat, beating me to it. "Sooo...talk to me. How's the art going?"

"Good." *Good? Really?* I winced at my pathetic attempt at conversation.

We made the second-to-last turn, my time running out, as he gave a single nod in reply.

Buck up, Kiki. You either want him or you don't. Stop being a pussy. "Actually, it's a smaller sculpture. A single orchid sprouting from a rocky riverbed."

He glanced my way. "You work with metal, right?"

"Yeah." I leaned back, staring out the windshield, finally calming a bit as I thought about my art. "This piece is bronze. The lone color is the violet on the flower."

"Sounds cool." His voice lowered. He cleared his throat again.

Had he moved closer?

Impossible. He was driving. Behind the steering wheel, as always.

Yet our legs nearly touched. The rough denim, tight over his thigh, had slid over the tan leather seat to within an inch of my bared knee; he'd spread his legs wider.

The man already consumed most of the space in the truck with his commanding presence. But instead of moving away, I automatically drew closer. My thundering pulse throbbed heavier, warmer...lower.

I swallowed hard, attempting to find my way back to the conversation. "How did your night go?" Maybe his sound board was a medium for his art, like metal was for me.

"Good." The corner of his mouth twitched into a barely perceptible grin, then relaxed.

He dropped his right hand from the steering wheel and floated it in the infinitesimal space between us. Gentle pressure rubbed through the flimsy fabric that covered my upper thigh.

My gaze lowered from the dashboard at the exact moment the knuckle of his index finger trailed in slow motion up the skin under my hem.

I held my breath.

I haven't *been imagining things.*

But then his hand suddenly lifted and fisted. His expression hardened as he stared straight ahead. We made the final turn onto my street, and he eased off the gas, letting us coast. The ride I'd been waiting all night for—six long months and two failed attempts for—appeared to be over.

We rolled to a stop in front of the white picket fence that surrounded the darling butter-yellow Victorian. Then he shifted the truck into park, letting it idle.

Refusing to give up, especially when I sensed him struggling with an attraction we both knew was real, I made a final direct attempt. "You don't have to drive right off. You could come in for a drink."

"No, I can't."

"Why not?" The two words tripped out flippant in my pitiful effort to sound nonchalant.

"You're Cade's little sister."

"No, I'm n—" I blinked.

The pad of his finger pressed to my lips. Warm. Firm. Suddenly, I thought of nothing else. My whole world became our tantalizing first contact.

He didn't move. Simply stared at me.

I closed my eyes. My head eased back against the headrest, but the contact remained as my lips pursed into the gentlest kiss against his fingertip. I wanted to flick my tongue out, taste him. But then he pulled away.

I blinked my eyes open.

He'd half-twisted on the seat toward me. "You deserve better than a one-night fuck, Kiki."

"What I deserve," I muttered, then snorted.

Damn right, I deserve better than that.

But one night was all I could handle.

"Doesn't matter." What I continued to tell myself. "What

I want right now is you." There, I'd said it. Out in the open. Bold and direct.

"What you deserve *does* matter. Don't ever forget it." His voice hardened with every word. His dark brows furrowed to the point a deep crease marred the tanned skin between them.

Without thinking, I reached up and pressed my thumb along that vertical line, massaging until his face began to relax.

He stared at me with renewed intensity. "What are you doing?"

"Trying to get you to chill out." I let my thumb slide a fraction to the right until I found a pressure point, then I spread the rest of my fingertips across the line of his eyebrow. "Is it working?"

"No." The corners of his mouth twitched again.

"Liar."

"Okay. A little."

"Seriously, though," I continued as if I hadn't been distracted by his impressive scowl. "I'm an excellent one-night fuck."

He jerked his head away, then lapsed into a coughing fit.

I arched a brow. "What? Don't think so?"

He shook his head. "No." His mouth fell open. "I mean, I'm sure you are." He blew out a heavy sigh, cheeks puffing from the effort. "You just..."

"Unnerve you?"

"*Yes.*" He thrust a splayed hand into the open air between us with the curt word. "Are you trying to kill me?"

A smile began to curve my lips. "No, I'm just trying to—"

"Don't say it."

The word hung on the tip of my tongue. "You know I'm thinking it."

"Stop thinking it." He took a measured breath, his chest gradually rising, then falling.

Enjoying the loaded tension between us, I remained still, waiting.

When he turned toward me again, I leaned closer and deeply inhaled his earthy scent. "Look. This doesn't have to be complicated just because I'm Cade's sister. You're an adult. I'm an adult. Aren't you attracted to me?"

Every telltale sign he'd shown suggested that he wanted me. But I'd never encountered so much resistance in a guy before. Then again, I'd never had one in my sights so long before either. I ignored the implications in that.

"Of course I am." He draped an arm along the top of the seatback.

His warmth lured me in, and I edged even closer until my entire side crushed against his. He made no move to stop me and didn't flinch away, but his lengthy pause indicated that he resisted committing to anything.

"All it has to be is one night," I whispered, my lips nearly touching the warm skin of his neck.

Another heavy sigh ruffled the hair above my ear, shooting chill bumps down my side. "You gotta know, if I could...I would. It *is* complicated. I can't explain. But no matter how badly either of us want to, this can't happen."

I blinked, confused and lost in uncharted territory. Never had a guy not taken the bait I'd offered. And he was being so nice about it. My mind couldn't process what was happening. "You want me."

"Fuck, yes. I mean, no." He growled in frustration. "God-dammit, Kiki. Just get out of the truck. Please."

I pulled away from him and straightened in my seat, almost laughing at the desperation in his tone. Then I dared a glance at him. His expression grew tortured. A tiny part of me felt bad for putting him in a position I didn't understand. The rest of me beamed that I wasn't the only sexually frustrated one in the vehicle.

Not yet willing to admit defeat, I gave him a smile and grasped the cold metal door handle. "Thanks for the ride, Darren."

I wouldn't ask for one again. But I didn't need to. The seeds had been planted. My work was done. Either he wanted me enough to get past whatever obstacle was cockblocking his way, or he didn't.

Meanwhile, I'd go back to the life I'd been trying to forget, once my mind-numbing buzz wore off.

I wanted to glance over my shoulder as I unfastened the painted wooden gate, double-check to see if he was still watching, but I fought the urge.

The low hum of his idling truck engine remained unchanged. But had his mind?

This lonely girl can only hope.

———

Enjoy the rest of the romance...
Heartbreaker

**Sneak Peek of the final installment in our Highland Legends
series**

Found in Flame and Moonlight

Eight minutes was all Chelsea Smith had. All she needed. *Hopefully.*

The heavy wooden door to Professor MacLaren's private office snicked closed behind her. With a subtle suggestion from her mind, the tumblers reengaged within its lock, a deadbolt she'd "picked" with similar mental ease mere seconds ago.

On her next inhale of cooler undisturbed air, the distinctive scents of age washed over her: that certain spice of centuries-old leather, a mustiness of layered dust, the sweetness of yellowing paper in a prized collection of ancient books.

The room's furnishings echoed its owner's passion for antiquities. Within a sizable entry, a vintage coffee-colored Chesterfield sofa with matching wingchairs hovered at the edge of a burgundy-and-gold Aubusson carpet. Along the side and far wall, relics from exotic locales perched from various niches between precisely stacked scholarly tomes in massive bookcases. And beyond a sizable polished wood desk and its stately leather chair, within tall display cases that flanked a large window, treasured discoveries from historic digs rested on glass shelves.

Yet one particular artifact stood apart from the rest. The

sole reason for her break-in. And the item occupied the nearest corner of his polished wood desk, exposed. No bookcase niche. No protective case.

"Such unfathomable *power*," Chelsea murmured toward the rectangular object, at once fascinated and intrigued. More than she'd been about anything in her first twenty-two years of an immortal life hiding-in-plain sight among "normal" humans.

Her excitement even eclipsed what she'd witnessed from the other side of that window while walking to MacLaren's lecture less than an hour ago.

Though her mind still reeled about that discovery as well.

Because something very *not human* had stood near that power-drenched box, partially transparent, as if not fully materialized into the human world. And that shirtless muscular something had resembled artistic depictions of male angelic warriors, only skewed darker and more sinister with its dusky olive skin, inky black wings, and blue-green prismatic eyes.

And the enigmatic creature had stared directly at her, eyes narrowing, puzzlement twisting his sharp features as Chelsea blatantly stared back. He'd seemed surprised. That she could detect him? Or perhaps that their paths had intersected in the first place.

Yet inside the professor's locked office, no sign of the dark angel remained.

Seven minutes.

The forceful vibration of the artifact's unique power was what had caught her attention from the other side of the window. It had radiated an exhilarating and complex energy, beckoning her like a siren's call.

"Invitation accepted," she whispered.

With slow breaths, Chelsea banked her excitement. Not hard to achieve. Her kind, further evolved humans, born-and-bred assassins, had been trained through millennia to suppress emotion.

"Yeah." She let out a soft snort. "Look how well *that* turned out."

Members of her race had recently evolved again. And an underground faction had organically formed. One that no longer sought to squelch their emotions. That strong minority yearned for something greater, a deeper meaning to their eternal life.

Months ago, Chelsea had been secretly contacted by them. The founders had detected her tendency to operate on the fringe of acceptability. Of course, she'd joined their cause without hesitation.

In the hours and days following that pivotal decision, she'd eased the cognitive restraints that had hobbled her. They had warned her that she would suffer unimaginable internal struggle. Yet nothing had prepared her for the cascade of emotions. One in particular had caused an enormous dissonance with her inherited vocation.

Empathy had bled into her black-and-white world.

An *assassin's* world.

And that problematic emotion had caused a thunderstorm of chaotic gray.

Six minutes.

Focus, Chelsea. She took measured steps toward the charged artifact, noting its unusual features. A foot long, half that wide and tall, a rectangular box sat encased in layers of elaborate metallic latticework. The gleaming designs that adorned its corners and edges were comprised of various metals from differing artistry. But beneath those ornate motifs, simpler flat sides were fashioned from a beautiful bluish-silver metal with a slight sparkle to its sheen.

Indirect bright light glowed in from the large window, but as Chelsea approached, an aura of energy haloed around the box. Infinitesimal particles glittered beyond its surfaces, flashes of silver and gold visible to her preternatural eyes.

Five minutes.

Which meant MacLaren's lecture in his beloved Advanced Theories in Archaeology had concluded. Earlier, Chelsea had obediently endured the graduate-level course with fifteen other classmates until she'd politely excused herself at the last and most opportune moment. A correct amount of respectful time from a valued student. The perfect window of plausible deniability should her burglary plans go awry.

Students typically waylaid him after his lectures, but to be certain, she extended her superhuman hearing. Down a wide sidewalk between buildings, across a grassy quad, and into the cozy window-lined room that the tenured professor claimed as his own, she detected the voices of eager students who had indeed detained him. Which enabled him to wax eloquent about the week's series and his latest obsession: prehistoric artifacts handed down by gods, breadcrumbs to the secrets of mysterious civilizations.

"But you've been keeping the biggest secret of all right here in your office, haven't you?" Chelsea murmured as she paused within reach of the object.

Four minutes.

Plenty of time to abort, to walk away without detection.

"I don't *need* to be here." Sound reason.

And yet, need had become relative.

For in the months following her recent evolution, an

undefinable hunger had begun to grow that nothing satisfied. A craving for a deeper purpose. Not the deadly one mandated by her ancestry. Not even the glimmer of hope that her emerging faction offered.

"Something personal," she murmured, staring at the box. She'd been hunting a cause that matched her sudden passion for life. Unique and special. Sparked by her newfound awakening. "Worthy. And all my own."

Because every action she'd taken in life, from actual missions to basic periphery cover, had been by her race's directive. Even attending university. Particularly MacLaren's courses.

But for the first time, she operated on her own volition. Because before that morning, she hadn't been privy to any details of *why* MacLaren had become a person of interest. Until one shining detail had made itself known, flashing its undeniable energy straight toward her.

Therefore, the risk of exposure? While investigating an object as exceptional as what she hoped to discover about herself?

More than acceptable.

While she continued to listen, the distinct voices of six fellow grad students dwindled to two hardcore disciples. They peppered the professor with questions, theories, and offers of assistance on his next expedition. Groveling, as usual. But MacLaren had their number. And only a couple of minutes remained of his scheduled patience.

Chelsea drew a deep breath to calm her riotous—clearly *not* suppressed—emotions.

Instinct screamed the intricate box held her destiny. Even if she had no idea why.

But as she took a final step and reached out a hand to touch, its unique power reacted to her proximity with accelerating vibrations of energy—plenty of evidence to back up that gut feeling.

Three minutes.

MacLaren shooed out his fan club with his parting excuses and locked up the classroom.

Right as Chelsea hovered a hand over the artifact.

Energy emanated upward from that bluish-silver top, charging the air with electrons that sizzled and sparked. Warmth bathed her palm. Friendly. Inviting. *Intoxicating.*

Until a sense of grave danger spiked in those scant inches between the mysterious metal and her skin. And an unfamiliar feeling of trepidation tripped down her spine. Like some cosmic warning.

Chelsea paused, then blinked heavily, thrown by the sudden unfriendliness of the box and her own emotion about it. She wiggled her fingers within the box's charged aura and considered her impulsive actions. And their unknown ramifications. With the artifact. And MacLaren.

An extensive list of potentialities scrolled through her advanced mind. But the calculations magnified when she removed the laws of the known universe and input alternate realities. Involving energized boxes. And dark angels. And supposedly regular professors that capture the attention of a race of assassins.

Ninety seconds.

"So many possibilities," she murmured about the upside. *Too many variables to calculate.*

Chelsea snorted and shook her head with a slight smile. "I've never been afraid of anything in my life." Headlong into the adventure. The only way she saw the world.

The leather heels of MacLaren's loafers clicked down the nearest sidewalk.

Less than a minute. Before her trespass was discovered.

Urgency fired through her veins. She tensed her arm and lowered her hand, ready to touch no matter the outcome. To finally complete some circuit she'd begun to sense, as if the dark matter hovering between the spaces in the universe needed her help.

The charged air rippled with a stronger dose of caution.

Chelsea narrowed her eyes at the box.

Are you trying to communicate with me?

That the inanimate object had sentience, as opposed to some other force out in the ether, gave her pause. Deadly animals and insects often displayed vivid warnings of their lethal venom.

But why lead me here with such clear invitation? Do you not want me to touch?

The warning vibration wavered back and forth in response as the additional questions crossed her mind. Not quite a yes, not quite a no. That it wanted her there, perhaps. But not to touch? *Orrr…*

"Not yet?" Barely an inch existed.

A hot glow sparkled into existence between her and the artifact, golden and shimmering. The box's energy extended an exquisite representation of agreement in its special language.

"Fascinating." Mesmerizing.

The artifact's seductive power continued to astound.

Have you taunted MacLaren with such scandalous invitation?

No sooner had she posed the mental question, than an answer rippled forth. Only that message vibrated not from the artifact, but from somewhere out in the ether. *No.* Crystal clear. Not as any legible word, but a negative in resonance.

The energized box did not wait on that desk for the professor.

At that moment, the artifact existed for a singular purpose: to join its immense power with hers.

MacLaren's footfalls began to click down the tiles of the building's corridor.

Energy spiked from the box again. Even while its power rippled another caution: *Not yet.* The message clearly vibrated from the object, not the ether.

But unraveling the mysteries of a higher consciousnesses in matter and space had to wait.

Adrenaline surged through her. "Out of time."

Golden sparks fountained up from its metallic top, singeing her palm. *Not yet!*

"When?" Chelsea choked out a laugh at the box. "*After he has campus security cuff me?*"

MacLaren's key slid into the lock.

Her pulse raced, the thump of her heart a drumbeat in her ears.

Now or never! she argued to the unseen gatekeepers.

Tiny clicks echoed as tumblers released in the lock's mechanism.

The door edge scraped over its frame, the only means of a clean escape swinging open and her window of opportunity closing right along with it.

Half-assed alibies spun through her mind, all utterly ridiculous: *I followed a burglar in, I needed to lie down and only your pin-tucked sofa would do, I saw a black-winged angel with sparkling blue-green eyes staring out your window.* Voicing that last factoid? Bordered on certifiable insanity.

But at the last split second between clean infiltration and utter discovery—right as her anxiety skyrocketed—a powerful vacuum slammed her hand down that remaining inch.

A scorching current charged up through her palm from the metal. Blinding power and incredible pleasure flashed through her being.

MacLaren's office vanished.

And a realm of absolute nothingness descended.

———

Gawain Brodie sucked in a stunned breath as the inside of his chest...*boomed*.

Thunder? Confused, he frowned but refused to break stride. He raced down an earthen footpath in the shadowy forest to rejoin his warriors; he'd been ambushed while scouting. And since no cloud marred the late-afternoon sky, he shook off the jarring sensation.

Faster! Scant seconds remained. Clan Brodie had been exposed. Their castle's centuries-old secret somehow breached.

Blood from three attackers speckled his arms and chest. Yet the last one's dying words bore evidence of the exposure: *Your magick castle is ours!*

A tang from the skirmish coated his tongue, pungent earth and the coppery taste of blood. Anger churned in his gut. Ferocity pumped through his veins. Single-minded determination overcame burning muscles as he sought to vanquish whatever enemy they faced.

Intent on cutting time, he broke into a sunny glade, ran across rippling purple blooms of heather, then rejoined the well-worn trail. Yet as he rounded the gnarled trunk of an ancient yew, a sudden awareness made him veer wide in the turn.

Alongside the path, lacy fronds of bracken trembled. Then a blur of motion burst forth.

Dark garb registered in his peripheral vision. As did the gleam of a swinging sword.

He unsheathed his own sword, then blocked a strike meant to cleave his neck.

Never pausing his momentum, Gawain twisted his body and shifted forward, swinging his weapon over. Then he tightened his blade down at the last moment for the killing blow.

To his surprise, the swords clashed. Punishing vibration jarred his bones from hand to arm, shoulder to neck, till they rattled a final quiver down through his teeth.

The attacker—a male with flaxen hair, of similar height and breadth to the threesome he'd more easily dispatched —merely sounded a low grunt.

With greater determination, Gawain thrust.

In equal measure, his opponent parried.

Fury darkened his attacker's eyes.

Exhilaration fired through Gawain's veins.

Their deadly battle-dance continued with strikes and blocks, thrusts and parries. Each next metallic crash rang out with echoing menace.

"At long last, a worthy opponent," Gawain murmured.

Gawain arced his sword back around, but once the tip swung skyward, he twisted, tucked, then thrust from a lower angle.

The soldier deflected then stepped aside, just as well trained, equally gifted.

"Aye. An 'opponent' who'll impale yer bloody arse like a stuck pig," the soldier replied in an English accent. A sick hunger gleamed in his eye.

Amused, Gawain relaxed his stance and drew back his weapon. He tilted his head and narrowed his eyes. "Why eat pig when you can dine like a king?"

The man's expression fell. As did the tip of his sword while he gave a heavy blink and furrowed his brow. "What're you on about?"

In the next heartbeat, Gawain lunged with incredible speed. The tip of his sword led the way, piercing the man's heart before he was able to draw a full gasp of surprise—or reengage his sword.

"The differences between us," Gawain whispered into the ear of the dying man.

Severe lack of emotion and abundance of wit.

What Gawain possessed and most did not.

With a quick jerk, Gawain freed his sword. As the body crumpled to the ground, he swiped both sides of his weapon on the cleanest patch of the soldier's woolen tunic. He believed in letting fallen men keep their blood. *Off my sword.*

English! The revelation of how far and wide their exposure had traveled still stunned him.

No time! He charged back toward the footpath and raced on.

After another few hundred yards, the clear sounds of combat filtered into the dense forest: the clatter of weapons, shouts and grunts from men.

Seconds later, he burst upon a greater battle. Or what little remained of it.

His brethren carved and sliced through their own tenacious dark-garbed attackers. One Brodie to five English. But the last of their foe fell in rapid succession, one after the other, none prepared for the skill of the unique clan of Highlanders.

With no immediate threat left to eliminate, Gawain sheathed his weapon.

A second strange thunder boomed through his chest.

And its fading vibration carried the aftertaste of something imminent...*weighty*. As if an event of great import was about to transpire. *Involving me?* Or the clan.

Dismayed by the inexplicable and unnerving sensation, Gawain stared toward the western horizon as a fiery sun dipped below jagged mountain peaks.

Two warhorses suddenly appeared below his line of vision, one snow white, the other coal black. Both materialized seemingly from nowhere. And knowing their riders as Gawain did, they likely had.

Another powerful vibration reverberated through Gawain's chest so hard, he stifled the urge to cough as his family approached.

Astride the white mare was Isobel Brodie with her long blond hair flying back in the wind. Clad in her custom deerskin hunting outfit, she braced her toddler son between her arms.

On the black stallion rode Iain, Isobel's husband, Gawain's older brother, and Laird of Clan Brodie. He cradled their lad's twin sister with a father's protective hand.

Clutched in Iain's other hand was a magickal box whose surface sparkled even in gloaming's waning light.

Yet that box had *never* left Brodie Castle.

Not in all the years of Gawain's life.

Nor in any of the legendary tales of generations past.

An unmistakable sense of foreboding washed over him as his fellow warriors gathered to watch their leader and kin draw near.

"*All* approach the battlefront?" their commander, Robert, inquired to his right.

"With the wee ones?" Duncan asked at his left.

The warriors were part of Iain's elite guardsmen. Twelve in total. Closer than brothers.

"Nay." Naught was as it seemed. A great change had begun. Those facts rang true with every heavy beat of his heart. And he'd somehow landed in the center of its shifting tides. "They'll be but a moment," he murmured.

Even if Gawain failed to comprehend *how* he knew what was about to transpire, he sensed why they'd come.

Fate had descended upon him. Though the circumstance made little sense.

"I'll not take your place!" Gawain objected to the notion. The magickal box may as well have been scepter, orb, and crown. For of the many powers it wielded, foremost among them had long been to ordain the next Brodie male as chieftain of their clan.

"*Aye*, you will." Iain lifted the hallowed box high, reaching back.

"You remain hale and whole." Fit to rule. No reason to shift the obligation.

"We've no time to explain." Isobel tightened her legs to bring her mount alongside Iain's as she glanced at her husband. "Danger abounds. And we've been summoned"— at the last word, she directed Gawain a pointed look, heavy with meaning—"*away*."

Gawain sighed. *Away through* time itself. *No explanation needed.*

A strange feeling quivered in his gut. Akin to uncertainty. And a more familiar one: dread. Of the unknown. Of the burden of a reign he had never expected to shoulder.

The obsessive focus of battle had served him well all his life, had helped him overcome childhood demons. Even to the detriment of relations with close family. Namely his sister, Brigid, who he'd wrongly blamed for the cause of those demons so long ago. But Gawain had already come to accept how he'd done Brigid a grave disservice and labored to make amends.

Of late, he'd grown more noble. Worthy of the reign.

And his brother well knew it.

"'Tis the way of it," Iain bellowed for all the guardsmen to hear in witness of the historic moment. "You'll lead the clan through."

"*Aye.*" Gawain gave a clipped nod to his brother in dutiful acceptance of the role.

Iain dipped his chin with satisfaction, punched his arm forward, and released his grip.

The box arced through the air.

With narrowed eyes, Gawain thrust his hands up to catch it.

Yet at the exact moment his fingertips made contact with its cool metal sides, several monumental events happened at once, in plain sight of their guardsmen.

A bright bolt of lightning shot from ground to sky with a true boom of thunder.

Isobel touched a hand to Iain's shoulder and Clan Brodie's former ruling family vanished, warhorses and all.

Heat sparked from the box to his fingers and flashed through his entire body.

And a raven-haired woman appeared out of thin air. Vibrant blue eyes stared straight at him. Her slender hand rested atop the box.

"*Nay!*" Gawain growled, furious.

In his disgruntled shock of becoming laird, he'd forgotten the *other* burden the ancient box bestowed.

A soul mate.

Enjoy the rest of the adventure...
Found in Flame and Moonlight

ACKNOWLEDGMENTS

A team of people were involved in the making of *Two Bar Mitzvahs* and are mentioned below; however, any errors within the published novel, whether existing there intentionally or not, are ours alone.

Enormous appreciation goes to Kristi at Picky Editor, editor extraordinaire.

Gratitude goes to Lillie at Lillie's Literary Services, for beta reading *Two Bar Mitzvahs* as her first No Weddings Series book and giving it her stand-alone stamp of approval.

Huge thanks to Heather and Misty, our close friends and cheerleaders.

To our social media friends, fans, supporters, readers, reviewers, and bloggers, both those we've interacted with thus far and those we look forward to meeting—we are immensely grateful for all you do. Your unending enthusiasm for reading our stories fuels our excitement to write them.

Stone, what in the world could I say here to cover the depth of my gratitude to you? Not enough. But I will say that I'm so glad we took a wild idea over pizza out one night and turned it into a labor of love and laughter. I'd shout out some of the hilarious moments to make you laugh, but I have a feeling you're already thinking about them...and smiling.

Kat...Wait, what? Is this like wedding vows? You know

what you mean to me. The journey. The love. The laughter. *Squirrel!*

ABOUT THE AUTHOR

Kat Bastion won several awards for her bestselling debut novel *Forged in Dreams and Magick*.

Kat & Stone Bastion's bestselling first novel *No Weddings* and the No Weddings series were named Best of 2014 by multiple romance review blogs.

When not defining love and redemption through scribed words, they enjoy hiking in vivid wildflower deserts, ancient tropical forests, and historic urban jungles.

Join our Bastion Family Adventurers!

Be in the know with preorder alerts, exclusive bonus gifts, and occasional free stories:

katbastion.com/email-subscription